VERSES OFF THE BEATEN TRACK:
A Narrative Exploration of the Pairing Assistance Programme in China's Poverty Alleviation

He Jianming

New Classic Press

2024

NEW CLASSIC PRESS

Published by New Classic Press (UK) *

5th Floor, 99 Mansell Street, London, E1 8AX, UK,

Great Britain * Established in the year 2008 *

Seeking business opportunities worldwide

VERSES OFF THE BEATEN TRACK: A Narrative Exploration of the Pairing Assistance Programme in China's Poverty Alleviation

Written by He Jianming

Translated by Margaret Hillenbrand

Edited by Fernando Arrieta

Copyright © Ningxia People's Publishing House Co., Ltd

First published in China by Ningxia People's Publishing House & Fujian People's Publishing House

This English Edition Published in the United Kingdom of Great Britain and Northern Ireland by New Classic Press Limited in 2024

"This town of Minning has opened up for us a bright new road. We must spread this valuable experience throughout the whole country."

Xi Jinping

Contents

Preface
My Heart Trembles

Xihaigu, Saying Goodbye to the Title '*Poorest in the World*'

That faraway place, very far indeed, has ever since been in my heart. That place is Xihaigu.

The Liupan Mountains in Xihaigu.

For mostly everyone who could recognise the name, 'Xihaigu' meant nothing more than a poor region somewhere far. Even the local people of Xihaigu would say this about the land where they lived: 'If there are such things as an afterlife and reincarnation, there's no way I'll choose this place again to be my mother.' But, as everyone knows, there's no choosing one's mother.

Because it has carried that title, of the poorest place in the country, Xihaigu became famous, and because of that fame its poverty would also be exaggerated by the imagination, to the point of being used as shorthand for poverty in China more generally. In other words, 'Xihaigu' became synonymous with 'poverty'.

But I often asked myself, if Xihaigu is thus so 'unsuitable for settlement', as it was often said, how come there were still people living there, and people living there for hundreds, if not thousands, of years to boot? But this was in fact a silly question to be asking, because the place the ancestors of the modern-day dwellers of Xihaigu moved to was in no way poor and barren. Quite the opposite, it was a rich land plenty capable of feeding and clothing the people who lived in it. It was only much later that things changed, for the most part as a result of natural climatic changes, but also due to war and other disasters, in other words, calamities that humanity can hardly avoid. Something else that needs considering is that human dwellings are somewhat like trees. Once the roots are fixed in place, they cannot be easily uprooted and taken somewhere else. This means that, no matter how harsh the conditions are, how inclement the weather or how brutal the circumstances, people will resist leaving the land where they live. That is the reason why the people of Xihaigu, despite the unspeakable hardships they went through, would not give up on the land to which they were linked by birth.

As for myself, I grew up in the lush and prosperous Suzhou, and I have now lived in Beijing for more than forty years. I have long been used to hearing the name of Xihaigu being mentioned, and I have been in the past several times on the verge of setting off to visit the region, only to let the opportunity slip away. There was in fact only one reason I wanted to visit Xihaigu in the past, and that was to see for myself how poor the people there really was and how the so-called 'people without water' there lived. How inconceivable their lives might have been for people like us, used to living in a moist world with water aplenty!

Perhaps there were in my mind way too many things I had labelled 'inconceivable', so many indeed as to give me a distorted idea of Xihaigu and of Ningxia more broadly. In fact I know I was not alone in making that mistake.

But then the opportunity came up! And so, in the summer of 2019, with my heart filled with a mix of curiosity and nervousness, I boarded the plane that took me to Yinchuan, and from there I began my journey south, passing through places such as Wuzhong and Tongxin, till I eventually made it to my destination: Xihaigu.

A week on the road isn't what one can call a 'cursory trip', but it wasn't enough time for a 'thorough inspection' either.

That week on the road, however, going from place to place and stopping at each place for just a short while, time and time again left me speechless.

Was what I saw Ningxia? The land of the barbarian reed flutes, north of the Great Wall, where, according to the record left in history books, 'the solitary smoke column rises straight up from the desert's vastness upon which the Long River meanders towards the round sun'? Was that the old and poor western frontier, that old base of the Revolution, and homeland to minorities? I stood there, at the beginning of my visit, looking into the distance at a land I was seeing for the first time, and it perplexed me. There was the high-speed rail, which, however, does not reach the entirety of the province's territory. But in Ningxia you can now also use an extensive network of motorways that allow for a very smooth ride to any small village or town, not to mention the many neat and tidy new cities along the way, which are also growing fast... My hosts weren't very particular about the route to follow, and, starting at Yinchuan, simply took me in a southward direction to give me an overview of the landscape of today's Ningxia. And what I saw began to undo the old ideas I had about Ningxia and the western regions in general. Out of my mind went all those things I had earlier labelled as 'inconceivable'.

How could what I saw be that *barren* Ningxia?

How could that be the 'border region' where one is *always treading on dry rocks* and where *all fear the wild beasts*?

Where I looked there were rippling clear waters, birds singing sweet songs, and reeds swaying in the gentle breeze. To both sides of the road I could see myriad flowers blooming, their names unknown to me. But they seemed to be all issuing forth, indefatigably, love and admiration for one another... Then there were the fruit farmers appearing here and there along the road like little stars along the Milky Way, holding up their fragrant produce and waving to attract your attention. They were bound

Beita Lake in the City of Yinchuan

to enchant you and make you stop to smell and taste the sweet fruit they offered. You'd even feel a little inebriated, lost in that experience, and you could not believe that what you were seeing was Ningxia, *that* Ningxia of which you already had an image in your mind.

What I saw over a long stretch of road outside the city of Yinchuan almost deceived me, and I was even mumbling to myself and asking, how come I'm back in Suzhou, with all those lakes and all that water around?! Indeed, how could that place be more graceful, its climate milder, than Jiangnan, that land of lakes and canals south of the Yangtze? And yet that's what I saw, large expanses of viridescent and rippling waters, a landscape of luxuriant reeds and birds rising up in the air in large flocks, no different from the land I come from. Ah, so that was the fabled 'Jiangnan north of the Great Wall'! That was true after all, there is a Jiangnan north of the Great Wall, and one even better than the original!

Although I am a native of Jiangnan myself, I could not help but look around with great admiration at the beautiful northern landscape before my eyes. I had no words to say, but within my chest rose waves of emotion that I could not repress, and that was because Ningxia was thoroughly changed! And those were very exciting and most remarkable changes!

Today's Ningxia thus looked absolutely nothing like the Ningxia I had previously carried in my imagination. After visiting the county of Tongxin, in the prefecture of Wuzhong, and the county of Yanchi with its new city of Hongsibao built in the middle of the desert, and also Yuanzhou, Xiji and Haiyuan, all in the region of Xihaigu, and seeing their new streets, buildings, civic plazas, libraries, schools, and parks with flowers in bloom, I was left speechless. And then my heart trembled again as I realised that, in terms of their overall appearance, those places were in no way inferior to the cities of my native southern Jiangsu, cities that appear among the top positions in the official list of the top 100 cities in China.

But the most astounding is that Xihaigu has since antiquity been described as an arid land suffering from chronic water scarcity, also, as registered in the local annals, as a place with an average annual precipitation 'lower than 180 millimetres'. And that aridness has been consistently confirmed over history by the people of Ningxia themselves. And yet on the 21st of July of 2019, through the whole night before we left Xiji, in Xihaigu, to travel to the county of Tongxin, it rained torrentially. The next day, as we arrived in Tongxin, county chief Ding Wei told me with great delight that it had rained no less than 168 millimetres. In a single day.

'Isn't this about as much rain as you used to get here in a whole year?' I asked him, very much amazed myself.

'Yes, it is!' county chief Ding replied cheerfully and nodding repeatedly. 'In these past few years, it's been raining more and more each year.'

'Has Nature really been that good to you?' I asked him, not quite convinced yet.

Chief Ding nodded some more:

'That's been absolutely the case.'

That was a transformation ordained by Heaven, I told myself, and there'd be no one who could simply fake it. The locals, nonetheless, seemed to smile at me to express how proud they were about it.

During my 'tour of inspection' of the region, short as it was, I came across many other such things that amazed me as well, so I naturally had to keep reminding myself of the main purpose of my trip to Ningxia. I was there to observe and study the poverty alleviation work carried out there and to conduct interviews with families that had already been lifted out of poverty through that work.

'Are their living standards really acceptable now?' That was the question weighing down in my mind like a rock, and it was for that question that I was eager to find the answer.

The first visit I paid to a household in the region was after interviewing an official in charge of poverty alleviation work in the district of Yuanzhou. I presented the request to him rather abruptly, in the middle of our interview. As soon as I told the official that I wanted to see for myself some of the local families now lifted out of poverty, he took me directly to the home of an old man named Wang Pengyao.

In 2014 Wang's household was assessed and formally categorised as a 'poor household'. Wang's family at the time had a total of five members. Besides himself and his wife there were also their son and two daughters. This family's poverty was mostly due to the burden the cost of their three children's education placed on them.

Wang's house was located on a hillside two or three hundred metres away from the village committee's building. It came into view as we walked past a small cornfield, and just outside the house's courtyard there were a few apricot trees that gave it a rather festive air. Pressing against the wall of the courtyard there was a cowshed with three head of cattle and seven or eight sheep inside. The courtyard was quiet, spacious, and it was also kept very clean and tidy. The house itself had been rebuilt. The owner explained that it had been rebuilt with the help of a 25,000-yuan subsidy to poor families the government had offered, specifically for that purpose.

'Our three children are already grown up. They all finished middle school and left to find work far away from home. There are only the two of us now, old husband and wife, here at home working the land...' said Wang Pengyao, exactly sixty years old and in seemingly good health. He told me also that in his farmstead he cultivated twenty or so *mu*[1] of silage corn.

'We now have a calf born every year, and we can sell it for seven or eight thousand. It is one calf a year now that we sell, but in two years we'll be selling two, three calves a year... That comes in addition to the money our kids send back, and it is for sure enough for us not to have to worry. A year from now we reckon we'll have about ten thousand in savings. Compared to how it used to be, I can say I'm very happy!' Wang Pengyao said, completing this last sentence of his with a large smile.

Standing inside Wang's spacious courtyard and lifting my gaze to look around at the leafy tree canopies above, listening also to birds singing and smelling the sweet fragrance of the flowers, I couldn't help but take a few deep breaths and let out an emotional sigh:

'This place is much nicer than the place where I live in Beijing,' I said. 'Even if I compare it to my old home in Suzhou

---

1   One *mu* corresponds to 1/6 of an acre.

A peony oil production complex in the district of Yuanzhou, Guyuan prefecture

it'd be a very tough match!'

'Really?' Wang Pengyao asked with wide-open eyes, expecting me to confirm it, also turning a little red in the face.

'Air quality and the environment here are much better,' I told him in earnest. 'And you still get to enjoy a much freer lifestyle.

'Ha ha!' Wang Pengyao laughed merrily in reply, and you could tell that it was a laughter emerging from the bottom of his heart.

About a hundred metres beyond Wang Pengyao's home was Gu Chengzhong's courtyard, that of another once formally 'poor household'. And yet Gu's home was very obviously even more stylish and better off than Wang Pengyao's. Not only was Gu's courtyard more spacious, but his animal shed also contained more animals than Wang's, eight head in total, all Angus cattle.

Gu Chengzhong, who was sixty-two years old, told me that back in 2014, when his family was officially classified as a 'poor household', his family had a total of eight people: himself and his wife, plus two sons, two daughters, and two elderly individuals. Back then they owned a single ox to till 60 *mu* of land they managed to keep cultivated through loans. 'After a whole year of hard work and paying for the loans, we barely had enough to keep our stomachs half-full,' he said. 'Life was very hard…'

As Gu Chengzhong spoke of the past, tears welled up in his eyes.

'My parents left this world having gone through nothing but suffering,' he said. 'Had they lived just two or three years longer they'd have experienced something totally different.'

After the government introduced poverty alleviation programmes, Gu Chengzhong was able to get a subsidised loan and purchase three head of Angus cattle. Through his hard work he also managed to grow silage corn in his 60 *mu* of land. He then went from three head of cattle in his property to eight, while all his children managed to find work and started making money.

'Now the cattle alone make me twenty to thirty thousand

a year!' he said. 'We no longer need to worry about not having enough to eat or not having what to wear. And if we feel like splurging a little on better food, we just do it…'

The faces of Gu Chengzhong and his wife were telling me all I had to know. Theirs was a peasant family no longer in poverty, but now enjoying a life of plenty instead.

'If there are seven or eight head of cattle in a household, that family should be able to make from them a stable income of over 30,000 a year,' said the village official standing next to me.

'And in addition to what they make from cattle they'll also have income from other sources, such as chickens and orchards… All combined those can make for a very comfortable life.' I noticed that, from the moment I stepped into his courtyard, Gu Chengzhong could not stop smiling. That expression of happiness was only changed when the topic of the premature passing of his parents was touched upon. At all other times during our conversation, he was nothing but smiles and laughter.

But what impressed me the most was that the common people there were all very mindful of hygiene and the general cleanliness of their homes. Tables, cupboards, windowpanes, everything was kept spotlessly clean and tidily organised. There were, moreover, fragrant trees laden with fruit outside every home, and spacious areas both inside and beyond the courtyards, areas with plenty of shade from the trees and with plenty of cool and fresh air… When Gu Chengzhong and his wife, holding some pieces of cantaloupe and hot water ready to make tea, invited us to take a rest under the trees in his courtyard, we readily accepted the invitation. After eating a couple pieces of melon and savouring the tea, I took a few deep breaths of that fresh air and raised my head again to look around at that countryside which, no matter the direction I turned my gaze, always looked like some wonderland in a painting. I couldn't help but to feel emotional. Could such a life in such a place not be enough to anyone?

'We're going to another village, Mr He, and there you'll surely witness many other such touching scenes!' said the official from Yangzhou sitting next to me, and already filling me with anticipation.

'People here are so charming and we're already talking about leaving?' I said, wondering how I could simply get up and leave, revelling as I was in that wonderful rustic environment.

My friend from Ningxia then smiled and said:

'Are you not particularly interested in seeing the *Guyuan* of Guyuan?'

'I am,' I said.

'Well, the next place we have to visit is the *Guyuan* of Guyuan...'

'Really? Where is it?'

Visiting the poorest village in Xihaigu was the idea I had original put forward to that comrade there in charge of poverty alleviation. He then told me that the place I was looking for was in the prefecture of Guyuan. He formulated it that way, the *Guyuan* of Guyuan, because the place I wanted to see was supposedly the *poorest* of the poor.

'The place is only a short trip further down the road,' he said, and then towards the end of another short car ride going round hills and through mountain passes, the poverty alleviation officials pointed out to me a brand-new village with a few white walls and red-tiled rooftops. 'That village is under the jurisdiction of the county of Xiji, in the prefecture of Guyuan… It used to be called Lannitan[1], but in 2017 its name was changed to Hanjiang.'

'Hanjiang?!' I exclaimed. When I heard that a village that used to be known for its poverty had its name changed to a new one suggestive of a place with rivers and lakes aplenty, I had to stop and think about it. 'Is it because water is no longer scarce here?' I finally asked.

---

1 The name 'Lannitan' can be read as literally 'mud banks'

'Ha ha, Mr He, you're not too far off the mark,' one of the local officials laughed. 'But we'll have to keep the answer to that riddle to till after we have visited some of the formerly poor families here.'

'Ha, it seems like those *mud banks* have plenty of stories to tell!' I said, referring to the village's old name, but not really giving much thought any more about how the place's renaming had come about. Instead, my eyes just kept looking curiously ahead, past the hills and the pass, and at the village itself, a place in Xihaigu, a region commonly said to be 'barren' and once described as 'most unfit to human settlement'.

'You see, every cave at the foot of those hills there, either big or small, used to be the home of a villager…' said the local official to me, stretching his arm outside the car's window and pointing at a series of connected caves at the base of a large mountain.

'When were the villagers moved out of those caves,' I asked, unable to hold myself back as I saw along the way caves not unlike those Stone Age men used to inhabit.

'Not that long ago!' one of the officials, a man in his forties, rushed to answer me. 'We used to live in caves like that when I was a kid…'

'So that means people were living in caves like that as late as the 1970s and 80s?' I asked after doing some basic arithmetic in my head.

'Yes, that's about right,' he said. And just as he said it, the car stopped on a slope in front of some kind of ruins. 'About two or three years ago this used to be the village of Lannitan. Let's get out to look around!'

So I and my friends of the Yellow River Publishing and Media Group who accompanied me in the trip stepped off the car and walked towards some abandoned houses and courtyards under some trees. I saw then for the first time and in person the kind of place the people of Xihaigu would still be living in up to 2017. Each farmstead was composed of three or four dwellings, those were built with mud walls and broken tiles making up the roofs. Some of them were roofed instead with a sort of screen made of plastic and straw. Of the rooms inside the dwellings themselves, about half of them were in fact caves, dug into the

A house in the old village of Lannitan

mountainside, and the other half were built outside of the mountain, but leaning against the rock face. Because they were abandoned, weeds and shrubs grew wild all over the courtyards, making the dwellings look like they had been left uninhabited for centuries.

'If it weren't for General Secretary Xi Jinping's call for the whole country to support the poverty alleviation work we do here, it is most likely that people from our generation would still have to live in that kind of dwelling their whole lives!' one of the officials accompanying us said.

'Now there are neither one of you nor any poor people living in this kind of dwelling?' I asked, particularly interested in the answer to that question.

'Not any more,' said the official. 'And by the end of 2020 there will be no one in Xihaigu living in a dwelling like this! They will all be moved to new houses, with new courtyards!'

'You say so?' I said, unable to hold it back.

'I say so! That's how it is!' said the official, tapping his chest loudly.

'Very good!' I said, making another slapping sound with a fist against the other hand and then waving. 'Let's go. I want to see the new houses where the villagers live now.'

The Renaming of Lannitan

'Let's go! Let's go! That's three more minutes on the road…' said that official, already in a very upbeat mood from the moment we all got into the car.

'There was in Lannitan nothing but bitter wailing in the past, but Hanjiang is now a village with great joy to last…' intoned the official. 'Mr He, my little verses may be rubbish, but when you see for yourself this new Lannitan your eyes will be opened!'

'Was the change really that impressive?!' I asked, indeed sceptical.

'Believe it or not…' he said, and as he spoke the car reached a stretch of road over surprisingly flat land. After going up and down for such a long time, being on a stretch of flat road cleared our heads and had a refreshing effect on our ideas. It also put us all in much better moods. All around us we saw potato flowers and different types of mountain flowers for which I had no name. They clustered around the mountains, and seemed to rise, like a newly formed army contingent full of enthusiasm and zeal, placed there to greet us… The cool breeze blows gently and caresses our faces, getting our spirits even higher. The blue sky and white clouds above the valley touch and become one, turning into a Peach Blossom Valley, the sort of place where one forgets all about one's own thoughts and worries. Standing in the middle of a place like that, how could one not feel happy and light-hearted? How not to indulge in daydreaming?

'Here! Here! Come in and take a seat! Please!' we were greeted. After a long journey, and as we were still taking our deep breaths to recover, that warmth and sincere friendliness swept us almost like a hurricane into that peasant family's home.

'This is the home of Mr Su Xiaoping. A few years ago, his household was well-known in the area for just how poor it was. Look at his home now...' said the local official guiding us into Mr Su's home, a house shaped like an inverted L. It was a very spacious house inside, with the main room having perhaps something close to a hundred square metres. In that main room there were a TV set, a refrigerator, a wardrobe, basically everything needed for a complete living area. I noticed also two details in particular. The first was that the clothes hanging on the walls of Mr Su's home were all new and not of inferior quality, and the second was the brand-new small heater, undoubtedly meant to keep people inside the room warm during the winter. 'This heater was provided by the government. Every household now has one,' they explained it to me. And Mr Su was out working in the village, Mrs Su added while she cut some pieces of watermelon for us.

'How's life for you now?' I asked, wanting to know whether the Su family had really been lifted out of poverty.

'Very good! And it gets better every year!' Mrs Su replied very enthusiastically. She seemed to be an expert on every kind of housework. 'Our babies are both studying now, because the government has given them an exemption from the school fees. We also have nine head of cattle and a dozen or so sheep here. We have plenty to eat and plenty to wear! In addition, we also grow potatoes and some other things. Things are getting better and better! Since I got married more than ten years ago, we moved houses three times, but now we don't need to move… We were very poor before, and because of that we were always moving. But now we don't have to move any more! Look, isn't this house a good place to live? Just a few days ago some university students from Shanghai came and told us they wanted to rent our house. They were painters and said they could pay some tens of thousands a year. Some of them said they wanted to stay here to paint, some others that they just wanted to live here with us. Don't you people have nice places to live in big cities like ours here?'

'No we don't, not at all!' I told her without hesitation. 'We have nothing like what you have here, two houses in a plot of land as big as a football pitch, and this beautiful scenery around, this fresh air... Not even a vice-minister could dream of living in a place like this...'

'Vice-minister? What vice-minister?' she asked.

'Any of those national government leaders we see on TV day and day again... Not even they can live in places as nice as this one here!'

'Ha ha...' Mrs Su laughed loudly, bringing her hand to her mouth to cover it and even bending her trunk down a little. 'You're making fun of me, right?'

'It's true,' I answered her in a serious tone. 'This nice environment you have here, such good living conditions, it's definitely not something just about anyone can have.'

'So I'm the luckiest person in the world now I guess?' Mrs Su concluded joyfully.

'Maybe not the luckiest of all, but a very lucky one for sure!' I told her.

'Then I have to thank President Xi! Also thank the government, thank Fujian, thank Hanjiang...' Mrs Su said, suddenly breaking out in a stream of thanksgiving.

'Fujian? Hanjiang? What's up with those?' I asked her, a little confused. 'Why thank Fujian and Hanjiang?'

'The changes we see in this village today are a result of the

Cooperation on Poverty Alleviation Between Fujian and Ningxia that comrade Xi Jinping started when he was in office in Fujian. The cooperation of our district with the district of Hanjiang in the prefecture of Putian in Fujian was what transformed this village. So that's also the answer to the question you asked before, as to why the village changed its name from Lannitan to Hanjiang,' the local official told me, providing an answer to that mystery at last.

'I see!' I said.

'Folks, y'all know that the nice life we all enjoy today is thanks to the great kindness of President Xi Jinping and the people of Fujian, right?' I provoked them all, directing my question at Mrs Su, who stood right next to me.

'I know! I know!' Mrs Su said. 'Were it not for President Xi we wouldn't have such a good life! And if it weren't for the help of the people of Fujian our lives couldn't have improved so fast! That's why last year people here in the village suggested that we change the village's name, and everyone raised their hands to agree with that. I raised both hands, he he he...' Mrs Su laughed, bending her trunk forward again as she did so.

'Now tell me, how exactly is your life different from what it used to be?' I asked her.

She answered me apparently without stopping to think about

it:

'I came to Lannitan right after I got married. At that time I was always digging and digging and digging inside those *yaodong* caves. I dug all year round. After that I moved to Huaishulin, and life there was just getting stuck and tripping in the mud all the time. But now? Now I can wear clean trainers and walk on paved streets. That's so much more comfortable…'

'You do make a good picture of it,' I said with sincerity, and then I waved at the local officials. 'Let's go! We have to see how those *mud banks* of Lannitan were turned into Hanjiang!'

'Let's visit the village committee then,' they said, and we all started moving towards the door.

'Hey! You can't go! Can't go yet!' Mrs Su intervened, suddenly catching up with us in the courtyard and grabbing me by the arm to make sure I wasn't going anywhere. 'You come here, don't eat anything, and then just walk away? Come and eat something, then you go!'

'It's… uh…' I mumbled, at a loss as to what I should do. I wanted to break free, but Mrs Su, true to her enthusiastic hospitality, clung firmly to my arm and would not let me take even one step away from her. I realised then that she wholeheartedly wished for our group to stay and have a meal at her house.

Mrs Su enthusiastically inviting the author and the rest of his group to have a meal at her house

My schedule of interviews, however, was very tight, and so I couldn't stay for the meal she offered us. But no matter how much I tried to explain this to her, Mrs Su would simply not let me go, so I was 'stuck' there for the time being. I leant my body a little aside, meaning to leave, but when I did so Mrs Su grabbed my arm even more firmly and dragged me back inside the house… That short scene greatly amused my Ningxia colleagues who were there to witness it. One by one they took out their mobile phones and started to take pictures. Afterwards a picture of me being 'forcibly drafted' was posted to Wechat Moments and received a boatload of 'likes'.

The common people are often extremely generous in their hospitality, so it was only after the local officials had explained the situation over and over again to her that we managed to untangle ourselves. But just as our group was about to leave Mrs Su's house and get back into the car, we realised that Miss Yan, one of the members of our travelling group, was nowhere to be seen.

'Miss Yan! We have to go!' someone called out. And then we saw Miss Yan stepping out of another house of the Su family's farmstead. With her right hand she offered support to an old lady who, notwithstanding, seemed to be still very firm and healthy. That was a very heart-warming scene, particularly more touching as a result of the redness around Miss Yan's eyes. We were all also a little emotional at seeing that, and more so when Miss Yan said:

'This place is so nice! People here are so nice! I don't quite feel like leaving…'

In fact, none of us really wanted to leave. Wouldn't it be a very happy existence to live without worries in a place like that? As our car drove away from the Su household and the little village it was a part of we were all a little sad to be leaving. The car moved ahead, but our gazes all kept turning back…

Later, as we approached the site of Hanjiang's village committee, we were greeted by the sight of a very modern rural village and its new centre of social life in the form of a very wide main square. Reportedly every rural village in the prefecture of Guyuan now had a square like that one, featuring a broad open space for villagers to hold meetings and other cultural events, and also an area for the practice of sports and physical training, complete with all the equipment suitable also for both children and the elderly to exercise. That served us as a reminder that people in rural areas were now enjoying lives that were on a par with the lives of people in large and mid-sized cities.

Just by looking at those villages and their brand-new houses one can know that Xihaigu is today a far cry from the poverty it was once known for. In its past the village of Lannitan was also part of a township. That was the township of Piancheng. A full reference to the village, when all the subdivisions it belonged to were accounted for, was 'the village of Lannitan, in the township of Piancheng, in the county of Xiji'. That long reference by itself tells a lot about the place.

The villagers told me that the village of Lannitan, which means *mud banks*, did not take its name from any regular abundance of rainfall. In that small mountain village, located up a very windy road, a drop of rain was as precious as oil, and people had in fact to travel five kilometres to fetch water, which they carried on their backs on the way back to their village. Bringing back a load of dirty brown water with the help of an ox or donkey meant spending hours on the road, and because it was such an arid place, whenever there was a sudden torrential downpour all the bends along the road became massive quagmires, nothing but soft mud traps that rendered the road impassible. That's how Lannitan, or "Mud Banks", got its name.

'Of the 330 families living here before 2016, 192 moved out due to poverty. Some went to Xinjiang, others to Inner Mongolia, often relying on relatives and friends to help them settle down in a new home, find work, and basically survive. Back then there used to be a saying that circulated among everyone in the village that said that "if you can pull yourself out of this bunch of sheep guts that is this place, you'll be able to see the golden path outside..." But our roots are here after all, in the land of our ancestors. Even if one of us leaves and goes somewhere very far, ties of affection will remain in place and make the person homesick, thinking of the family they left behind. Those ties will keep pulling them back to this place. Experiences such as that often made the people of Lannitan heartbroken...' explained Qin Zhenbang, first secretary of the local village committee, his eyes turning red as he told me of how much poverty the villagers used to have to endure.

'We really have to thank Xi Jinping! And thank the people of Fujian!' Qin Zhenbang added, and as he raised his tearful gaze again his eyes beamed with gratefulness and joy. 'Lannitan was transformed in only three or four years. It is like one of those people who live away from their hometown for a very long time, and when they return to visit their relatives no one can recognise them any more... You see, now there is a broad road connecting the village to the rest of the world, paved with concrete. Traffic can flow freely both ways, and cars no longer need to stop to give way. It used to take a long time to get here, but now it's only ten minutes or so on the road. Every house now has running water. The arrival of running water not only put an end to a struggle the common people from this place had been dealing with for centuries, but also caused many of those who had been planning to leave to change their minds. If the village of Lannitan could be lifted out of poverty in only two years it was because there was now running water and a road!'

When I heard that I opened wide my sceptical eyes:

'Two years? There's no way!' I exclaimed.

'That's the truth I'm telling you,' Qin Zhenbang smiled. 'We have to thank also, of course, all the help we received from Fujian's district of Hanjiang during those two years. With their help taking this place out of poverty was like hopping on an helicopter and taking off…'

It was only later that I found out what that help from Fujian's district of Hanjiang consisted of in concrete terms. They gave the village a main paved road connecting it to the outside world and also other paved roads connecting every household in the village, granting easy access to motor vehicles. They also provided water supply connections to every household and interest-free loans for cattle purchases and greenhouse construction. They built a 'poverty alleviation workshop' for those families unable to start their own independent businesses or line of work. And so on. The help provided included in total more than ten such measures.

'And all of that came in addition to the local government's implementation of the central government's poverty alleviation programme, which included providing credit for the remodelling and rebuilding of residences, creating pension schemes for the elderly, and providing subsidies for the children's education. That's how it was possible to completely transform Lannitan in just a little over two years…' Qin Zhenbang told me with pride as he took me to visit the local administrative services centre.

Next to the building of the local village committee there was a small building with 50 or 60 square metres, inside of which

there was not only a small supermarket, but also a citizens'
services centre providing assistance on all sorts of government
programmes, and a separate counter serving as a local branch
of the Xiji Rural Commercial Bank. Moreover, there was a big
slogan on a wall that caught my eye. It said: *'No need to go far
to manage life's small matters, all services are right here next to
you'.* I found myself wondering whether even city people would
have access to that level of convenience? And yet the common
people of that small village in the mountains, a village that used
to rank among the poorest in the country, could now have a taste
of modernity in their lives that is very much like what people in
large cities experience.

In the poverty alleviation workshop, a white building roofed
with blue tiles, I found about half a dozen workers making
electronic components. They told me that their working hours
were quite flexible since they used a piecework system. That way
workers were free to make their own schedules. I saw on a wall
the pictures of 22 of those workers, and nearly all of them were
women. 'Our male villagers all work in the village making even
more money. Women have to be home to take care of children
and do the house chores, so the flexibility of work here suits
them better,' Qin Zhenbang explained.

'How much can you make in a month?' I asked one of the

women working there. The woman, who looked a little over thirty, raised her head, blushed a little, and said:

'Fifteen, sixteen hundred!'

'Is it enough?' I asked, and no sooner had I asked that than felt quite stupid for asking.

'How can I say it...' the woman began to reply. 'It's a little less than what people can make in other places, but I'm working less than 300 metres from home. I can come here any time I like, and if I need to go back home to take care of the children or do something in the house I can just go. It's really worth it.'

The mild tone of the woman's voice as she answered my question sent a wave of warmth billowing up inside my chest. It was the warmth of a home that came from these women, who were already wives and mothers. And how important that warmth is for a poor woman living in a remote mountain area! Many are those who have lost their children, have lost their families, and ultimately themselves, because they lacked that warmth.

That poverty alleviation workshop was not very large. But as I walked out of that place, perhaps of a kind unique in the world, in my heart stirred countless different emotions. How could a country, with the largest population in the world and also with a large part of that population living in poverty, be raised out of poverty in no more than a few decades? It could only be because on every front, such as Party, government, armed forces, educational institutions, and business, from the central government down to the local level, people were fully mobilised in that direction and moved with great impetus, so strong in fact as to wash away all the obstacles hindering the progress of our nation, and then change reality and transform the land. But it was also because this all started from the simplest, most ordinary goals and aspirations in the day-to-day lives of common people, who went on to strive for the humblest aspirations and for the things dearest to their hearts. It was that way that the largest battle against poverty in history could be won.

And just as we left the small village of 'Mud Banks' another heavy downpour started to fall over Xihaigu, moving from south to north and lasting for several hours. Only when we reached Tongxin, our next destination, did the clouds clear up and the blue returned to the sky. The sun shone brightly again on the Liupan Mountains, illuminating both flanks of the verdant hills, bestowing on them in an instant vivid colours and exuberance. In that fresh and clear air, my mind went back to a fact that had long been common knowledge among the people, namely the poverty alleviation programme that Xi Jinping had started while serving as deputy secretary of Fujian's provincial Party committee in 1996, and with which he had been involved ever since, that programme was the Cooperation on Poverty Alleviation Between Fujian and Ningxia. In Beijing, in Ningxia, and in many other places, I have heard people sing the praises of that Cooperation, and tell me about how it truly transformed Xihaigu and Ningxia… So yes, now I have seen it all for myself. I have seen that transformation, those inconceivable changes, and they left me speechless. And everything that I saw made me extremely happy.

That was poetry, that was song.

That was sunshine and hope, happiness and beauty.

And it was there to be seen also the brilliant faith of our Communist Party members, their lofty aspirations, and also that slow-flowing warm-heartedness that comes from understanding the common aspirations of the people.

Chapter 1

The Tears of the Mountains and the Longing for the Waters

A Place Where Once 'People Ate People'

There are two major mountain ranges in Ningxia: The Liupan Mountains and the Helan Mountains. The latter is embraced and irrigated by the Yellow River, producing what is known as 'the Jiangnan north of the Great Wall'. But the Liupan Mountains are a different matter. They are at a great distance from the waters of the Yellow River, and have, as a result, always been associated with barrenness and extreme poverty. Many Chinese have formed the idea they have of the Liupan Mountains from the following poem by Mao Zedong:

Liupan Mountains

> *- to the tune of Qing Ping Yue*

The sky is high above us, the clouds are pale,

we watch the wild geese vanish in the south.

Men are we not if we don't reach the Great Wall,

we who have travelled twenty thousand li.

Up there on the crest of the Liupan range,

red banners have fluttered in the west wind.

Today we hold in our hands that long rope,

when will we tie up the Grey Dragon?

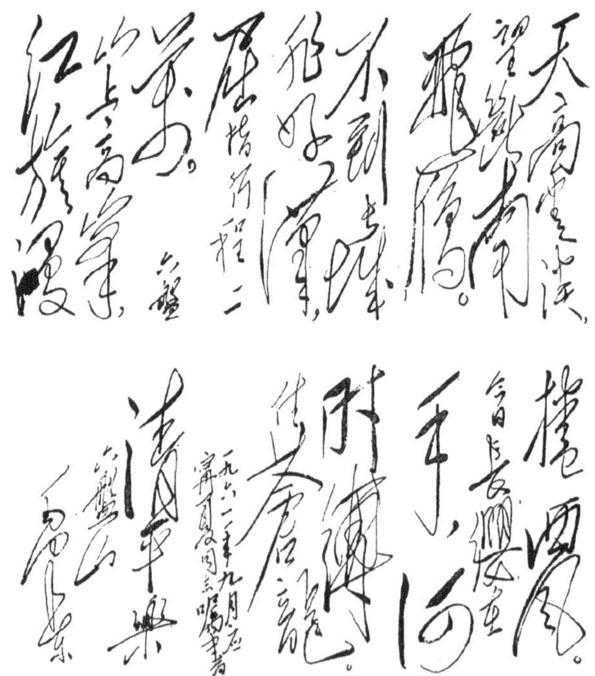

Through the eyes of Mao Zedong in his poem the Liupan are revolutionary mountains, and in them are embodied a spirit of daring that can conquer all geographic features of a landscape.

I have learned both from history books and from still extant ruins that the 'Great Wall' Mao Zedong refers to in that poem corresponds in fact to the most ancient fortifications to receive that denomination, namely the Great Wall of the Qin Dynasty. It enters the county of Xiji in Ningxia from county of Jingning, in the province of Gansu. Then it moves north along the east bank of the Hulu River, passing through the villages of Dongpo, Baolin and Mingrong in the township of Jiangtaibao, also in the county of Xiji. From there it takes a turn to the south-east in the township of Jiangtaibao before taking a turn to the east and entering the town of Malian. After that it follows the course of the Malian River in a north-easterly direction, going through the township of Zhangyi in the district of Yangzhou, crossing the Didi Valley and reaching the southern part of Sunjiazhuang. It then assumes an easterly route again, traverses the Haizi Gorge, and reaches the north of Wuzhuang, then going around the township of Guanting in a section known as the 'Great Wall Liang' and going through Mingzhuang and Guozhuang till it reaches the western bank of the Qingshui River… On the 5th of October of 1935, Mao Zedong led the First Front of the Shaanxi-

Gansu Unit of the Chinese Workers' and Peasants' Red Army out of Jieshipu in Jingning, province of Gansu, and marched east through Jiangtai and Malian in the county of Xiji, setting up camp that night in the village of Shanjiaji, in the town of Xinglong. On the 7th of October, Mao Zedong and the Red Army crossed the last mountain range of the Long March, the Liupan Mountains. He was at the time greatly inspired by the fighting spirit of the officers and regular soldiers of the Red Army, who, despite being faced with countless difficulties, still managed to attain victory. So he expressed his feelings in the poem titled *Liupan Mountains – to the tune of Qing Ping Yue*, manifesting in vivid verses his revolutionary fervour and his certainty in the ultimate victory. And so, in the minds of the Chinese people, the Liupan Mountains remained ever since associated with the Revolution.

But, for the people of Xihaigu, what kind of mountains are the Liupan?

The more well-read people of Ningxia, particularly those from Xihaigu, will tell people, with a gleam in their eyes, that their land is 'one of the cradles of Chinese Civilisation' and that 'the Yellow Emperor once conducted a tour of inspection in the Jitou Mountain'. This 'Jitou Mountain' is the one mentioned in Sima Qian's *Records of the Historian*. The *Encyclopaedia of*

Ningxia (*Ningxia Baike Quan Shu*) also includes an entry that reads: 'In the Liupan Mountains, inside the county of Jingyuan, we find the source of the Jing River. (…) And because the crest of those mountains looks like a cockscomb, they took in antiquity the name of *Jitou*, meaning "chicken's head".' During that time, on both sides of the Jing River, 'vegetation was luxuriant, and a moist breeze blew over the cliffs'. In Gaoling, in the province of Shaanxi, the Jing River joins the Wei River. And from historical times we have inherited the saying that 'the Jing is clear, while the Wei is turbid' (*jing qing wei zhuo*), meaning that, because the Jing flowed from the verdant Liupan Mountains, its waters were limpid, viridescent and rippled, whereas the waters of the Wei were turbid because of all the sediment they dragged from upstream. And so today we can read songs and verses such as this one from the *Classic of Poetry*:

> *The muddiness of the Jing comes from the Wei,*
> *but its bottom may be seen around the islets.*
> *You feast with the wife you just married,*
> *and think me not worth of your company.*

But after thousands of years of incessant erosion by northerly winds and of suffering the flames of war, those 'Loong

Mountains'[1] gradually turned barren and desolate, and so did the lands around them, to a point when they became as described in the following verses by the Ming poet Li Mengyang:

> *Water turned salty and the grass died, horses could neither eat nor drink,*
> *travellers passing by cried bitterly under the shadow of the Great Wall.*

That once abundantly irrigated and fertile land turned arid and bitterly impoverished, a change that brought with it endless suffering to the people. The sky dried up, the land was in distress, and people died young. Those were then the 'three basic motifs of the Ningxia of old', used in the making of a great number of outstanding 'frontier poems', poems that depict much of the sorrow and pain experienced in the history of the Chinese nation.

> *In a cool autumn of the eighth month along a desolate mountain pass,*
> *the howling wind breaks the dead grasses on the*

---

1 Pronounced in Chinese the same way as 'Mount Long' (*Long Shan*), a mountain on the border between Shaanxi and Gansu.

Heavenly Mountains.

(…)

*I will send you my dear sir amidst the plaintive cries
of the reed flutes,*

*to stand on the Qin Mountains looking into the
distance at Mount Long.*

Those verses, of a poem titled *Hujia Ge*, or '*Song of the Reed
Flute*' were sung by the Tang Dynasty poet Cen Shen as he bid
farewell to a friend. They invite people to a heartfelt appreciation
of that touching sadness and sorrow of the frontier, also
expressed in one of the verses towards the end of the poem:

*Every night in the remote towns of the frontier many
are the melancholy dreams.*

The sorrow and pathos of the Liupan Mountains and of
Xihaigu are like stars hanging in the starry night sky of the
Chinese nation. Or like dust obtained from crushing and
grinding every stone of the ancient fortifications at the Xiao Pass,
dust that now floats among the words inside history books.

At the same time as new soldiers and officials were
constantly being called up for duty to relieve other ones at the

border garrisons, the borders themselves would move, and the territory of the empire would grow and shrink, growing in times of prosperity and shrinking in times of decline. Only the local people of those border regions, who lived there, remained rooted to the land and never went anywhere. It was, for that reason, always the local people who suffered the most whenever conditions took a turn for the worse, either because of natural disasters, or due to social and political upheavals. To fully grasp this point and the great suffering experienced in that land it is not necessary to look for events that took place millennia into the past. It suffices to take as an example the Haiyuan earthquake that happened on the 16th of December of 1920, merely about a century ago, which was dubbed the 'tremor that went round the globe'. It was so called because, reportedly, the seismic waves unleashed by that event reverberated around the entire globe twice, being captured by all 96 seismic stations that existed all around the world at the time. The effects of the tremor reached level 12 on the Mercalli Intensity Scale near its epicentre, and level 10 or above in an area of about 100,000 square kilometres around it. That meant that basically the entire district of Xihaigu was severely affected by the tremor. About a year later, *National Geographic*, the American magazine, referred to that earthquake as one of the most devastating tremors in world history, and also as one of the most tragic disasters to have ever taken place. That publication, in an article titled *Where the Mountains Walked*, thus reported on how the local people, victims of the disaster, described the earthquake: 'Mountains that moved in the night; landslides that eddied like waterfalls, crevasses that swallowed houses and camel trains, and villages that were swept away under a rising sea of loose earth...'[1].

The Haiyuan earthquake was a disaster of a kind seldom seen in the history of China, both in terms of severity and of the size of the affected area. Its severity was such as to pose a challenge to the imagination of an ordinary person. According to some contemporary reports, the tremor shook electrical light fixtures as far off as Beijing so violently as to make people feel dizzy. In Shanghai clocks stopped, their oscillating mechanisms brought to a halt, and hanging light fixtures also swayed from side to side. In Guangzhou roof tiles flew off rooftops and bricks fell off buildings. Also in Hong Kong it was reported that the tremor was felt by most people in the city. In Kuanzhou, a place north of Xi'an and hundreds of kilometres away from the earthquake's epicentre, more than 400 coal miners were buried inside a mineshaft that collapsed; and in Guanyuan, in the province of Sichuan and nearly a thousand kilometres away,

---

1   *National Geographic - May 1922*

more than a thousand people were either swallowed up by huge crevices the earthquake opened up in the ground, or else crushed to death as the buildings they were in collapsed on them... It can thus only be assumed that by the tremor's epicentre, in the district of Xihaigu, the devastation was of an even more frightful scale! A local villager who survived the disaster reported that he was walking along the street when the earthquake struck. He said that he suddenly felt as if someone had very abruptly shoved him down to the ground, sending him rolling for over ten feet and making him lose consciousness right there where he lay. By the time he came round and looked, the houses on both sides of the street had all been reduced to rubble and a thick layer of dust had risen and covered the sky. The whole town around him was then dead and quiet. Another witness of the disaster thus described the events: when the earthquake struck, strong gales suddenly blew, bringing in a thick fog that darkened everything, the ground let out a reddish glow and thundering sounds rolled and rumbled under one's feet. The intensity of that earthquake can be grasped from the fact that many Chinese references to it make use not of simple adjectives, but of expressions that are in fact descriptions of concrete scenes, expressions such as 'moving mountains' (*da shan zoudong*) and 'rivers changing course' (*heliu gai dao*). When I visited Xiji to conduct interviews, members of older generations drew my attention to the barrier lake that still exists to this day in their grieved land. That barrier lake was formed by a landslide at Dangjiacha, triggered by the earthquake, and serves as a very concrete illustration of the expression 'rivers changing course'. As to that other Chinese-language expression, 'moving mountains', in Xihaigu a large number of overlapping rock fractures can be found just about everywhere high up in the more mountainous areas and serve to illustrate it. A friend of mine, also a writer and originally from Haiyuan, gave me an extra piece of information: he told me that since he was still a child he knew that the people of his home village were generally unwilling to talk about the earthquake of 1920, the reason being that the tremor, according to the people of Haiyuan themselves, killed 59% of the population living in their county at the time. Mortality was so high, my friend also told me, because, at the time, the region had gone through over a year without rainfall, what made the walls of the *yaodong*, the traditional cave dwellings of the region, unusually loose and brittle. 'Therefore,' my friend said. 'When the big earthquake hit, the walls and ceilings of the caves collapsed inwards all at once, towards the centre of the caves, coming in like giant fists that suddenly clenched tight, crushing people to death inside them.' This my friend heard from his grandfather, who was one of the lucky survivors of the disaster.

Just by trying to imagine that scene, indistinctly as one might, it is possible to picture how devastating a blow that earthquake was for the people of Xihaigu at the time. And how many people died in that earthquake after all? That remains a mystery to this day… The old Chinese government later claimed in the papers that the death toll was about 250,000 people killed, whereas foreign news sources put it at 'no fewer than 300,000 people'. The exact figure of how many people died, however, is still unknown. We can take, nonetheless, a report from a local county record of the time that stated that, because the death toll was so high, three months after the earthquake there were still scattered around a particular town 934 unburied bodies, left so unburied due to a lack of manpower. And there were many other reports such as that one. Most tragic of all, because the area affected by the earthquake was too large, the government was unable to provide assistance to all who needed it, leaving in the disaster area many people who were alive, but who 'lack clothing, lack food, have no place to live and roam about the land aimlessly, a dread sight to see, terrible even when only hearing about it'. And so came the reports of 'the living eating the dead', 'the strong killing the weak', and other such tragedies…

It has been a century since the earthquake, and so still

living survivors of that disasters are very few indeed. But for the people of Ningxia, and particularly for the people of Xihaigu, the Haiyuan Earthquake, as it became known historically, is still a topic that instils great fear. Not long after the earthquake, an American reporter paid a visit to the region of Xihaigu. With tears running down her cheeks she very succinctly described the devastation she had witnessed, mentioning only the complete desolation seen just about everywhere. That reported was Anna Louise Strong, whose name would later become very familiar to the Chinese.

Anna Louise Strong would also later visit Shaanxi and Yan'an, and she certainly must have heard that, from the winter of the year after her visit to Xihaigu to the spring and summer of the year after that, and before Xihaigu could recover from the effects of the earthquake, a drought even more devastating than the earthquake itself ravaged once again that already utterly destitute land. That was from the end of 1928 to the middle of 1929, and during that time every inch of land in Xihaigu was shedding tears and blood...

According to the records of the time, the apricot trees in Xihaigu bloomed twice in the year of 1928, but produced no fruit. That same year each stalk of spring wheat also produced two ears of grain, but harvests still failed. For several months, from the winter of 1928 to the summer of 1929, there was no rainfall anywhere in the region of Xihaigu. The land became so dry that it developed cracks. Crops died, trees lost all their leaves and withered, and even the stones on the Liupan Mountains were subject to such intense heat that they also cracked. A famine as never seen before ensued, and it affected all of Ningxia, from the Liupan Mountains in the south and all the way north around both flanks of the Helan Mountains. Even the Yellow River was reduced to a trickle 'as thin as child's urine', as it was described. According to the official statistics of the time, the drought affected a total of 60 counties, and caused either the death or the forced migration of as many as one million people. In the wake of a tour of inspection, members of the China Huayuang Disaster Relief Cooperative issued a report that concluded that the severity of those disasters was 'unprecedented', stating also that it was 'not at all surprising that people have resorted to cannibalism'.

A scholar based in the county of Guyuan at the time penned a work titled *Notes from the Famine of 1929*, in which he stated:

'(...)The misery that has befallen the people in southern Ningxia as a result of the hunger caused by the disasters is too difficult to describe with words.

Some people fleeing the famine arrived in Guyuan willing to exchange anything for food. Even girls of marriageable age were given to strangers as wives in exchange for grain. Young and beautiful girls offered to work as domestic servants, asking for nothing more than food to appease their hunger in return. Middle-aged women, driven away from their lands by the famine, would rather become someone's concubine in order to have anything to eat at all. And also children, just about reaching an age when they could recognise someone as their father, expected only to be adopted by anyone, regardless of that person's value.

In Qingshixia, to the south of Guyuan, there was a widow of surname Sun who had refused to remarry and who had been taking care of her three young children all by herself. For four days in a row she had nothing to give to her children to eat, and so her three children remained around her crying without stop, to the point that she could no longer endure it. Seeing no other alternative, she took some soil and made some cakes with it, which she then put into a cooking pot, pretending to her children that she was making some pancakes for them to eat. Because the pot was covered with a lid, the children believed it and stopped crying. But a long time passed without their mother daring do lift the lid from the pot, so the children eventually gathered around that pot and started crying again, while trying to open it. The mother tried to stop them, but the children ignored her and grabbed the lid of the pot. At her wits' end, and overcome by extreme grief, the mother rushed to an apricot tree in her backyard and hanged herself. The children, having opened the pot with the "mud cakes" inside, nibbled and nibbled at them, but soon realised that they did not taste like food. They went out crying and looking for their mother, and found her in the backyard, already dead. They started pulling at her legs and cried so mournfully that even Heaven shed tears...

There was also a well-off man in a town north of Guyuan who had only one son, still a child. That only son of his was lured away and then strangled to death by two beggars. When that man heard about what had happened he went out immediately in pursuit of the beggars. But the beggars, fearful that the man would catch up with them and take the child's body away from them, started to bite at the body as they ran away, biting off pieces of flesh from the dead child's arms and legs. The man finally caught up with the beggars, and to his great astonishment the two beggars did nothing but kneel down before him and uttered nothing but a plea for a quick death. That well-off man had been known for his extreme stinginess, but on that occasion, confronted with two beggars who had murdered his son and eaten the flesh from the child's body, all he could do was let out a loud wail, swing his arms up in the air in despair, and then walk away. That's how helpless and shattered that man was!

Because too many people were dying from starvation in Guyuan, coffins and straw mats were in short supply there for some time, and the men whose line of business was to carry coffins and bury people saw a surge in demand for their services. Later it was discovered that there were many among those coffin bearers who simply decided to quit their work and commit suicide, preferring to go down to face the King of Hell. Because of that the corpses of the deceased began to accumulate in piles left on the streets, so many of them in fact that the authorities had no option but to issue a proclamation explicitly ordering "the burial of those who perished due to starvation". From that the severity of the misery famine caused that year can be fathomed.'

The misery and abject poverty caused by natural disasters thus have deep historical roots in Xihaigu. And that misery and poverty also extended northwards, towards central and northern Ningxia. How could the poverty and pain this land has seen even be described? Even prior to the great earthquake and the great famine, Zuo Zongtang had referred to Xihaigu at the imperial court as 'the most barren and poorest place in the world'. There is no knowing what that famous minister would have said had he seen Xihaigu in the wake of those two great disasters. I can only take the liberty to imagine his words for him, and they would be something like this:

'The suffering of Xihaigu is the greatest suffering in the world!'

Dreams are a 'Sea' Wider Than any Sea

Human civilisation, in the course of its evolution, has managed some radical changes to the face of the Earth, many 'man-made miracles'. But suffering and poverty are two things that humanity has always found very difficult to get rid of. All the turmoil seen in the world throughout history and to this date was largely a product of those two things. Karl Marx predicted that, among the ruling classes that preceded the advent of socialism, there would be no regime or ruling party capable of freeing a country or nation from poverty and suffering. And even a large proletarian party, a communist party, would have to struggle unrelentingly over a long time to achieve that.

So, under the leadership of the Communist Party of China, was Xihaigu really able to shake off suffering and poverty?

That is a problem mankind faces all over the world, and it presents a challenge to all Marxist proletarian parties, and to the Communist Party of China in particular. The first country in the world ruled by a communist party, the Soviet Union, was ultimately unable, under the leadership of Lenin and Stalin, to free itself from either poverty or suffering. Will China be able to achieve what they did not? Are we really able to do it? The members of the Communist Party of China, who run a country that was once home to hundreds of millions of the world's poor, also ask themselves this question. Their task is to lead the Chinese living in the poorest and most backward places out of that poverty and backwardness. Among those places there are large impoverish regions such as Ningxia, in which there is Xihaigu, once categorised by the United Nations as a place 'most unsuitable for human settlement and survival'. Can the members of the Communist Party of China take on the responsibility of making such a transformation happen?

'Even if you can't do it, you still have to bear that responsibility!' Comrade Mao Zedong once said, consciously taking upon himself as well that responsibility as he addressed leading Communist Party members on the day the People's Republic of China was founded.

In Ningxia, and particularly in the region of Xihaigu, banditry used to be a widespread social cancer alongside poverty. In the early years of the People's Republic of China, pacification of the land and the suppression of local bandits were among the highest policy priorities for the leaders of the Communist Party. Once pacification and the suppression of banditry had been achieved in Ningxia, the people's government set up by the Communist Party's leadership turned their attention to the questions of whether the people of Xihaigu had clothes to make it through the winter and of whether they had any food at all to put in their bellies (at the time the concept of being 'underfed' was not seen as relevant). After those questions were taken care of, the top priority became to provide drinking water to the people.

Xihaigu was a place where drinking water was perhaps more precious than life itself. The name of Xihaigu includes a character that is read as '*hai*' and that means 'sea'. Perhaps it is because of that 'sea' in the name of the place that the longing for water is so deeply rooted in the hearts of the local people. That is a sort of longing that never disappears, and so even after many generations people still carry in their hearts the desire to chase dreams that are in fact unattainable illusions. It is that 'sea' in the name of Xihaigu that takes hold of minds and makes children daydream in vain and cry till they have no more tears to cry, makes the breasts of mothers dry up and look like loose skin on a dead horse, and makes many old people leave this world without having realised their real dreams. That is also what makes countless people who want to leave the Liupan Mountains turn back halfway, and also people who would want to come to the Liupan Mountains hesitate and turn away.

There was a time when Xihaigu was for me only a place in Ningxia I had heard about. But then I met the writers Shi Shuqing and Ma Jinlian who had both grown up in Xihaigu, and who are members of a new generation of writers from Ningxia. Much of what I would later learn about Ningxia and Xihaigu I learned from their works, and also from conversations with them. I have also seen a picture Shi Shuqing has taken of the vastness of the desert. In that picture the only things we can see are the undulating outlines of the sand dunes and the contours made by the shadows of those dunes… It really looks like a picture of a rough sea with its mighty waves. But instead of being a blue sea, it is a sea of a dirty yellow hue, making people feel a great sense of oppression, of having one's emotions stifled. That is a desert, a place with hardly any vegetation, and where rainfall is a very rare occurrence indeed. And even on those rare occasions when rain does fall, it amounts to something like a small trickle from a barely open tap hitting our bodies, just about removing a little of the dust that has accumulated on it and revealing a very coarse skin and flesh underneath. The desert is like a dry sea where, for most of the year, the sun is shining. When the sun is high up in the sky, the vastness of the desert looks like a burning landscape, and you can't help but feel like you're being dried up with heat inside an oven, and even breathing becomes very difficult.

This is how Xihaigu usually is. And in the eyes of the local people and the local writers, this Xihaigu is properly a '*hai*', that is, a 'sea'.

It was a rough sea, with ferocious waves.

In the endlessly powerful roaring of this sea world everything seems to be in constant turbulence, while also immersed in a deep, wide, and everlasting loneliness.

Amidst that tempestuousness one is lonesome and

self-contained, and in that loneliness there is an irresistible tempestuousness.

Shi Shuqing is from the county of Haiyuan, in Xihaigu. It is his belief that his hometown is the place 'where the sea originally was, the source of the sea, and the original sea'. He explained it to us:

> *Only those who have been here will understand how unworthy this place is of its name.*
>
> *This is the driest sea in the world.*
>
> *Many of the people who live here go through their entire lives without knowing what a real ship looks like. Many, of course, have also never seen a fish.*
>
> *Not only there are no fish for as far as the eyes can see, but there are also no trees in this vast and distressed stretch of land. There is nothing but those bare mountains allowing not vegetation, but only hopelessness to grow. There is nothing but this huge expanse of dry sea…*

Shi Shuqing left Xihaigu after making a name for himself, and has seen a real sea. So he is in a position to use the metaphor of a 'dry sea' when talking about the '*hai*', the 'sea', in the name of Xihaigu. That's a piece of wisdom that comes from having left the place. It is not, however, how the people who have never left Xihaigu would picture that same 'hai', that same 'sea', in their own minds.

'The sea? It's just sweat from the rocks coming together in one place!' a child who had never attended school once told me. There was no television in his home, and the only world he had ever seen ever since being born was the world of endless sand dunes outside his home and of the bare mountains.

'The sea is… a place where there's no echo when you scream!' a girl told me. She then pointed at the endlessly rolling dunes and whistled loud and clear with all her might, even bending forward a little as she did so. And, indeed, no echo came back. I did as she had done and let out a loud whistle of my own. Once again, no echo returned.

This is how the children of Xihaigu imagine a 'sea'!

But what about the grown-ups? How do adults in Xihaigu imagine the 'sea'? Today as in the past, it remains the case that most of the people in Xihaigu has never seen the real sea. Nonetheless, the understanding adults have of the 'sea' is not only more sophisticated than that of children, but also much more 'sacred'.

I met an old lady in Xihaigu, perhaps 70 or 80 years old.

Her eyes lit up and her expression brightened up like a withered flower suddenly revived when I asked her how she imagined the sea. This is how she answered me:

'Many times I have walked a long way over mountain roads, turn after turn, to find, behind some hills, a spring of clear waters. I would fill a few buckets with that water and load them on my donkey. Then I'd go back home, and then return to bring a few buckets more. While I was on the road, carrying that water, what I had in my mind, and also in my eyes and even in the ground my two feet stepped on was the sea...'

The understanding that old lady had of the 'sea' astonished me. It turned out that, for her, as it was for many generations of people in Xihaigu, the 'sea' meant that mixture of joy and anxiety one felt when going on a journey to search for water somewhere far away, then actually finding that water, and bringing it back home!

What a truly noble way of thinking of the sea! Could there be any idea richer and more deeply permeated by the flesh-and-blood relationship between people and their real lives than this 'sea'? People who have moved away from that 'sea' and retreated to 'dry land' have already forgotten all about the true meaning that 'sea'. But the people of Xihaigu have a much deeper and meaningful understanding of it than even people like us, who have lived our lives by the literal sea.

That is what amazes me!

Xihaigu! Oh, Xihaigu! How great and sublime is that '*hai*' in you, your 'sea', in the eyes of the people! How magnificent and holy it is! It is a sea not made of water, but formed purely from the crystallisation of spirit, thoughts that blossom, inquisitive souls, and from the sublimation of minds!

Now there is also this dry sea by the side of the Liupan Mountains. The sea that has hastened the birth of many children, harrowed the local people, torturing them for generations. They suffered in silence, living without water for centuries and yet surviving, as if constantly reborn from the dry ashes... It went on and on, seemingly till the end of time, as the stars above went round and round the sky, and the four seasons repeated themselves over and over again...

There were not many people from other places, however, who could really appreciate the long struggle of the people of Xihaigu. It was only after the People's Republic of China was founded that big changes started to occur. It was then that the policymakers inside Zhongnanhai and the representatives of the people started to think about the people of Ningxia, and, more specifically, about the people of Xihaigu and their old longing for water.

As a first measure the Army sent quilted clothing to the people for them to make it through the winter, then food for the children for the following year was delivered. But the problem that the people of Xihaigu had not received a single drop of clean drinking water in nearly 30 years remained to be addressed. Then, shortly after the Chinese New Year in 1972, at a meeting at Zhongnanhai, the Minister of Agriculture and the leader of the Ningxia Hui Autonomous Region both presented reports to Premier Zhou Enlai on the work they had been carrying out.

With some difficulty, the already-emaciated Zhou Enlai straightened up his body on the sofa he was sitting on, wiped the sweat off his forehead with a small towel, and then posed the following question to the leader of Ningxia:

'How much was the average peasant's income in Ningxia last year?'

'Forty-seven yuan,' the leader of Ningxia replied.

'That's three yuan and ninety-one cents a month, or thirteen cents a day,' Zhou Enlai said, frowning as though he was merely thinking aloud by himself. 'I guess that's not even enough to buy half a bowl of flour and a bit of salt.'

'Mr Premier, when I was in Xihaigu what the people there feared the most, as they told me, was not going hungry, but having no water to drink… And for them to be worried about water it means that they don't have enough even of that muddy water they keep in those holes they dig in the ground!'

'Water, water… Indeed, how can people live without water!?' Zhou Enlai exclaimed while reaching for a glass of water for himself. He ended up, however, just holding the glass in his hand for a long time without drinking and finally putting it down back on the tea table. 'In any case, we have to solve this water problem the people of Xihaigu is facing as soon as possible,' he said. 'You must come up at once with a plan and with all the steps to be taken! The Central Committee will convene a special meeting to discuss the problem of Xihaigu.'

'Work at Xihaigu must start with the comprehensive implementation of the policies towards ethnicities and the handling of the now expanding rebellions. Only after solving the political issues, the ideological issues, and the issues concerning the officials will we be able to fundamentally solve the problems of the common people's livelihood and the water issues they face,' Zhou Enlai said at the meeting. And as the meeting ended, he once again issued an exhortation to the leader of Ningxia: 'You should go learn more about that water problem to get a firm understanding of it. Ask the experts on the issue for advice and also to come up with solutions.'

'Understood Mr Premier. We will implement your

instructions at once,' replied the leader.

Once the leader of Ningxia had returned to the city of Yinchuan, he proceeded quickly to do some research and to devise a plan of action. He appointed Wu Shangxian, a water conservancy expert, to lead a working group that was sent to Xihaigu to implement the changes.

As a result, in the summer of that year, the people of Xihaigu witnessed the arrival of groups of doctors and of drought relief teams from all over the country. But, naturally, most exciting for the local people was the fact that Wu Shangxian and his team of expert were talking about 'bringing the Jing into the Qing'. 'The Jing and the Wei are clearly separated' (*Jing Wei fen ming*), is a saying most people in China are familiar with. Its meaning is the same as that other saying, 'the Jing is clear, while the Wei is turbid' (*jing qing wei zhuo*). The Jing River is the 'mother river' of the people of Xihaigu. It originates in the region of the Erlong River[1] and the Laolong Pond[2] in the south-west of the Jingyuan county, in Ningxia. From there it runs to the south-east through Pingliang and Jingchuan, in Gansu, then enters the Wei River in the county of Gaoling, in the province of Shaanxi. In ancient times, the basin of the Jing River was said to have

---

1   lit. 'Two Loong River'
2   lit. 'Old Loong Pond'

an abundance of water and a large number of rapids, making for beautiful landscapes, much like paintings. Natural climatic changes and earthquakes reduced the river and its basin to a third-class tributary of the Yellow River, a tributary less than forty kilometres in length. And despite that downgrading, the Jing River remained Xihaigu's most important source of water.

Wu Shangxian, who was born in the year of the Great Haiyuan Earthquake, was not only a water conservancy expert, but also a native of Ningxia. As such, he was very familiar with the role the longing for water played in the lives of the local people. After graduating from the Department of Hydraulic Engineering of the National Central University in Chongqing in 1946, he returned to the land where he was born to serve as an assistant engineer within the Ningxia Engineering Corps of the Yellow River Water Conservancy Commission, taking part in a survey of the area irrigated by the Yellow River in Ningxia. After the establishment of the People's Republic of China, Wu Shangxian then served as a technician in the hydraulic engineering division of the Northwest Field Army. And after the creation of the Ningxia Hui Autonomous Region, Wu Shangxian was put in charge of all water conservancy projects in Ningxia and became known as 'Ningxia's walking dictionary of hydraulic engineering'.

When talking about Wu Shangxian, people from Ningxia always mention his role in the construction of their province's first new canal after the foundation of the People's Republic. Wu Shangxian had been transferred to his native Ningxia, a transfer that, officially, was temporary, and there, as soon as he had settled down, he started working on the widening of the Qin Canal and on the construction of the First Farming Canal. This First Farming Canal is a canal 31.6 kilometres long built using many new techniques and materials selected by Wu Shangxian. After it was open and water started to run on it, the whitish alkaline soil of the regions it crossed were turned into rich landscapes with plenty of trees and rice fields and criss-crossed by smaller irrigation canals. It turned into a prosperous agricultural land full of the fragrances of rice and of other cereal crops. The First Farming Canal still functions to this day.

Following the completion of the First Farming Canal, Wu Shangxian and his team spent the next two years working on the straightening of the Tanglai Canal upstream from the Ximen Bridge in Yinchuan, in the process shortening it by more than ten kilometres. It significantly improved the flow rate and thus increased the volume of water transported by that old canal. It also provided Ningxia's Department of Water Resources with a successful experience to be used as reference in future retrofittings of old canals. After that, Wu Shangxian moved to the region of Xihaigu and led the implementation of the water conservancy projects for the Qingshui River, the Hulu River, and the Jing River. In Xihaigu he also led the construction of reservoirs up in the mountains. While working on those projects, he took also his team of hydraulic engineers to live a very rustic life with him, sleeping in *yaodong* cave dwellings, eating sticky millets meals, and drinking bitter water. Having not shied away from those hardships, he spent his time rushing from each river system he was working on to the next, and in only about eighteen months he managed to have built the first complete system of reservoirs in the area of the Liupan Mountains, bringing much relief to the common people of the region in regard to the water shortage problem they faced. In 1960, after the cofferdams for the construction of the Qingtongxia Water Control Project were completed, water levels on Yellow River rose, which allowed for water to be diverted through a newly excavated canal to the drought-afflicted areas on the eastern foothills of the Helan Mountains. That was how the Xigan Canal came into being. The Xigan Canal was also a project that Wu Shangxian had proposed, and which he was put in charge of. The construction of that canal required the traversing of a very mountainous region, which made it particularly difficult. The project Wu Shangxian adopted involved the diversion of the water, its storage in retention areas, and then its discharge, in order to limit maximum water levels. That had the effect of turning mighty floods into effectively manageable trickles. After a whole winter and a whole spring of arduous labour, the Xigan Canal was completed with its 112.7 kilometres of total length and with a capacity to irrigate more than 300,000 *mu* of land. Wu Shangxian had completed another pioneering work of engineering, another 'first' in the history of hydraulic engineering in Ningxia.

Then, when new instructions came from Premier Zhou Enlai in Beijing, the new idea that the old 'water conservancy expert from Ningxia' thought of was a plan to make use of

Jing River Nature Reserve Area in Jingyuan county

resources found locally in Xihaigu. It was a plan for the diversion of the Jing River into the Qingshui.

'That is the only source of clear water in Xihaigu, and I will do my absolute best to have the people of Xihaigu drink some of that sweet water,' Wu Shangxian said in a meeting convened to discuss how Premier Zhou Enlai's instructions would be implemented, with the goal of solving the water scarcity problem in Xihaigu.

The plan he came up with consisted in diverting water from the Jing River, where it was plentiful, and channel it through the mountains to the Qingshui River. That would provide the water needed for both agriculture and for domestic use in the region of the upper reaches of the Qingshui.

'That's a very good plan, a very professional one,' the leaders of the autonomous region and of other administrative departments said at a meeting convened to make a decision on that issue. 'But it's also a pity! A great pity!' everyone complained, sighing and groaning.

What was a pity?

Does it really needs saying? It was a pity that there was not enough money! The autonomous region did not have the money, and the country did not have the money to undertake such a large engineering project either! The plan to divert water from the Jing into the Qingshui could indeed create an adequate supply of water to all of the more than one million people who lived in Xihaigu at the time. But due to a lack of funds, Wu Shangxian's plan was shelved for the time being.

'But sooner or later Wu Shangxian's water-diversion plan will be implemented!' declared the officials in charge of the autonomous region and of the local department of water resources. 'At the earliest opportunity!'

Wu Shangxian shed tears upon hearing the decision. He was 56 years old at the time, and that also happened to be the year of Zhou Enlai's passing. 'I haven't fulfilled the important task you have assigned to me… I will certainly die with a grievance!' Wu Shangxian exclaimed at a meeting convened to commemorate the late Premier.

But even after that setback, Wu Shangxian did not give up on his vision of 'revitalising Ningxia with water'. In spite of his age, he would later volunteer to go to Yinbei to take part in a project aimed at treating saline-alkali soils. And within two years, the team he led dug 6,000 wells, built 200 small drainage stations, restored 96 electrified drainage stations, built also more than 190 kilometres of drainage ditches for desilting and seven flood retention areas, effectively solving the problem of low agricultural productivity caused by the saline and alkali soil in the region of Yinbei.

In the spring of 1980, Wu Shangxian, then 60 years old, stood on a margin of the Yellow River with a lifetime of experiences on his back and bright joy on his face. That joy was because right by his feet the Dongsheng section of the Yellow River in the county of Yongning had just been remodelled in accordance with a plan of his, solving the recurrent problem of the river banks collapsing. Looking at the sturdy new river bank and then turning his gaze around to look at the beautiful scenery of his hometown, a beautiful landscape of green grasses and flowers in bloom under the spring sun, Wu Shangxian couldn't resist the inspiration that came to him and composed a poem titled *So Beautiful, the Plains of Ningxia*:

The plains of Ningxia, such a nice landscape.
The Great Wall links up with the Northern Desert,
and the Yellow River reaches the sky,
under the protection of the Helan Mountains.
Before my eyes I see:
an oasis to one of the sides within view,
village houses under the shades of trees,
a criss-crossing of interconnected canals.
The fields are irrigated during sowing and harvest.

With no droughts and no floods productivity is high,

and in the north-west it is highest of all.

Halfway up the mountains spring is late and autumn early,

days are warm, nights cool, fruit sweet.

Summer is not so hot as to make us wave a fan.

In winter fragrant coal keeps it warm indoors.

The legend of Jiangnan on the frontier is real.

The people all sing the praises of their homeland,

and so do I.

Who has seen this land of wonders?

So beautiful, the plains of Ningxia!

It is not like Jiangnan,

it surpasses Jiangnan.

Sir, take a look!

After reciting his poem, Wu Shangxian's expression suddenly turned grave and he stood there, looking at the distant south for a very long time. At long last he mused to himself:

'When will I see the clear waters of the Jing River flow into that 'sea' inside my heart…'

That 'sea' in Wu Shangxian's heart was no other than long-suffering Xihaigu, that large expanse of dry land at the foothills of the Liupan Mountains, that land of more than a million people who, for generations, have longed for a 'sea'.

In 2001, after passing at the age of 81, Wu Shangxian, Ningxia's 'walking dictionary of hydraulic engineering', was buried together with all his knowledge in the soil of his hometown. Although he did not live to see the waters of the Jing River diverted into the Qingshui River to then enter that 'sea' he held dear in his heart, fifteen years later, on the 8th of October of 2016 someone shouted the command and the main water gate of the Zhongzhuang Reservoir in Guyuan was opened. Immediately the clear water of the Jing River rushed forward like a bolting wild horse and traversed the tall mountains and the ravines through pipes and canals, flowing into the open country and then into the homes of common people who had longed for that water for thousands of years. It was a moment that condensed 'the aspirations of more than forty years of Xihaigu and of the people of Ningxia, an aspiration shared by a million people'. It was at that moment that the Water Security Project for Urban and Rural Areas of Central and Southern Ningxia officially became operational. For the 1.13 million people living in the towns and in the countryside of Xihaigu it was great news. Now for the first time they could proclaim that the water scarcity problem was no more!

Even though Wu Shangxian could not be there to turn that

page in Xihaigu's history, the people of Xihaigu and of Ningxia at large have never forgotten the shiny tears in the eyes of that hydraulic engineering expert who hoped with a determination as firm as the Liupan and the Helan Mountains that clear water would pour in and irrigate the lands around the Xiaoguan Pass.

Wu Shangxian most definitely occupies an important place in the hearts of the people of Ningxia, and especially in the hearts of the people of Xihaigu. His eyes were filled with that clear water, a feeling of love for that native land of his that always longs for a faraway 'sea'.

I know that in Xihaigu, and throughout Ningxia, there are many other people like Wu Shangxian. In fact, most people are like him in this regard. They all have a 'sea' in their minds, a dream, or rather a dream whose end is a 'sea' that they have never seen before...

Chapter 2
Mazu Looks Back at 'You' in the Distance

There is a song, called *Heartbeat*, that goes like this:

> *Heartbeat,*
>
> *My true heartbeat, heart that beats for you.*
>
> *Needs to move fast, my heart tinkling*
>
> *Touch won't be light, but won't be ordinary.*
>
> *Say to me: bingo...*

There is also another song about heartbeats:

> *Only you make my heart beat*
>
> *I look up at the sky,*

and fear dark clouds will come

Still I'm with you always,

only you make my heart beat

You're the rainbow I chase,

and I'm not just a viewer

Just want our hearts to connect

Make love complete,

and promise it will be forever

I want to be your shelter,

and hold your hand on every journey...

Some believe that love can only exist between people, but in fact all things in nature can love one another: east and west, north and south, the earth and the sky, the moon and the sun… There is love between all things, and because of this natural love, the Earth and the Universe can exist in eternity. For that reason, it also reminds people of that kind of love that exists between a *you* and a *me*. And so, would not a love between different places be also possible?

I believe that in this world where we live there are always two natural forces that give people the ability to engender love in each other. Those forces, once combined, acquire an immense and invincible might, and turn into great beauty. Those forces are like the sun and the moon, like day and night. Without the gentle moonlight we would not be able to appreciate the intensity of the blazing sun, and without the melancholy dimness of the night we would also be unable to appreciate the magnificence of bright daylight.

Perhaps among all the natural worlds and all celestial bodies, and also on Earth, the most intense and complete love connection between a *you* and a *me* is that special connection between the mountain and the sea.

The mountain and the sea, one is towering and lofty, the other flat. The rock faces of the latter are firm and majestic, while the water of the former is soft and pliant. When the waves of the sea hit the shore, their roar reverberate among a myriad of precipices and cliffs, and when some large boulders come crashing down from the mountain and hit the sea, they inevitably create great waves that rise to the sky.

Thus, both mountain and sea roar and thunder, the mountain in reply to the sea, mirroring the unit between Heaven and humanity. Those are the *harmony* and the *Tao* those sages of the past have spoken of. Since the *Tao* is correct, things will go as they should, be successful, and be perfect. The *Tao* here means that our actions must have a clear and proper direction and follow clear and proper standards. If there is to be coexistence between things for the good of all, harmony is key. If there is a state of imbalance, then both Heaven and Earth will be upturned.

The First Holding of Hands that Seals Love

The fight against poverty in China has so far managed to lift the largest number of people out of poverty in the shortest period of time ever seen in history. That move towards prosperity is a great revolutionary and historical battle. It's ultimate success or failure will be determined by what methods, that is to say, what *Tao*, is used.

Likewise, we can clearly see that in the 70 years since the establishment of the People's Republic of China, poverty alleviation and aid to the poor never ceased. That was determined by the very purpose of the Communist Party of China. However, the fact that that work never stopped does not mean that the union of the wills of Party and people has been fully realised. Maybe it is because the leadership of the Communist Party of China has a special concern for and also a connection with the broad masses of the people, particularly with those who have long endured poverty, that after the People's Republic of China was founded poverty alleviation and assistance to the poor have carried a special weight for the government and for Party members at all levels. That is a concern that has been firmly established in the minds of many leaders and officials. But some people and some regions in China have not yet been completely lifted out of poverty. This is mainly because our country is a very large one and had to start from very flimsy economic foundations. But it is also because, in the first two decades after the establishment of the People's Republic, economic development was intermittent, going through tortuous roads full of complications.

When the tide of history brought about that great change known as *Reform and Opening-up*, China's society and the pattern of its development were fundamentally changed. The coastal areas in the east developed at a galloping pace, and so the gap between the more developed east and the more backward west kept growing wider, to the point that they could be described as being poles apart. Under such circumstances, the Communist Party decided that balancing and coordinating the pace of development of the east to allow the people in the west to also escape poverty and improve their standards of living would be the strategy to be implemented.

For that reason also, former President Deng Xiaoping, the chief architect of *Reform and Opening-up*, once proposed the strategy he called 'two overall situations' (*liang ge da ju*). Events then unfolded in a very clear direction. They went the way the *Tao* went, and the *Tao*'s path is bright and leads very far. This is the path the new generation of Communist Party members needs to explore with dedication and with clear heads, and then move on to practice it.

For as long as there is this bright Way, the *Tao*, many people will want to follow it. But each person who decides to follow it may do so differently. There will be many who choose to walk hand in hand with others, and they will be successful, and will find happiness and harmony. But there will also be those who give up halfway, walk with a divided heart and forget the practice, starting their projects but not carrying them through to completion. Those will be like that creature in the proverb, which has a tiger's head but a snake's tail. Anything one can conceive can become reality. So how to achieve the goals of that struggle, make common aspirations real, and move towards a better future?

There is no question that joining hands and working together is the best and most admirable way of lifting people out of poverty, the many people of the most backward areas. In this world people have the power to enact all sorts of change. There can be creation or destruction, regressions or great leaps ahead. All those possibilities are within people's power. And among all the great powers that human beings have, no one is greater than the power of love that comes from the heart. No other power is more resilient, even indestructible, and no other power is more fruitful in the wonders it creates.

But how about *you* and *me*?

But who are *you*? And who am *I*? How are we both like? Can we come together to work as a team, with fraternal love and kindness towards each other, to create a better future together?

Heaven is watching, and the people are wondering...

And who are *you* really? That distant *you*, that *you* that remains alongside that great sea. People who live by the sea say that *you* are their protector spirit, and so that faraway *me* begins to recognise that faraway *you*.

Gradually, the children, the elderly, and myself, all begin to know *you*, because *you* are that sea goddess of our tradition, and every family who lives in the regions along the coast know *your* name. And everywhere around the world where Chinese people live, they know *your* name. *Your* name is full of kindness and love, *your* name is *Mazu* (and could we not understand your name and the characters that form it as *the first ancestor of kindness and love*?).

Only when we go to the coast we learn that *your* story is not at all fictional. *You* had also a worldly name: Lin Mo. *Your* father was Lin Yuan, a famous official of the Min Kingdom during the time of the Five Dynasties. Today in Fujian's Meizhou Island it is still possible to find evidence of the Lin family's sea enterprises, which took place over generations. According to tradition, there was a time when the head of the Lin family had just passed away, and so the task of going out to sea fell upon a son named Lin Yuan. But Lin Yuan's first sea voyage was very unsuccessful. It had turned out that it was extremely difficult to carry out business out in the seas without official protection from the government. Lin Yuan then understood why his father had to once purchase an official government position. Following his father's example, Lin Yuan then also spent a large sum on the purchase of an official position that could facilitate his business activities. Lin Yuan thus ceased to be just a commoner and became an official. As an official, not only was his family exempt from taxation, but he also enjoyed the privilege of charging duties on local shipping. Lin Yuan's sea trading business then grew very quickly, and so did his wealth.

Later Lin Yuan would marry a woman named Xiaohua. Within just a few years, Xiaohua gave birth to four sons, but for some unknown reason none of them was particularly outstanding in appearance and were also all of rather weak constitutions. Fearful for the future of his family, Lin Yuan decided to take his wife with him on a long journey to Mount Putuo, where he would make a vow to Guanyin[1] and ask the Goddess of Mercy for another son.

Guanyin had long been aware that the Lin family was kind and charitable, and also merciful and honest in their official dealings. She knew also that they had spared no efforts in undertaking their trip to Mount Putuo, so Guanyin called one of her disciples, a daughter of Dragon King Sāgara[2], and told her: 'You will reincarnate in the Lin family, to fulfil this destiny. And once you are there, you must give love first and foremost, and be of benefit to all living creatures. You will be able to subdue evil spirits at sea and do justice by Heaven's authority!'

The daughter of Dragon King Sāgara, puzzled by what she had just heard, replied:

'But master, the Lin family has asked for a son!'

'That's the Will of Heaven,' was Guanyin's answer.

The daughter of Dragon King Sāgara knew that it would not be proper to question it again, so she was reincarnated in the Lin Family. Lin Yuan's wife became pregnant again not long after the two of them had returned from their journey to Mount Putuo. And at noon on the 23rd day of the 3rd month of the following

---

1   Guanyin, the Bodhisattva of Compassion or Goddess of Mercy (Sanskrit Avalokiteśvara)

2   Sāgara is a dragon king in Mahayana Buddhism. His name comes from the Sanskrit word meaning "ocean".

year, a very loud sound was heard under the bright and clear sky, glittering red lights appeared both in front and behind the Lin family's home, and the home was also suddenly immersed in a very sweet fragrance. That happened because a 'precious daughter' had been born in the Lin family. Seeing that the girl was very cute, and that she was not very given to crying, the family named her 'Lin Mo'[1].

Once she had grown up, little Lin Mo often went over to the shore to pray for her father's safety while he was out in the sea on business. She also said prayers for all the other fathers of the village who were also at sea. Then the people there gradually discovered that Lin Mo had divine powers. She could predict storms at sea and knew when ships would be in distress. Those miraculous predictions started to multiply, and so the people who lived by the coast eventually all came to believe that there was something very special about Lin Mo. They started saying that she was a goddess from Heaven who had come down to earth.

During the reign of Emperor Xuanhe of the Northern Song, a certain court official was sent as a diplomatic envoy to Korea. On his return voyage he encountered a very violent storm at sea and nearly perished. But Mazu had granted him protection,

---

1   *Mo* also means 'being silent'

and so he made it through the storm and returned in safety to the Song Empire. That official later presented a memorial to the Song Emperor, petitioning him to issue and imperial edict conferring official recognition of the goddess Mazu. Emperor Xuanhe[1] had long been hearing about Lin Mo's miraculous deeds, so he conferred on Lin Mo the title of 'Goddess of Meizhou', and instructed that the characters for *shun* (順) and *ji* (濟), which together means 'to rescue those in distress and benefit the whole world', be written on a tablet above the entrance to her temple. The Imperial Court also dispatched envoys to Meizhou Island to oversee the construction of that temple.

Since then, the goddess Mazu and her temples have spread throughout China's coastal regions, and also to other areas of the world where Chinese people live. Mazu and her temples have even been embraced in other countries, where Mazu was also received as 'the goddess of the sea'.

But this name of hers, *Mazu* (媽祖), was not the one used from the beginning. It became widespread and accepted by popular usage over centuries. The name evolved from the earlier name *niangma,* which the Hokkien people who had migrated to Taiwan used to refer to her. *Ma* (媽) was a word used to either refer to a grandmother, or as merely a respectful term of address

---

1   Xuanhe's posthumous name was 'Huizong'

for an older woman. And in the Hokkien topolect that character has the same pronunciation as that of the character used for the word 'horse' (馬). According to one theory the word *mazu* back then simply referred to any female ancestor from one's father's family line, such as a paternal great aunt. Believers would have then used that form of address simply because what those who went out to sea longed for the most was a loving and direct form of protection from the goddess. Using that form of address meant that they sought to shorten the relationship between people and divinity by making an analogy with a relationship that should always be firmly based on values, a family relationship. As General Secretary Xi Jinping has once pointed out, national culture is what makes for a nation's peculiarities and what distinguishes it from others. Mazu is a quintessential part of the Chinese traditional system of virtue and ethics, and also a very important part of traditional Chinese culture. She embodies all the beauty of the very rich ethical tradition of the East, and the very profound love of that tradition.

Lady Goddess, the fragrance of the incense burned in your devotion rises in Meizhou.
Today the love of Mazu, spreads far and wide and reaches very distant places...

Mazu has become the most widely spread symbol of Chinese culture, a symbol filled with the love and charitableness of Eastern civilisation. It has long taken roots in the West as well, to the point that Mazu is even often compared to other female divinities of Western tradition. What people might not realise, however, is that our modern-day 'Mazu' has already extended her affectionate gaze and reached out with her gentle and fragrant hands to that distant *you* more than 20 years ago.

And who is that distant *you*? It is the colossal 'son of the Yellow River', the 'brother to the Qin Mountains', no other than the Liupan Mountains!

A poem by Tan Sitong, a reformist and activist of the late Qing period, uses very powerful words to depict the Liupan Mountains in a grand and emotional style:

> *The horse has a sprained leg, the cart's axle is broken,*
> *the driver is tripping and falling.*
> *The mountains are high and perilous, and northern*
> *geese honking mean snow is coming!*

Tradition holds that the Liupan Mountains were originally called Yupan Mountains, or, literally, 'Jade Plate Mountains'.

Tradition also holds that they are of imperial lineage, being regarded as the northern child of the Jade Emperor. But the local people preferred to call the gigantic mountains next to them the 'Lupan Mountains', or, literally, the 'Deer-Goes-Around Mountains'. This latter name comes from the following legend:

Tradition holds that a long time ago there were three frontier generals leading their troops on a punitive expedition to the west, and they were crossing some very tall mountains in the midst of a bitter winter. As their troops reached the base of a tall peak, snow was blocking the road. The place was deserted, and there was not a single soul around one could ask for guidance. But right at that hour of peril, the generals heard a wild deer calling three times. The generals raised their heads to look around, and saw, standing on a mountain spur nearby, a plum blossom deer staring back at them. One of the generals took his bow and shot an arrow at the deer, hitting it. Injured and with the arrow still stuck to its body, the deer fled. With no clear path open to continue their march, the three generals gave chase to the deer, and would not give it up. And so it happened that, in less than half a day, they had led their troops to the other side of the tall mountains. The deer, however, was nowhere to be seen. As it was already getting dark, they decided to set up camp and stay for the night at the place where they were.

Then, in the middle of the night, as the three generals slept, a big man in armour and with a dark grey face appeared holding a knife. He struck the head of a bed three times and announced to them: 'I turned into a deer to take you across the great mountains.' And after saying that he strutted away. The three generals woke up with a start and in confusion, and rushed out to ask the soldiers: 'Did any stranger enter the camp during the night?' All the soldiers replied that none of the like had happened. The three generals then talked with each about any dream they might have had the night before and realised that all three of them had dreamt the exact same dream. 'Ay Ay Ay!' the three generals exclaimed in great surprise, then sat down together to discuss very carefully who that big fellow who had appeared to them might have been. It then dawned on them that the big man was no other than Zhou Cang, the companion who stands by the side of Emperor Guanyu, the God of War! The deer they had seen the day before had been in fact Zhou Cang, who had morphed into a deer to lead them and their troops out of the great mountains! As soon as the three generals realised that they immediately turned their gaze up to Heaven and then knelt down to prostrate themselves. Once they were done with their obeisances, the generals led their troops through the same route the plum blossom deer had led them and had their soldiers dig through mountain sides and fill in ditches to build a simple road for both horses and travellers on foot. It was a road with six great turns going around[1] mountains on the way up and six great turns going around mountains on the way down... Later people started to call those mountains the 'Lupan Mountains', or the Deer-Goes-Around Mountains.

Lupan Mountains, the mountains where a deer shows the way out. What a very beautiful and poetic name indeed! And I know also that those great mountains were not only made of precipitous cliffs and lofty peaks in the past. They were in fact a kind of wonderland with waterfalls, birds and other animals rejoicing in their natural environment, and luxuriant vegetation with blooming flowers of myriad colours. It was a fragrant and splendidly bewitching place where delicate fruit were wrapped in a gossamer misty spray... a wonderland like no other!

---

1   *"Liu pan" in Chinese*

Still within the borders of Ningxia, the Liupan Mountains have an equally lofty and majestic 'full brother', the Helan Mountains.

According to the *Yuanhe Maps and Records of Prefecture and Counties* (*Yuanhe Jun Xian Tu Di*), 'the Helan Mountains are located 93 *li* west of the [Baojing county] and count with a large number of forested areas, which makes the landscape look like a dappled horse, so that northern people call their dappled horses *helan*.' Later on, a number of historical works such as *Essentials of Geography for Reading History* (*Dushi Fangyu Jiyao*) and *Records of the Northern District* (*Shuofang Dao Zhi*) started copying each other in stating that the Helan Mountains take their name from some word meaning either 'dappled horse' or 'fine horse', even going so far as to affirm that *helan* means 'fine horse' in the Mongolian language.

A horse at full gallop on Mount Long, and a god-like deer turning its head to look back with eyes full of affection... How can those concepts, those images, not attract that distant *you* living by the sea?

'Come! Come! Revered visitor from that distance place, come!'

In early November of 1996 the weather in Fuzhou was still sunny and pleasantly warm. 'It is truly a blessed place! We're already freezing in the snow there, but here it is still balmy as spring! It's really good fortune, we're really blessed to have that partnership with Fujian!' said a member of the delegation of the Ningxia Hui Autonomous Region as we were being driven from the airport to city of Fuzhou. They were in Fujian for the first time to attend a joint meeting of the Cooperation on Poverty Alleviation Between Fujian and Ningxia. Everyone felt a sort of exhilaration at being there, an exhilaration that boosted our energy, both mentally and physically.

The next day the first joint meeting of the Cooperation on Poverty Alleviation Between Fujian and Ningxia was held in Fuzhou. Chen Mingyi, Fujian's provincial Party secretary, thus described the Cooperation:

'Although there is a great physical distance between our two provinces, the impulse of Reform and Opening-up and the modernisation drive it entails have long brought us close together. In accordance with the dispositions issued by the Central Committee and the State Council, our two provinces are now paired together and are meant to cooperate and help each other. This is an important step towards achieving our goal of a common path for development and shared prosperity, and we will certainly achieve that goal by combining our efforts towards the elimination of poverty.'

Bai Lichen, who served as chairman of the Ningxia Hui Autonomous Region at the time, offered words of sincere gratitude for the generosity and selflessness of their counterparts in Fujian and also emphasised that, under the leadership of the Central Committee and thanks to the combined efforts of government and Party officials and the common people, Ningxia had achieved remarkable results in only a few decades. He had, nonetheless, to also remark that there was still much work to be done towards the goal of eliminating poverty across the entire region. But now, with the central government as intermediate and planner in establishing a partnership with Fujian, there was much greater confidence in Ningxia that the goal would be achieved. And he thought also that the people of Ningxia had also gained much determination and greater ability towards that goal now that they counted with the support from Fujian, a support akin to what one could expect from a close family relation.

'Comrade Xi Jinping assumed the post of head of the leading group in Fujian in charge of the cooperation on poverty alleviation with Ningxia! That's great! Shows how much importance they all attached to it! Moreover, Comrade Xi Jinping has served as county Party secretary in Hebei, and has also held important positions of leadership in Xiamen, Ningde,

Fuzhou and many other places. Now he also serves as the deputy secretary at the provincial Party committee in charge of official and agricultural affairs. He has plenty of experience, and this is great news for the cooperation between our two provinces!' said the comrades from Ningxia, overjoyed from learning at the meeting that comrade Xi Jinping would be in charge of the cooperation on poverty alleviation from the Fujian side.

'How much was given?'

'Fifteen million yuan!'

'Wow, such a generous first-meeting gift!'

That 'first-meeting gift' given by the Fujian side on the occasion of the 'first handshake' between the leaders of the two sides was such as to leave the comrades who had come from Ningxia electrified for quite a while. But there was still someone who muttered:

'I'm not saying that what was given is small change, but once the sesame seeds are released, they will have to be put into bags, and there are so many poor regions back in Ningxia that I have no idea how those 15 million can be divided between them…'

'Don't go blabbering like that!' scolded a leader from Ningxia after hearing his colleague muttering like that. 'First time showing up in front of a friend and having hungry mouths wide open like that! Aren't you afraid you're going to scare people?

Moreover, look at the "delivery slip" our comrades from Fujian have given us, no small thing for sure!'

The subordinate who had been muttering fell silent at once.

'And take a look at this,' the leader said, placing a document still smelling of fresh ink in front of the members of his delegation. 'Are you still unhappy?

'What is this?'

'The list of the eight administrative subdivisions in Fujian with their counterparts in the cooperation. Look! These counties and cities are among the ones that made the most progress so far through the process of Reform and Opening-up!

'I see! The city of Fuqing in Fuzhou is partnered with Yanchi County in Ningxia, the city of Changle, also in Fuzhou, is partnered with the county of Longde, the city of Jinjiang in Quanzhou is partnered with Guyuan, the city of Shishi, also in Quanzhou, is partnered with the county of Tongxin, the district of Kaiyuan in the prefecture of Xiamen is partnered with the county of Jingyuan, the Tong'an county, also in the prefecture of Xiamen, is partnered with the county of Haiyuan, Putian county is partnered with Xiji county, and the city of Longhai in Zhangzhou is partnered with the county of Pengyang! See? That's quite an impressive line-up Fujian has put together!'

'That's so incredible! The folks from Fujian have taken care of all the details concerning our cooperation, and with so much attention! Do you know who's in charge of this matter from their side?' the leader from Ningxia asked rhetorically, making a pause to add some suspense.

'Who?'

'Xi Jinping! The provincial deputy Party secretary!'

'That's great! That's great! I heard that he's especially close to the people and their needs, and, more to the point, I heard that he got quite a lot done to alleviate poverty while in Ningde!'

'That's how lucky our Ningxia is!'

And so, the discussion among the members of the delegation from Ningxia was shifted to the topic of the person of Xi Jinping, a topic they discussed very passionately.

'Boss, can we invite Secretary Xi to visit Ningxia some time?' someone asked. 'That would be of great benefit to our cooperation on poverty alleviation!'

'Yes, we should definitely invite Secretary Xi and other leaders from Fujian to come to Ningxia to take a look around. No doubt this will be of great benefit to our cooperation...'

'Don't you worry! At this joint meeting leaders from both provinces have already reached a very important agreement. A joint meeting will be held every year with all the important leaders of both sides in attendance. As a matter of fact, this year we and our other comrades from Ningxia have come to Fuzhou, but next year it will be the turn of the Fujian comrades to travel to Yinchuan to attend the meeting in Ningxia with us. What do you guys think of this arrangement?'

'Very good!'

'It couldn't be any better!'

'There's nothing that can't be done here in our country provided that Party committees and leaders deem it important!'

'That's right,' another member of the delegation said, and followed up his remark with a question: 'So, as you said, it's possible that we'll host Xi Jinping and some other Fujian leaders next year in Ningxia?'

'If nothing comes up that prevents him from going, I believe he'll be there. He is the head of the leading working group in charge of cooperation with us after all!' the leader of the Ningxia Hui Autonomous Region said.

'I'll tell you why so many places by the sea have names that started with the character *fu* (福) for "good fortune". That's because they have the very good fortune of being close to Mazu! And now that we're here, we have to go see Mazu!' someone else said.

'This is a very good idea! If any one of you happens to have some free time go see Mazu at once, to bring her blessings and good luck back with use to Ningxia!'

'It is very easy to find Mazu in the coastal areas of Fujian. In virtually every city and town, and perhaps even on every street, one can find a temple dedicated to her. Those temples are also of every possible size, from the very small to the very large. But the devotees of Mazu in Ningxia say that you have to go to her hometown to find her…'

'Does Mazu really have a hometown?' someone asked, rather incredulous.

'Of course she does. Haven't you heard the story? Mazu was a real person who was later deified…'

'So how far was her home from Fuzhou?'

'Not very. I heard that it was in Putian, a little over a hundred kilometres away.'

'Let's go there tomorrow to see our "relative"!'

Having already taken care of all the business they were there to take care of, several members of the delegation were very enthusiastic about the idea.

So, the Ningxia comrades formed a travelling group and embarked on their journey to the hometown of that 'relative' they longed to see. That hometown was Meizhouwan, located on an exceptionally beautiful bay by the border between the prefectures of Putian and Quanzhou. Across the sea from it lies the beautiful island of Taiwan with its port cities of Keelung, Taichung and Kaohsiung. The harbour in Meizhouwan is itself a natural deep-water harbour with enough berths to accommodate many ships, a harbour like few others in China, and even around the world.

That is Mazu's hometown, a very beautiful town squeezed between the mountains and the sea. The majestic sights of Mount Hugong and the crystal-clear waters of Lake Jiuli, together with the classical elegance of the secluded and peaceful Meifeng Temple, and the gentle meandering of the Mulan River, combine to make Mazu's homeland by the sea a uniquely beautiful place. And, of course, the most striking sight of all there is the statue of loving Mazu, facing the sea and with her back to the ancient Mazu Temple.

'Oh, Mazu is so beautiful! Really beautiful!' someone said.

While the Ningxia comrades were immersed in the fragrance and the cool breeze of the sea, one among them suddenly took his hands to his chest and, while facing the colossal image of Mazu, began to chant loudly:

> *If I love you —*
> *I won't be like the trumpet creeper*
> *Flaunting itself on your tall branches,*
> *If I love you —*

I won't be like the love-sick bird,

Repeating to the green shade its monotonous song;

Nor like a brook,

Bringing cool solace the year round;

Nor like a perilous peak,

Adding to your height, complementing your grandeur;

Nor even sunlight,

Nor even spring rain.

No, these are not enough!

I must be a kapok tree by your side;

In the image of a tree standing by you,

Our roots clasped underground,

Our leaves touching in the clouds.

With every breeze

We salute each other,

But no one

Will understand our language.

You have your trunk of steel and iron branches,

Like knives, like swords,

And like spears.

I have my huge, red flowers,

Like heavy sighs,

And like valiant torches.

> *We share the burdens of cold, storms, lightning;*
> *We share the joys of mists, vapours, rainbows.*
> *We may seem forever severed,*
> *But are life-long companions.*

'Hey! Hey! What are you blabbering about? Come on, we still have to make it to Beijing to catch the plane back to Yinchuan!' some other member of the delegation said while pulling the chant-intoning colleague by the arm.

'Look, you don't get it! This poem I'm reciting is by Shu Ting, the greatest female poet of our times. She's from Fujian and this poem's called *To an Oak...*'

'No wonder it sounded familiar… But I don't think you recite it all that well!' the comrade pulling the colleague by the arm said, not giving up. 'What does Shu Ting's poem have to do with our poverty alleviation cooperation? Can we get moving?'

'You don't catch the analogy.' protested the other. 'This poem by Shu Ting is one of the most well-known love poems of the Misty Poets. It is about the love between two people. So it is very much relevant to the cooperation work in poverty alleviation between Ningxia and Fujian!'

'Really?'

'Yes, of course! Now listen to the last few verses of her

poem…'

And so, during the return trip, those verses from *To an Oak* were recited over and over again among the more poetically inspired members of the delegation:

> *This is the greatest of love;*
> *This is constancy:*
> *Love —*
> *I love not just your robust form,*
> *I also love the ground you hold,*
> *the earth you stand on.*

But can it not be that our Liupan Mountains, our Helan Mountains, our Xihaigu and the land of our Ningxia are nothing but upright and imposing physical bodies! Today Mazu and all places in Fujian have turned their caring gaze from the great sea and on to us and to our land. The people of Ningxia are truly blessed!

Mazu, bring your blessings upon us!

In early November of 1996, the delegation of Ningxia comrades returned home from Fujian, bringing with them the spirit of the first official meeting of the cooperation and a total of seventeen signed agreements. They also brought a donation of a million yuan from the Xiangjiang Group in Fujian to a Project Hope primary school in the county of Xiji, and the deep love and affection from Mazu and also from the people of Fujian. They were returning from a very fruitful journey, one that had opened a historically significant new chapter in the cooperation between Ningxia and Fujian on poverty alleviation. From that moment on, the people of Ningxia started looking forward to the coming spring, when sunshine would fall upon them with even greater warmth and tenderness.

A Spring Warmer Than in Prior Years

And so spring arrived! The spring of 1997 arrived earlier in Ningxia and felt warmer than past springs.

After the delegation's return from Fujian, poverty alleviation work in Ningxia also seemed to pick up the pace. Shortly before the end of the year, Ningxia's Military Area Command convened a very important meeting in Guyuan to celebrate the completion of the digging of 'a hundred poverty-alleviation wells'. In attendance at that meeting were leaders from the Department of Water Resources, the General Political Department of the People's Liberation Army, the Ethnic Affairs Commission, the Lanzhou Military Area Command, as well as leaders of the

Autonomous Region. They celebrated because the water that could now be obtained from those wells was water that the people of Xihaigu sorely needed, and for which they had long waited. In cooperation with all relevant organs, the Military Area Command of Lanzhou dispatched to Xihaigu troops of their water supply regiment. Those troops worked hard over a period of ten months and dug one hundred wells in total in the eight counties of the mountainous regions of southern Ningxia. Those were wells that reached depths of as much as 12,000 metres and provided as much as 104,000 cubic metres of water daily, enough to guarantee the supply of drinking water to 200,000 people and 2 million farm animals, while also securing the irrigation of 34,000 *mu* of agricultural land. For the mountainous regions of southern Ningxia, where, historically, water had been 'as precious as oil', the arrival of water in such volumes could only be seen as great news. Therefore, an official meeting had to be convened to celebrate the completion of those 'one hundred poverty-alleviation wells', and it had to be an extraordinarily solemn meeting. I emphasise this meeting also because it involves a fact that people in Ningxia may not be aware of, the fact that this water supply regiment of the Lanzhou Military Area Command is an advanced group attached to a division I used to serve. They are a unit of the Hydrogeological and Surveying Engineering

Corps, of which I have been press secretary back in the day. In 1983, when all the armed forces were streamlined, that group was transferred to the Lanzhou Military Area Command, and their mission was also changed. Their task was now to assist the people living in arid mountains areas by finding water sources and digging wells. That is in line with the main purpose of a people's army, which is to assist the people. I can imagine, in fact I know, all the hardships those soldiers went through while digging those wells there among the great mountains of Xihaigu, where water was 'as precious as oil', and then their joy at making

People from Xihaigu having a taste of the sweet water the project of 'one hundred poverty-alleviation wells' made available to them

100,000 cubic metres of clear water flow there every day.

I remember the piece I once wrote describing the work of that unit. To speed up the construction of the wells and bring water sooner to the people of Xihaigu, those troops forwent their winter training season and spent even the coldest days of winter digging out and moving away loess. Early mornings were particularly cold, and so to keep them warm, the military-political instructors had them jog in circles around the drilling rig before work started. They jogged till the sun rose and finally appeared in the east. That particularly touching story I later also included in an article I wrote for the *New Observer* (*Xin Guancha*).

Even though more than twenty years have now passed, the stories old comrade-in-arms tell me of the difficulties they faced while digging wells and looking for water in the Liupan Mountains still stir a few emotions within my heart. That was, in a few words, a place dry like few others, cold like few others, and poor like few others.

Now the people of Fujian had taken upon themselves the important responsibility of taking part in a cooperation for poverty alleviation and fully embracing the northwestern regions of our country. And people from all over the country, not least those from Ningxia, looked forward to seeing the results.

'We have to talk less and do more, get things done first!' people would say, and that is the way the people of Fujian work, the rule they live by.

And sure enough, on Chinese New Year's Day of 1997, the agreement for the first concrete cooperation project between the two provinces was signed in Yinchuan. It was a partnership on potato starch production between the county of Xiji, in Ningxia, and the county of Putian, in Fujian.

'I had no idea that the potatoes of Ningxia were so delicious!' the representative from Putian said shortly after signing the agreement and eating some of the roasted potatoes sent to him by the people of Xiji. 'These potatoes are so nice that I bet that if we took them back home, they could be exchanged for very fine sea cucumbers, one for one!'

That was the kind of praise the people of Ningxia most liked to hear. Potatoes are among the most important crops in the county of Xiji. Due to the high altitudes and the long stretches of cold weather, those potatoes also have a superior taste and are more resistant to being left in storage for long periods of time. That is why Xiji is known for producing the finest potatoes in all of China, a reputation that dates back centuries. In the county of Xiji potato fields cover an area as large as a million *mu* in total, with an annual yield of two metric tons per *mu*. Potatoes constitute between 80% and 90% of all farmers produce in the county.

When people from Fujian come to visit Ningxia, the local food they usually most want to try are the potatoes, just like when visitors from Ningxia go to Fujian, the locals are very eager to have them try their seafood.

The reactions potato crisps from Ningxia usually get are 'delicious!' and 'so much better than imported crisps!' In Ningxia potato fields can be seen almost everywhere, stretching as far as the eyes can see. It is only natural then that businesspeople from Fujian coming to Ningxia will turn their attention to them. That is how businesspeople see it, but it is certainly beneficial to both sides, and it is also the way public sentiment usually goes.

But when the leaders of Fujian turned their attention to every inch of poor and thirsty land in Ningxia, their intention was to deliver assistant to where it was needed the most. In March of 1997, even before the snow atop the Liupan Mountains had begun to melt, a group led by Lin Yuechan, a leading Party member in Fujian and a member of Fujian's provincial government, arrived in Ningxia. Lin Yuechan was also one of the deputy directors of the provincial office in charge of the cooperation on poverty alleviation with Ningxia.

'Comrade Xi Jinping has assigned to me the task of coming

over here to observe how the cooperation on poverty alleviation is being implemented, and to get an understanding of the situation,' Lin Yuechan told the comrades from Ningxia shortly after stepping out of the plane. During the following ten days or so Lin Yuechan, together with her team of inspectors, carried out the assignment given to her by comrade Xi Jinping, performing a careful assessment of each planned item of the cooperation work. Because of this comprehensive assessment work, her Fujian comrades got an understanding of the poverty situation in Ningxia, and of how it had to be tackled.

'The Yellow River is capricious, and Ningxia's fate hangs upon its caprices,' Lin Yuechan repeated a few times during my interview with her, not without a note of lamentation. 'But even the prosperity the river may bring is also not evenly distributed in Ningxia!'

In fact, Ningxia's geography means that it is divided into two very distinct areas. The north of the province is a plain irrigated by the Yellow River, whereas in the south we find the Liupan Mountains with all their aridness. Historically, the north has seen agriculture develop and flourish, particularly after the establishment of the People's Republic of China, and it is that region, often dubbed 'the Jiangnan north of the Great Wall', that produces the famous Ningxia rice. The south, on the other hand, is mostly arid and barren land, especially in the region of Xihaigu, where average rainfall is less than 180 mm a year. 'It's about as much as what the Heavens dump upon the coast of Fujian at a single go when a typhoon strikes during the typhoon season. What would be a wonder was if people and livestock did *not* die of thirst!' Lin Yuechan said upon hearing from locals for the first time how dry conditions were in Ningxia.

'And an especially dry year means total crop failure,' a local added.

'Really total failure?' she asked in reply, still a little incredulous.

'That's the way it is,' a native from the county of Tongxin told Lin Yuechan and her team. 'Not so long ago, in the three years between 1980 and 1982, a particularly bad drought resulted in 500,000 *mu* of land in our county producing absolutely nothing.'

'What did people eat then?' she asked, that kind of reality being inconceivable for someone from Fujian. But what startled Lin Yuechan and her colleagues the most was to learn that, during dry years like those, the people from the drought-afflicted areas had to pay more than ten yuan, or sometimes even more than twenty yuan, for a single bucket of drinking water.

'Oh, they are already poor, their crops have been lost, and they still have to pay such high prices for water to drink! How could they survive a time like this!' Lin Yuechan's team said upon hearing that, while also stamping their feet on the ground.

'Ah, somehow we made it...' said the local, twisting his fingers with embarrassment and lowering his head.

'We can no longer allow our brothers in Ningxia to live like this!' one of the members of the Fujian delegation proclaimed very gravely. And so, with a mind to present to the leaders of both provinces concrete projects to be discussed in the upcoming second meeting of the Cooperation on Poverty Alleviation Between Fujian and Ningxia, Lin Yuechan's team agreed with their Ningxia comrades that they had to focus on four areas. Those were the construction of wells and water storage pits, agricultural terracing, the settlement of sparsely populated areas through a policy known as 'lifting villages' (*diaozhuang*), and elementary schools of the Project Hope.

The drilling of wells had already been discussed, and several of them had already been built by the water supply unit of the Military Area Command of Lanzhou working in collaboration with the common people. Likewise, the construction of underground water storage infrastructure was also a measure designed to combat water scarcity. The idea was devised by teams of scientists working together with the local people of the drought-affected mountain regions. It consisted of digging water storage pits and channels inside mountain slopes to collect rainwater, snow, and even ice during the wetter season, water that would be later used in the irrigation of fields, and also as drinking water for both people and livestock. The construction of one such water storage pit cost about 400 yuan. In 1996, before the visit by Lin Yuechan and her team, but already after the project had been started, the people of Ningxia were very enthusiastic about the construction of those water storage pits. However, of the 420,000 pits planned for construction within three years, only about 100,000 were built. So, at all administrative levels, the government of the Autonomous Region was under great pressure, both in terms of time and of funding for the project.

'The amount of water one such pit can store is certainly not enough for one household, so the plan stipulated that five such pits would have to be built for each peasant household. The time and financial resources required for building five pits in each household was a problem that Ningxia had to contend with,' said a Ningxia comrade, somewhat apologetic, to his Fujian counterparts.

Now the resettlement of peasants, known as *diaozhuang*, or 'the lifting of villages', is a pioneering initiative intended to address the issue of Ningxia's poverty-driven migration. This programme was implemented with two different variations. In the first variation of the programme the villages, or, more specifically, the poor peasants thereof, would be relocated within the same county where they originally lived, leaving them under the same county jurisdiction they had been before. They would be allocated by that county two *mu* of arable land for each family at a location not very far from where they lived, but not be required to move straight away. Those two *mu* of land would come bundled with two farmhouses, a water storage pit, as well as a year's worth of food provisions, seeds, and fertilizers. By the second year, with provisions for both the family's livelihood and their farming needs already arranged, the entire family would then move to the new location and be formally registered as having settled down there. The second way the programme was implemented involved giving families a plot of land in a different county, at a location chosen by the government of the Autonomous Region. At this new location the peasants would form an entirely new settlement and would also take part in its construction and further development. In the end, however, they would remain under the same jurisdiction as they had been before, as their new settlement would then be formally attached to the county they had originally come from, becoming a part of it. Those two variations of the programme had a few things in common. The first was that, in both cases, the plot of land the family had originally come from would not be taken back by the government, and the family would be allowed to continue cultivating it as they did before. The second was that the peasant families would be allowed to try life at the new location and decide whether they wanted to stay there or else to go back. The third was that, in case all the members of a family were not in full agreement as to whether they should stay or go back, they would be allowed to split and to remain a part in each location, with both sides looking after each other even after the split. The fourth was that broader family connections and relations of neighbourly friendship would be preserved, with people allowed to move as groups of families and remain close to each other at their new locations. Ethnic minorities in particular were given the freedom to either maintain their traditional customs and ways of living, or else to adopt new ones.

At the time the construction of many new Project Hope elementary schools was also occurring throughout the country. No matter how poor a family was, their children could not go without education. That was the grand national purpose behind the creation of Project Hope.

'After seeing the conditions people lived in in the mountain regions of Ningxia, I proposed that the poverty alleviation work there should also include attention to health care and to education,' Lin Yuechan said, leaning her trunk against the back of the chair and moving about animatedly. 'While visiting those peasants up in the mountains, I made a point of talking to the women and girls there. I learnt from them that a disproportionately high number of the women there suffered from gynaecological diseases because of water scarcity and poor sanitary conditions. Even girls who had just about started having their periods suffered from those diseases... That situation caused me great anguish!'

'People will find themselves in poverty for very objective and concrete reasons, but there is no such a thing as a culture that will be forever unable to escape it. During my visit I discover that, although the nine years of nationally compulsory education was adequately covered in the region, secondary-level education was still very deficient due to a lack of teachers and a lack of sufficient qualifications among the teachers they had. That resulted in an increasingly smaller number of students enrolling at middle schools at the county level, and in a very small percentage of students entering university or even making it to senior middle school. Without a serious effort on the education front, it would be very difficult for poor families to really escape their poverty. So I submitted my report to the provincial government and to Secretary Jinping, urging them again and again to include support for health care and education in the Cooperation on Poverty Alleviation,' Lin Yuechan said. 'And to my great joy, secretary Jinping and the other members of the provincial leadership gave their support for including those two elements in the programme.'

Besides carrying out the assignment Xi Jinping had entrusted her with, Lin Yuechan's trip to Ningxia also had another important goal to achieve, namely, to make arrangements for the leaders of Fujian to come to Ningxia for the second joint conference of the Cooperation on Poverty Alleviation Between Fujian and Ningxia.

'They are coming! They are coming! Provincial leader He, deputy secretary Xi Jinping... They will all be here!' people said. And in the afternoon of the 15th of April the Fujian delegation arrived in Yinchuan. Theirs was the highest-ranking Party and government delegation from Fujian to be welcomed to Ningxia ever since the establishment of the People's Republic of China. It had 35 members in total, and, as their Ningxia hosts put it, 'our family from the coast has arrived to visit us'. And for those few days that fraternal atmosphere, filled with affection, would take hold of the city of Yinchuan. On the day following their arrival, the second joint conference of the Cooperation on

Poverty Alleviation Between Fujian and Ningxia was formally opened. Huang Huang, then Party secretary of the Ningxia Hui Autonomous Region, the Autonomous Region's chairmen Bai Lichen and Ma Qizhi, as well as Kang Yi, Zhang Lizhi, Zhou Shengxian, Wu Shangxian and other leaders of the Autonomous Region, were in attendance. Fujian was represented by governor He Guoqiang, by deputy Party secretary Xi Jinping, and others. At the meeting deputy secretary Xi Jinping, in his role of head of the leading group in charge of the cooperation work with Ningxia, delivered a very enthusiastic and emotional speech. Xi Jinping's speech is still fresh in the memory of many old comrades in attendance that day. They told me that his speech was very strong and in touch with reality, and that at no moment did they feel like they were being talked down to.

Xi Jinping told them that, at a working meeting convened by the Central Committee in September of 1996, it had been decided that Fujian and Ningxia would be partnered in a poverty alleviation programme. He also said that the Central Committee and the State Council had great trust in them and had entrusted to them a glorious task of great historical significance.

My Ningxia comrades told me that, as they listened to Xi Jinping deliver his speech, they noticed something very unique:

'For instance, when he uttered terms like "great trust" and

"a glorious task of great historical significance", which in other people's mouths would sound perhaps too boastful or clichéd, coming from him sounded sincere, genuine and forceful,' one of my comrades said. 'Did you notice how, in his speech, he mentions the words "trust" and "entrust", words that also bring with them the notion of responsibility? Could they not come from the sense of great historical responsibility that a leader of a party, a party that we respect and hold dear, feel deep in his heart?'

Great responsibility! Great responsibility! What a great responsibility! It is the great responsibility of lifting hundreds of millions of Chinese from poverty that befell the Communist Party of China and its members. Who could, in full conscience of the fact, place upon one's own shoulders that great responsibility, and then work strenuously to fulfil it?

Well, Xi Jinping that is! History has taken us to this day and has already given us this loud and clear answer. The goal of eradicating poverty throughout China by 2020 had been put forward by General Secretary Xi Jinping, and it was during his tenure as General Secretary and President that it was achieved. How can that not be enough to make us all understand what it means to bear a 'great responsibility'?

The ancients used to say that 'the greatest responsibility

Heaven has sent down and placed upon us is the people'. The mission of lifting China out of poverty can be said to have been 'sent down from Heaven' and placed upon Xi Jinping personally, and upon Xi Jinping as the core of the Central Committee. That is a choice History has made, and greatly fortunate for the Chinese nation.

In 1997 few people in Ningxia knew about, or understood, the significance of having a 'relative' such as Xi Jinping. All they knew about him was that he was deputy secretary of the Fujian provincial Party committee and head of the leading group in charge of their cooperation on poverty alleviation with Fujian. They knew also that Xi Jinping was still young (44 years old at the time). In fact, very few people in Ningxia knew that eight years prior to him becoming head of that leading group in charge of poverty alleviation, Xi Jinping had been Party chief of the Ningde prefecture in Fujian. From June of 1988 to April of 1990, the young comrade Xi Jinping acquired crucial experience working with poverty alleviation in the poor areas of Ningde, following the ethos of the one that 'gets the weak bird to fly' and of the 'dripping water cutting through stone'. Comrade Xiang Nan, an old revolutionary and former secretary of the provincial Party committee in Fujian, said in the foreword that he wrote to *Up and Out of Poverty* that Xi Jinping 'thoroughly did away with the current bad leadership habits of grandiose, empty, and formulaic speech', and that 'there is no doubt that the good conduct Xi Jinping practised has been an inspiration to his successors, as what exists today comes from the past'[1].

'Ningxia and Fujian are in very different geographic locations, and the geographic features of the two provinces are, naturally, also very different. Thus, the cooperation between them also has a very strongly complementary character. The two provinces, working together, can promote the economic development of poorer regions based on principles such as "complementary advantages", "mutual benefits", "long-term cooperation", and "common development". By understanding that securing the basic necessities of life to the people of poor regions is a very important task, we should be able to thoroughly develop a wide range of ways to cooperate on poverty alleviation, and thus promote the common development of both Fujian and Ningxia,' Xi Jinping said in his speech.

The speech Xi Jinping delivered as a delegate of the Fujian side in the morning of the 16th of April was, moreover, received by the representatives of the Ningxia side as if it was a gentle breeze caressing their faces. That was because Xi Jinping announced that, for the next three years, Fujian would

---

1   First page of the foreword of *Up and Out of Poverty* by Xi Jinping

allocate a budget of 15 million yuan a year to be destined to individual programmes of their cooperation agreement. Xi Jinping announced also that he was about to call on investors at the national level, at the local level, and also of the 'three types of investment' communities, namely overseas Chinese, foreign investors, and the Chinese-foreign joint ventures, as well as on private investors more generally, to step forward and invest on businesses and factories in Ningxia. 'Through extensive cooperation on the development of local economies and trade, support of main industries that help alleviate poverty, expansion of the exports of services, the development of natural resources and of the economic integration of mountain areas, the launching of new public welfare programmes, official exchange and training, it will be possible for us to develop the poorest regions of Ningxia and lift those regions out of poverty very quickly, promoting also a continued, fast, and healthy social and economic development of both Ningxia and Fujian,' Xi Jinping said.

'To be honest, the words of General Secretary Xi Jinping felt particularly refreshing for us in Ningxia. That is because ours was a rather backward region, economically speaking. And even though by 1997 Reform and Opening-up was already twenty years old, the pace of development in Ningxia was still very slow, especially regarding the goal of lifting the people out of poverty. So, to propose making use of economic incentives and to see things from a perspective of social integration felt almost like starting things anew. For that reason, General Secretary Xi Jinping's speech piqued our curiosity as well. His words were like clear water slowly pouring into our hearts,' said an old comrade from Ningxia's Poverty Alleviation Bureau.

'Speaking from the heart?' I smiled and asked him.

'Absolutely speaking from the heart,' the Ningxia comrade replied in earnest and loudly. 'Maybe you don't know, but there was another part of comrade Xi Jinping's speech that also felt very refreshing to us at the time, going straight to the bottom of our hearts… He said that "the provincial Party committee of Fujian, the provincial government and also all the people in the province had decided to spare no efforts to, together with all ethnic groups of Ningxia, work effectively towards the goal of eliminating absolute poverty throughout the whole country before the turn of the century, so that in the 21st century the Chinese nation would stand tall among all the other nations of the world, having fulfilled the solemn responsibility she had undertaken and having made to the world a contribution of great historical significance, according with the requirements put forth by the Central Committee and the Second Joint Conference of the Cooperation on Poverty Alleviation Between Fujian and Ningxia, and carried out with a spirit of unrelenting heroism!" My friend, those are the words comrade Xi Jinping said more than twenty years ago! And listening to them today can still make one's blood boil with righteous indignation, because back then those partnerships called Cooperation on Poverty Alleviation were just getting started across the country, and people were still asking themselves whether it'd be really possible to lift out of poverty utterly destitute people like those living in Xihaigu, here in Ningxia. Deep down people were still very sceptical, to the point of not believing in it at all. That kind of mentality was very common at the time, because, just like it was the case with Xihaigu, poverty alleviation work did not start in the 1990s, it started shortly after the establishment of the People's Republic of China and has continued ever since. In reality, however, that work had also for a long time been rather ineffective, and people's lives were not changed in any meaningful way, with poverty remaining a very serious problem. Would this new cooperation on poverty alleviation between Fujian and Ningxia turn out the same way? Or would it work this time? We could only wait and see. Nonetheless, comrade Xi Jinping's speech really raised our spirits! Especially when he spoke of a "spirit of unrelenting heroism" and of the strong determination necessary to help lift our Ningxia out of poverty. It was that kind of confidence, of spirit, that kind of determination not only to speak but also to act, to carry out the mission to the end, to have the will and sincerity to move forward in the face of adversity, how could it not move us and encourage us here in Ningxia? It was for that reason that we used to say at the time here in Ningxia that our dear relatives from Fujian had come to visit us, and that the spring of that year would be much warmer than in years before. That's how I felt, I felt that the people of Fujian, and comrade Xi Jinping, had come to warm us with their sincere hearts…'

The heart is the most sensitive of all organs in this world. In this world it can tell true and false apart, it knows what is beneficial and what is harmful, and also what is beautiful and what is ugly. And this is the greatness of the human heart, that besides all that it can also make the clearest distinction between warmth and coldness. The true feelings of comrade Xi Jinping and of the people of Fujian touched Ningxia and its people and brought them real warmth.

In the spring of 1997, all of Ningxia was immersed in that warm spring breeze. It was warm, and especially bright and beautiful. The snow on top of the Liupan and the Helan mountains seemed to have thawed earlier that year than in previous years. In the pale light of an early morning in April many were the people craning their necks in expectation of the arrival of their esteemed guests. They waited for their guests as if waiting for the rays of the spring sun to shine upon them…

Chapter 3
Dispersed Sunlight on a Golden Beach

'Lifting Villages' – A Revolution in Poverty Alleviation

'The Yellow River's water is sweet, and the Communist Party is dear to us.' When I first began hearing those words from people in Ningxia who had been lifted out of poverty, I was a little confused by them, and even a little sceptical. But later I understood them and could not but agree. And the more I heard them, the more pleased I was to hear them. In fact, only when you are emotionally close to them you can feel that gratefulness that springs from the bottom of the hearts of the people of Ningxia.

Perhaps that phrase can become a very well-known verse in a song such as 'the East is red, the sun is rising'. And then again, a friend from Ningxia told me in their local dialect:

'Ay, that's it!'

I do ask my readers to follow me in trying to grasp the true meaning of that phrase.

One Ningxia, many layers of Heaven and Earth! If you have never lived there, you might need quite some time to fully come to understand what sort of place Ningxia really is like. Along both banks of the Yellow River, in the region east of the Helan Mountains, the landscape is flat with plenty of canals and irrigation ditches, the oxen are robust, and the sheep are fat, and there grow fragrant fruit. That is the region the people of Ningxia often refer proudly as 'the Jiangnan north of the Great Wall'. And, in fact, by looking at this region, one would have a hard time associating it with the word 'poverty'. In central and southern Ningxia, however, there is a vast dry belt, and then there are the Liupan Mountains. If you drive from Yinchuan towards those central and southern regions, you will soon start to feel like you are in a completely different world from the one you departed. And then it won't be much longer on the road before you reach the world-famous tombs of the Western Xia dynasty. There you will find out that landscapes in Ningxia can be very similar to what can be found in the Gobi Desert in Inner Mongolia and in Xinjiang. That is the kind of place where winds howl and dry tumbleweeds roll, and where the eagle and small white clouds keep each other company in flight high up there in the sky, to be seen from every direction. The Western Xia dynasty has left their very distinct mark in the history of Chinese civilisation, and in that land we can also find very concrete evidence of their existence in the form of the many royal tombs they have left behind.

The royal tombs of the Western Xia dynasty are indeed magnificent and are regarded as among the greatest royal tombs ever built in China. Their greatness resides largely in the fact that they have existed in the wildernesses of the Gobi Desert for nearly a thousand years, and that in those nearly a thousand years they have had virtually no human help in withstanding the constant assaults of the harsh environment in which they are located. In contrast with the well-protected and maintained Ming and Qing imperial tombs in the outskirts of Beijing, the Western Xia tombs can only count on their purely 'earth-like' qualities to continue in existence. That is consistent with the spirit and the innate character of the people who built them, a brave and fearless people who never blinked in the face of pain and death. Most admirable about the people of the Western Xia, was that, when under assault from inclement winds or the stone projectiles of trebuchets, they put up resistance with nothing but their bare torsos.

The Western Xia dynasty was established in the early 11th century by the Tangut people, a non-Han people, as a separatist centre of political power in what is today China. It came into being as a separate realm when, in 1038, Yuanhao was proclaimed emperor in the prefecture of Xingqing (today's city of Yinchuan, in Ningxia). The Western Xia had a total of ten emperors before they were finally vanquished in 1227 by the Mongol invaders. Their territory went 'from the Yellow River in the east to the Yumen Pass in the west', and 'from the Xiao Pass in the south to the open vastness of the desert in the north', over distances of 'more than 20,000 *li*'. In fact, at their peak, the Western Xia occupied an area of about 830,000 square kilometres, a vast territory that included today's Ningxia, most of Gansu, the north-east of Qinghai, the western regions of Inner Mongolia, the northern part of Shaanxi, as well as the southern parts of today's independent state of Mongolia. They coexisted in their early period with the Northern Song and the Liao dynasties, and with the Southern Song and the Jin dynasties during their middle and later periods. They were described in the literature as 'existing when the world was divided in three, and controlled valiantly the north-west for two hundred years'. The creation of the Western Xia state resulted in the partial unification of the north-western regions of today's China, representing an important contribution to the economic, social, and cultural development of those areas, and to the eventual formation of a multi-ethnic society. The two most conspicuous elements of the culture of the Western Xia still visible and recognisable today are their writing system and those royal tombs built on the eastern foothills of the Helan Mountains, in the western part of today's prefecture of Yinchuan.

The tombs are built on an open country that stretch out as far as the eyes can see, but the landscape there is littered with small stones and covered with the sand of the Gobi Desert, and you can even feel on your skin the loose grit blown by the wind. The tombs are all inside a demarcated perimeter with an area of 58 square kilometres. Scattered inside that area are a total of nine imperial mausoleums and 271 smaller tombs still standing. This is one of the largest and most complete imperial burial areas in China, but those tombs are also an impressive sight due to their location between the imposing Helan Mountains to one side and the open vastness of the Gobi Desert to the other. Mausoleum no. 3, which is open to visitors, is the largest and tallest among all the Western Xia tombs. It is also known as *Tailing*, or the 'Tai

Mausoleum'.

The Tailing is nearly a thousand years old. Despite the structures within it having suffered considerable damage over time, the bases of its gate towers and of the tomb itself are still largely intact. The 'divine' wall, the gate towers themselves, and the bases of the corner towers are also in fairly condition, so that it is possible to make out the overall arrangement of the complex. Being guided in my tour by the site's personnel, I was lucky enough to come very close to the tall burial mound and touch that ancient tomb made fully of rammed earth and weathered

A local farmer tending grapes in today's Yuquanying Farm

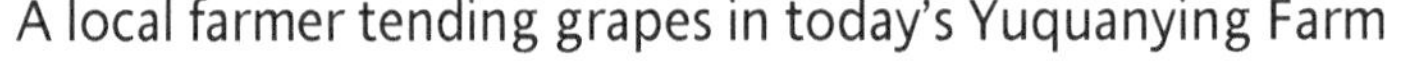

by the sand the wind unrelentingly blew against it. There was indeed a sense of sacredness and solemnity about it, so strong as to make one feel the aura of true heroism and nobility!

But when taking one's eyes from the imposing tomb and turning one's gaze to look at the horizon, one cannot help but to feel pained at the sight of the land. Besides the sand and the rocky ground there's nothing except a few shrubs here and there. For tens of kilometres into the distance one can't spot a single thing that could properly be call a tree, much less a village or even the outline of a human being. After taken a car and driving away for a while, however, one can finally see a few houses surrounded by low walls.

'This used to be a base of the armed forces' farming units, but it's been abandoned since 1974,' a local government official told me. Only later did I learn that, for several hundred square kilometres around the Western Xia tombs, there was no human presence at all up to 1969. That was the year of the Zhenbao Island Incident, a flare-up of a border conflict between China and the Soviet Union, as a result of which the Military Area Command of Lanzhou was deployed to the area of the tombs to set up a 'combat readiness farm' and open the land for agriculture. Five years later, the Army withdrew, and the farm was placed under the responsibility of the Department of Agricultural Reclamation of the Ningxia Hui Autonomous Region, with the relatively nearby Lianhu Farm, a state-run farm also under the jurisdiction of the Department of Agricultural Reclamation of Ningxia, formally assuming control of the site. Four years later it was incorporated into the area under the administrative control of the Yuquanying Farm, which is located in the southern part of the Xixia[1] district of the prefecture of Yinchuan and covers an area several times bigger than the central urban area of Yinchuan itself. But although Yinchuan is in an area irrigated by the Yellow River since ancient times, benefiting also from the water carried by the Xigan Canal, most of the land in the Yuquanying Farm is in fact arid and barren. There is a saying locals use to describe the contrast: 'Though all in the same Yinchuan, difference is like Heaven and Hell'. The same metaphor is also applicable to the contrast between the landscapes of the more urbanised areas of the prefecture and its desert areas. Perhaps because of that, and also because of the modern trend of contracting out land management, the Department of Agricultural Reclamation of Ningxia decided to contract out the work necessary to develop the Yuquanying Farm and the vast area of wilderness they had received from the Army, an area where, as the saying goes, 'no wolf take a crap'. In

---

1 The name means, literally, 'Western Xia'

practical terms it meant asking John Doe, hey, John Doe, do you want to grow something on that piece of land? If yes, great! Here you go! And then asking Joe Bloggs, hey Joe Bloggs, do you want to grow something there too? Sure enough, take that land next to John Doe's! And just like that John Doe, Joe Bloggs, and just about anyone could become a 'landowner'.

'But what sort of landowner is that!? You can give me everything under Heaven to grow something on that land and still all I'll have to eat will be the wind… I'll give this land to whoever wants to come and take it!' one of those new 'landowners' would say. That way a labourer from Xihaigu, waving his hands, subcontracted more than 400 *mu* of land, state-owned land he had been assigned to by the Department of Agricultural Reclamation, to some other person from the region he was from.

But the subcontracting was not the sticking point here! The sticking point is that the man had 'resold' land at 120 yuan per *mu* to a fellow villager, a villager from up in the mountains who had never in his life seen a piece of flat ground before.

'One hundred and twenty yuan per *mu*, spending that kind of money can mean death to half of my family!' said the person who took it. 'But for all of us to survive we have to put all we have together and come up with a way to get our hands on that land!'

The perseverance of the people from Xihaigu is as big as a mountain. Once they've made a decision, they won't go back on it, and what they have agreed upon cannot be changed! It is set in stone, and going back on one's pledge is the same as being careless about one's own life!

But one day those villagers who had already spent their money, seen the land, and who are ready to move their entire families a few hundred kilometres to the north to grow their crops and settle down, are simply told that the land is state-owned, that it is illegal for anyone to subcontract it, and that they cannot work on it!

What? We have paid that much money and now we can't work this land? How can this be fair? This is too cruel!

Let's go! Let's go make our case! And the angry villagers come down to the city of Yinchuan to present their grievance to the Department of Agricultural Reclamation and demand to 'be granted' their 'right to till the land'.

'We want to eat!' and 'We want to work the land!' say the banners they unfurl, powerful battle cries. Some of the angrier and more exalted among them begin to storm the building of the Department of Agricultural Reclamation. 'Give back our land!' and 'We want to eat!' they shout.

An army of petitioners of a kind seldom seen has shown up in the city of Yinchuan. For a city known for having always 'been content with their lot', the arrival of the petitioners sounds like thunder ripping through the winter sky.

The leading government figures of Ningxia come in person, naturally furious, and order the Department of Agricultural Reclamation to handle the cases adequately and as soon as possible. However, as the Department 'handled' the cases, more and more petitioners arrived. They were thirty or forty people at the beginning, but later their numbers increased to over a hundred, and then again to several hundred... They had become a dense crowd very nearly surrounding the grounds of the Department's building.

'This is terrible! We can't handle it even if we work non-stop! Go ask the leaders for help!' some official says.

'Help? What kind of help? Come and take a look for yourself... My comrade, the entrance to the regional government's building is also full of petitioners!' says one of the leaders. 'They've been here since last November making nose, almost half a year... Now even the *Voice of America* is talking about what is going on here! You tell me how you think I can help you!'

That exchange between officials of the Department

of Agricultural Reclamation and of the government of the Autonomous Region makes it very clear how serious an affair the buying and selling of land at Yuquanying turned out to be. But that man-made storm in the middle of the spring also resulted in a total revolution in the history of poverty alleviation and migration in Ningxia. That revolution was the now well-known 'Village Lifting Revolution', the *Diaozhuang* Revolution!

It can also be described as a 'revolutionary storm' because of some of its characteristics. The first of those is that it was born out of a movement of people who saw themselves forced to fight for their basic rights, the second was that both Party and government were aligned with the aspirations of that movement and supportive of the people, and the third is that, after it was decided upon, the migration and poverty alleviation programme known as 'village lifting' saw unprecedented development and went on to achieve great successes. And that 'revolution' must be successful, for only a successful revolution can be a part of China's struggle towards the eradication of poverty!

Now a member of the first generation of villagers from Xihaigu who were resettled in Yuquanying told me with great pride that, after they had persisted with their petitioning for a long time, around the May Day national labour day of 1990 the Party and government leadership of the Autonomous Region instructed the Bureau of Civil Affairs and the Petitions Bureau to act in coordination. The General Offices of the Autonomous Region's Party committee and government were then instructed to bring the leaders of the counties of Xiji, Haiyuan and Guyuan together with the Department of Agricultural Reclamation of the Autonomous Region, so that they too could act in coordination to handle the complaints.

The best solution turned out to be also the most realistic: to allow the people who had paid money to 'subcontract' land in Yuquanying to settle down there in a planned fashion and open the land for agricultural development.

The question that remained was to whether their residency registration, or *hukou*, would be changed, placing them under a different jurisdiction, or whether they'd maintain their association with their counties of origin.

It was the local administration of Yuquanying that raised this issue:

'We have no way of managing them. It's not easy to survive in those state-owned lands and, as individual farmers, they may become a "hot potato" for us if we can't handle them adequately. It's best to let their counties of origin continue to manage them.'

But the Party committees and the local administrations of every county in Xihaigu objected:

'They've moved a million miles away. How can we manage them? That's not an easy task!'

'Yes, but if you can't manage them, you can't leave that burden to us either. Then the best solution would be for you to take the people back,' was said in reply.

'That must be a joke! If we could take them back, would we have come down to Yinchuan? And please consider this too: the land up there on our mountains is barren, and we can't even take a few stalks of corn or a few potatoes out of it… Now those people have left and made up their minds to stay at that new place. You please have mercy!'

'Well, that's right. If they can stay and work the land there for a full eight or ten years maybe they'll be able to turn that desolation into another "Jiangnan north of the Great Wall". That'd be great!'

'That's it. Let's work together to make that happen!'

'Yes! Let's work together for that!'

The 'hosts' from Yinchuan and the 'guests' from Xihaigu sat down together in the offices of the Autonomous Region's Party committee and of the local government and together they presented a proposal to the leaders. The proposal consisted of delimiting a portion of the land in Yuquanying and assigning it to those farmers from Xihaigu who wanted to grow their crops there.

There was, apparently, no serious objection that could be made to that proposal. The Gobi Desert in the south-western corner of Yinchuan was just as desolate and empty as anywhere else, so if there were people capable of settling down there and cultivating the land there, that would certainly be of benefit to everybody. Since ancient times no past dynasty has ever been able to achieve this. But now our people's government will be able to do it, a virtuous accomplishment for the ages! The leaders of the Autonomous Region were very happy to hear that.

But then one of them asked:

'What if those people work there for a while, then decide to leave? What if they want to go back? Will you people back in Xihaigu be able to handle their return?'

'It's very simple,' the leaders of the counties in Xihaigu replied without hesitation. 'They can come and go as they please. They are *our* people after all.'

'Great, freedom to come and go, stay or leave as they see fit,' one of the leaders of the Autonomous Region nodded.

Then another one asked:

'But assume people come in large numbers to Yuquanying and decide they want to settle down there for good, how do you think you'll manage their *hukou* registration? I heard you folks here in the city of Yinchuan weren't very keen on being in charge of that?'

But a comrade from Yinchuan smiled and replied:

'Let's hear what our comrades from Xihaigu have to say. I guess they've already thought of a good solution to that problem.'

'Oh, Xihaigu comrades, please do say it!' a leader of the Autonomous Region said, turning his gaze to the leaders of the counties of Xiji, Haiyuan and Guyuan.

'We can report to our leader what our thoughts are: These people come from our counties, some may decide to move with their entire families, while others may decide to only bring part of their families for the time being. For instance, sometimes the children may want to move, but their old parents my prefer to stay. In cases like that, placing the family under the jurisdiction of Yinchuan is certain to cause a lot of trouble. So we think that, in those cases, it's better to leave their *hukou* registration unchanged and keep us responsible for them.'

'And how do you plan to manage people living hundreds of kilometres away?' a leader of the Autonomous Region asked, raising another key problem that also needed to be addressed.

'We have already thought about this issue and decided that the solution is to dispatch officials from the relevant departments in our counties to manage things on site, so that the management structure can be replicated there. Each county will also appoint a deputy county head to be specifically in charge of the matter. That way there will always be people to be held accountable, and so things are guaranteed to go well. And the leaders here of the city of Yinchuan have also thought of an even more promising idea. If we can implement it, it will be excellent to everyone! We hope that the leaders of the Autonomous Region will approve of it.'

'What idea? Come on, tell us and we'll be glad to hear it,' a leader of the Autonomous Region turned to his Yinchuan comrades and asked.

'Well, we thought of the following: Aren't all those regions by the coast in the east setting up 'development zones', 'special zones', and the like? Perhaps we should also think a little outside the box and take a lesson or two from them, maybe turn the area in Yuquanying assigned to settlement by those poor folks into a special 'economic development zone'… Meanwhile, our governments could also provide the financial support and specific policies as required for their development needs. That way maybe a 'little Shenzhen' will grow out of that land!'

'Ha ha ha… That's a good idea! Very creative! Very well, the Party committee and the government of the Autonomous Region will study and implement the relevant policies as soon as possible, so as to give to those folks who are willing to move here both the opportunity and the ability to shake off poverty and become prosperous! They'll be able to count with the Autonomous Region's full support, and maybe this will mark a historic turning point for poverty alleviation in Ningxia!' said joyfully the leader of the Autonomous Region. 'And indeed, this kind of thing is like lifting a bucket full of water and carrying it to be used somewhere hundreds of miles away, how could this be called? A village lifted and taken to some other village, you, modern day Zhuge Liangs, think up a name for that!'

'This "lifting", and villages, ha ha, that's quite interesting.'

'Since it's about lifting villages and moving them about, why not call it "village lifting"?'

'Village lifting? That's an interesting name. How about just calling it that?'

'Great, "village lifting" it will be!'

And now this word, *diaozhuang*, or 'village lifting', is a household name in Ningxia, finding a place also in the hearts of millions of poor peasants in the region, and becoming also synonym with hope and good fortune…

That word makes countless people get lost in dreams and makes the faces of countless people wet with tears.

Following the Path of the Great Mountains

Go, go, go far, far to that distant place

My heart is troubled and it is like a knife

Yo-heave-ho-hey

This song's tears flood my heart...

Go, go, go far, keep going farther and farther

The guokui loaves in my bag get lighter

Yo-heave-ho-hey

But the sadness in my heart gets heavier

Heavier, this song's tears fall to the ground.

The scene in that song probably took place in the twilight of an evening more than 80 years ago, when the air in that desolate wilderness was filled with sand being blown by the winds. There a lonely young man trudged forward along a gully path meandering between loess hillsides. Suddenly he heard, coming from behind him, a resounding and very slightly hoarse voice singing a *hua'er*, a folk song. It was a sad song, and the voice belong to Wu Duomei, the lady owner of an inn for travellers and for their horses and carts. It was a send-off song to that young man on his long journey away from home.

The moment the young man became aware of the singing and turned in the direction from where it was coming, 'tears rolled down his face and moistened the front of his jacket'. That young man was Wang Luobin, who would later become known as 'the best singer of the west'.

> Ay ye ye ah, woman is that peony growing in the garden
>
> Ay ye, this man's darling she is
>
> That other brother is the phoenix in the sky
>
> Ay ye, spinning around, spinning around, and not in vain!
>
> Lifting himself up above that white peony tree ay!
>
> Woman, my heart is also lifted up there in the air ay!
>
> Wandering about without rest ay!
>
> Without rest ay...
>
> The lifted village has taken away my darling
>
> and lifted her to the edge of the sky ay
>
> Woman my heart has no rest ay
>
> my heart has no rest ay...

In a spring thirty years ago that love song was often heard through the valleys and up the hills of Xiji, Haiyuan, and other such places on the Liupan Mountains. It was a melancholy song that was part sadness and part hope for the future. It made many a migrant on the road walking away from the mountains stop and turn back to look after each step.

Scenes such as that in the song are among the most tragic and unforgettable impressions taken from the long fight against poverty in Ningxia. They are like a prelude in history to that method employed in that fight and known as 'village lifting'. The great migrations that the 'lifting of villages' entailed will themselves turn into a very important chapter in history.

'But who were, after all, the first migrants to leave the great mountains and become the first migrants of a 'lifted village'?' I asked.

And, as I come today to Yuquanying, now a new 'oasis north of the Great Wall', the officials and villagers living prosperous lives in new houses all tell me with a smile:

'We all are…'

'You all are?!' I ask.

'Yes, we all are.'

I smiled back. They all were those first migrants, no question about it… Because there were in the first group of migrants,

400 families in total. And in those 400 families there could very well be as many as a few thousand people. After those first few thousand people came a few thousand more, and then there were also the women who were pregnant at the time. Those must also be counted among the first people who left the mountains and became inhabitants of 'lifted villages'.

'But if you really want to get to the bottom of this, we can tell you this much: *We* were the first ones to leave the mountains.' It was three people who told me that, all of them already retired. Their homes, however, were in Xihaigu.

Really? Could it really have been them? When I made enquiries at the local Party committee of the county of Guyuan they confirmed it to me. Those three guys were telling the truth. Ding Jianyi, Ma Qiang and Xie Junqing were the first three people to leave the mountains of Xihaigu and move to Yuquanying. But they were not counted among those 400 families of the first group of migrants. In fact, they had arrived at the wilderness that was the 'migrant area' of Yuquanying a full two months prior to the arrival of that first group.

They were the 'advanced official group' assigned to serve that first group of migrants in their new 'lifted village'. The Party committee of Xiji and the county's government had turned them into a work unit in their own right. That unit was called the 'Base Office of the Migrant Lifted Village of Xiji County in Yuquanying'. Thus, they were indeed 'new migrants' who had just been 'lifted' to a new location. The fate of those three officials then became inseparably intertwined with that piece of land and with the whole project of the migrant's 'lifted villages'.

Ding Jianyi is a former deputy mayor of the town of Xinglong, in the county of Xiji, Ma Qiang is a former deputy director of the Agricultural Construction Bureau of the county of Xiji, and Xie Junqing is a former Party branch secretary for art troupes, also in the county of Xiji. Unfortunately, I could not find an old leader of Xiji to ask him why his county had chosen those three in particular to move away and start a 'lifted village'. But the three of them gave me their own modest attempts at an answer to that question. There would have been a couple of reasons why they were chosen. The first reason was that the county expected that, if the 'village lifting' programme was successful, having a township-level unit for those poor families and transferring three deputy-level officials to staff that unit would allow them to learn from that experiment, meaning that the whole thing could be used as a test bed for new ideas. The second reason was that the three tranferred officials were all from different work units. Ding Jianyi had been deputy mayor, and so had administrative experience. Ma Qiang came from the Agricultural Construction

Bureau, and so had plenty of knowledge about the fundamentals of construction management in rural areas. And Xie Junqing, who had some experience as a Party branch secretary for art troupes, was, in a general sense, capable of carrying out ideological and political work. Those were the reasons the three of them gave for why they were chosen. And, in fact, that might as well have been what the Party committee of Xiji had in mind at the time.

Following the episode when petitioners came en masse to Yinchuan, the Party committee and the government of the Ningxia Hui Autonomous Region, together with their counterparts in the prefecture of Yinchuan and in the various counties in Xihaigu, decided to coordinate their efforts to conduct a careful evaluation of the matter, which was then discussed at a special meeting presided by the then chairman of the Autonomous Region, Li Chengyu.

From that meeting came out a decision that was issued in the name of Autonomous Region's government. The 10th and 11th work teams of the Lianhu Farm, which was under the jurisdiction of the Autonomous Region's Agricultural Reclamation Bureau, would be relocated, and 26,000 *mu* of land would be demarcated to serve as a base for the 'lifted village' for migrants coming from Xiji, while another plan would also be devised for the peasants coming from the counties of Haiyuan and Guyuan who had also gone to Yinchuan to petition. The relevant documentation stipulated that the boundaries of this 'lifted village of Yuquanying' would be set to the east by the Xigan Canal, to the west by the Yanshan Road, to the south by the limits of the Lianhu Farm, and to the north by the border with the county of Yongning. That would mean a distance of 5.2 kilometres from its western to its eastern end, and 3.75 kilometres from its southern end to its northern. The total area would be 29,200 *mu*, of which 21,100 *mu* could be used for development. Of that development area, 17,800 *mu* would be used for crops, of which 9,800 *mu* to the east of the main railroad crossing the area and 8,000 *mu* to the west of it. Moreover, the approved documentation also stipulated that, after the completion of the crucial Yanghuang poverty alleviation project (a water project pumping water from the Yellow River), 40% of the developable area in Ganchengzi, in Qingtongxia, that is 18,000 *mu*, would also be assigned as land for a 'lifted village' for peasants from the county of Xiji. The area of the 'lifted villages' of Yuquanying would be expanded twice more later, in 1995 and then again in 1996, growing to a total area of 60,000 *mu*. That included areas in Yuquanying, the Lianhu Farm, the Huangyantan Farm, the city of Qingtongxia, and the county of Yongning, and the plan was for it to accommodate as many as

10,000 migrants.

'Lifted village' migration was a creation, a poetic saga, of the people of Ningxia. It became part of history through its innovative spirit and after being implemented by successive governments and Party committees of the Ningxia Hui Autonomous Region, all working under the guidance offered by the central authorities and motivated by the vision of a victorious fight against poverty. Nonetheless, the most touching verses of that poetic saga were written by the migrants themselves, those who left their homes in the mountains, and by workers who fought hard to implement poverty alleviation measures on the ground.

'Tomorrow you are going! Make sure you don't forget anything you may want to take with you, because once you've left, you can't turn back. You three are officials, and also Party members!' the county chief said to Ding Jianyi, Ma Qiang and Xie Junqing. Besides the county chief were also present other leaders of the county, including the deputy chief, the local Party secretary, and a representative for the Standing Committee of the National People's Congress.

'That's a very important mission,' said the secretary of the local Party committee. 'And also a glorious one. The leaders of our Autonomous Region have their eyes on you, and so do the tens of thousands of people of our county. In other words, you have to keep forging ahead, never to retreat! For generations our people here in Xiji have lived very arduous lives, because our land is not fertile enough, and because people were always too many for that land… So now we have to "lift" the first group of people out of here! And after that first group is lifted and gone, we'll lift some more. And once those first people to be lifted achieve prosperity, others will follow suit. For this reason, I say that what you're carrying on your shoulders is not simply the responsibility of a job you have, but also the hopes and the future of our people of Xiji, and of people all over Xihaigu!'

Ding Jianyi, Ma Qiang and Xie Junqing did not hesitate to speak up their minds:

'Dear secretary and county chief, you don't have to worry. Even if our bones are to lay to waste there, we will build that "lifted village" for our migrants! Let's get those first people to lay down roots there and find prosperity… And then we'll take group after group there!'

Then, on the first working day after Chinese New Year in 1991, the Party committee and the government of the county of Xiji had a special meeting with the newly assigned administration of the 'lifted village' to make decisions regarding staff transfers.

'Right away we began making the necessary arrangements for establishing our base in the 'lifted village' in Yuquanying, hundreds of kilometres away,' Ding Jianyi said. His title was also changed from 'deputy town chief Ding' to 'director Ding', or, in full, 'director of the base office of Xiji county in the migrant lifted village at Yuquanying'. His two colleagues also became deputy directors, each officially in charge of different matters.

And so Ding Jianyi and the two others hurried with their preparations. They hurried because the county chief had told them to be ready to leave 'as soon as the notification arrived'.

'We were like soldiers at the time, ready to get moving as soon as our orders were issued. Moreover, there wasn't really any more preparations that still needed to be done… What could our bureau have at the time? We couldn't have things like typewriters or photocopiers. Telephones also needed cables, and those cables would still take several months to reach our location. If we wanted to make a phone call to report on our progress, that required a trip to the city of Yinchuan,' Ding Jianyi told me.

'Do you know what all our belongings were at the time?' he asked me, then proceeded to tell me that all of their team and all their belongings fit inside an old Jiefang truck that had been especially assigned to them for the mission. 'Besides some food and blankets we had brought for ourselves, there were also in that truck about 30 plain board beds we had borrowed from the local county Party committee, some desks and some benches for sitting. That was all we had to start that 'lifted village' endeavour.'

'There was no motorway from the mountains in the south to Yinchuan at the time,' he said. 'And the provincial road that did exist was a very rough and bumpy ride. The weather was also cold and windy for an entire month at the time, so it took us two full days to reach Yinchuan in our Jiefang truck. I remember that it was already dark when we reached Yinchuan, and we had to put up at a small inn on the outskirts of town. It was only early the next day that we would be able to report at the Agricultural Construction Committee of the Autonomous Region. And then it was already dark again by the time we reached the location of the Lianhu Farm's 11th team. The original plan was that, as soon as we had arrived, the farm would vacate an old house to accommodate our team. But when we made it there, we were told that they knew nothing about those plans, and that no one had notified them. What could we do? Well, we *had* to stay for the night!'

Ding Jianyi told me also that, for the rest of his life, he would remember how they spent that night. The winds in northern Ningxia in January were so cold they reached down to your bones, and temperatures dipped below -10°C. 'We had the food we had brought with us, so there was no worry on that regard. But we had no water!' Ding Jianyi said. 'We had to go to a small shop nearby and buy a few metal buckets. Then we dispatched four of our officials to cross the Xigan Canal to fetch some water. Those four men going out to fill four buckets with water took four full hours to be back, and in the end they returned with only two and a half buckets' worth of water. The road was very uneven to walk on, and they also had to go after it was already dark, so bringing back even that little water was no easy feat! With the problem of water out of the way, the problem now was getting to sleep. We were in the middle of a bitter winter. In the middle of the night temperatures dropped below -20°C. I dispatched a few more officials to go dig up some wormwood for us to start a fire with. We then piled up some bricks and heated some water in a pot on top of the fire, so that we could drink the hot water and keep ourselves warm inside as well. But the cold winds were too strong, so that the fire blackened the new aluminium pot, but the water would still not boil. We had to make do without it! And so, in order to get some sleep, we took a few board beds from the truck and arranged them in a circle. Everyone sat down on the bedding… and we all remained like that till dawn.'

That was the first night of a 'lifted village', a night that really foreshadowed the difficulties 'lifted village' migrants would come to experience themselves. But that was how the many months and years of the struggle against poverty really started, a struggle that would eventually succeed.

Theirs was a group of working officials capable of enduring great suffering and of achieving great things. Ding Jianyi's team then took only twenty days to demarcate the 20,000 *mu* of land that would become the base of that first 'lifted village', surveying its geography, natural conditions, the quality of the soil, the availability of natural resources, and the overall potential for development. And, while lying in beds that were full of the sand that was blown by the wind, they penned works such as the *Report on the General Plan for the Construction of a Lifted Village from Xiji County in Yuquanying* and the *Report on the Relocation Plan*.

Soon enough the county of Xiji, the county of Haiyuan and other such counties with plans for 'lifted village' resettlements came up with a unified arrangement for the transfer of people and for their general administration. That arrangement consisted of the following points:

1 – The Lifted Villages Office will be responsible for helping the migrants settle down and for all other administrative questions concerning them. Resettlement locations will be

assigned by that Office within the approved areas, and in accordance with information provided in the migrants' transfer notifications and personal identification cards. Each household will receive half a *mu* of developable area for the purpose of setting up a residence. Peasant families whose documentation is incomplete will not be accepted in the programme.

2 – A total of 32 residential areas are to be delimited within the Lifted Village, and each is to receive 55 families, for a total of about 275 people. There will be one villagers' committee for every four or five villagers' group, that is, for every four or five residential areas. And in order to preserve the customs and ways of life of the migrants, those groups will be divided in accordance with ethnic affiliation.

3 – Once migrants have been assigned to their areas of residence, the Lifted Villages Office will divide the arable land and the developable forest areas among them in accordance with family size as verified.

4 – Resettled families will not be allowed to buy or sell the land or else transfer it by any method.

5 – The 350 *mu* of land that is already cultivated, including the forest area and the orchards within that area, will be collectively managed through the Lifted Villages Office.

6 – If a peasant family fails to build a house in the land

allocated to them for that purpose within two months from being notified, the people's government of their place of origin will be notified and asked to arrange for another family to take their place. If within six months still no house is built, the corresponding resettlement quota will be nullified, and the spot given by the Lifted Villages Office to another village or township.

7 – Resettled peasant families must follow the administrative directives and the unified leadership of the Lifted Villages Office. When dealing with those who seize land unilaterally, start their own cultivation arrangements, disrupt the order of the resettlement process, thus affecting the people's production and livelihood, the Lifted Villages Office has the ultimate authority to cancel the resettlement decision concerning those people and to send them back to their places of origin within a determined time frame. Any losses should then be the responsibility of those who caused them, with circumstances being taken into consideration for punitive measures. If the circumstances are serious enough to warrant the involvement of the organs of public security, those will mete out the appropriate administrative punishments. And in case of a criminal offence, the judicial organs will ascertain any criminal responsibility in accordance with the law.

8 – As the resettlement process advances, the Lifted Villages Office will also establish new basic organisations to strengthen

education and improve the administration of the resettled families.

9 – All contracts to develop and grow crops on lands already under cultivation that the Lifted Villages Office reassigns to resettlement will be terminated within three years. During that time all contractual obligations will still have to be performed.

The arrangement above also stipulated that the Autonomous Region would require from the county of Xiji and from the resettled families that progress be made on a set schedule, establishing a clear plan for the creation and upgrading of organisations and infrastructure serving the resettled families. Between 1991 and 1995 water infrastructure was implemented, together with a small hospital, a primary school, a services centre for peasants, a forestry station, a veterinary station for farm animals, a cooperative for the buying and selling of necessary goods, a local police station, a township government headquarters, a granary, and other such facilities. That was the beginning of the first great battle in the history of 'lifted village' migration, a pioneering and innovative struggle like never before seen in the history of Ningxia and Xihaigu.

'My child, you are leaving. When will mother be able to see you again?' said the mother standing by the entrance to the village while clinging to her son, who was about to whip his horse and leave.

'Oh, mother! Once I have set up a home there, I'll come back to fetch you and dad!' the son said.

'You will take us there? What should we do with our home here?' the mother asked in confusion.

'We'll get rid of it!' the son laughed.

The mother sat down on the ground and cried:

'Mother won't go! And you also can't go!'

'Ah, that's enough! Life will be good! Go, go, go!' the son said, whipping his horse. The animal took off at a gallop and went up the mountain road, leaving behind a trail of dust. Since very early in the morning the entrance to the village had been filled with dozens of horse carts, flatbed carts, and tractors, forming a powerful stream, a 'lifted village' stream! Next to the lofty peaks of the Liupan Mountains, however, it looked like no more than a streamlet flowing through a ravine. And yet it continued to flow, tirelessly, always advancing towards a future in that distant place...

Near the entrance to another village a young woman waited at a deserted place, out of sight behind a mountain ridge. She waited for the tractor to appear round the bend.

Finally, the loud chugging of an engine vibrated inside her

chest.

'Stop! Stop!' she shouted as she rushed out from behind the ridge to the road and slapped the front of the tractor. She carried a little cloth bundle on her back, which she then pushed onto her guy's lap for him to hold it. She also left behind the same promise:

'I'll write back as soon as I'm settled!'

'That's right. Just wait and see!' the guy's voice reverberated through the valley and against the mountain sides, like a never-ending love song that she will foolishly listen to night after night while standing on a ridge.

And by the entrance to that same village there was something else unusual: a dozen or so flatbed carts filled to capacity. Those belonged to five different families, and each group of carts carried three generations of people, the oldest seventy or eighty years old, the youngest four or five.

'We don't want to return! We fear the misery! We just want to… just want to go there... even if it is to live just one good day in our lives! We don't want to stay in these poor mountains far away from everything any more!' said an old man, his goatee trembling as he spoke. And because he was of that mind, no one in his family of nine stayed behind in their old home.

And the people travelling together with his family were

fellow villagers, people who had always faced the same hardships. Even the quilts the People's Liberation Army had sent them the year before, and which they had kept in their *kang* beds, were now full of holes from so much use. Those were all very poor families who had almost nothing to their names. It was possible that, had they stayed another winter in their old home, the elderly among them wouldn't survive, the children would go hungry and would end up eating mud, and the men and women would all end up fleeing. So it was better to hurry up and move to a new place with the family still whole. That way at least they would stay together!

Thus, the families got together and decided to rush to a distant place in the north they had never been to before. That future home was for them at the time still nothing but a dream. But having a dream meant having hope, and it was hope what gave them the necessary strength to keep moving forward.

It was a strength coming from the hearts of long-suffering people living on dry mountains. Because of that strength that people could leave behind the land and homes of their ancestors and move, out of the mountains and to a place they had never seen before. How much courage and determination would that not take!

'It was only because it was impossible to continue living

where I was born! I had to leave and look somewhere else!' many told me. Most of the migrants who joined the 'lifted villages' programme felt the same way.

An old leader of the county of Xiji confessed to me that, back in 1991, most of the peasant families in his county were living in poverty and had, on average, just three- or four-hundred-yuan worth of belongings. On a single cart they could load everything they owned in this world, he told me. 'This is hard to hear, but at the time there were girls who, despite having just got married, would consider going away with an outsider if offered just a few hundred yuan… And if the wife just left, wouldn't the family collapse?! The elderly were just waiting for death, the children were going hungry, how could the men be able to carry on without their wives? That was the hard reality many people in our Xiji, in our Xihaigu, faced at the time!' he said. And what he said was the truth.

He also told me that the situation would be particularly difficult for a family if there was any among them sick or disabled. It was a reality to bring tears to anyone's eyes.

The people of Xiji were suffering, the people of Xihaigu were suffering, and they were desperately seeking for a path that could give them a hope of survival.

'Yuquanying? Great! Only by hearing the name I already

know it's a wonderful place! Sign me up!' one said.

'Our family also wants to sign up!' said another. 'Yuquanying, just by the name I can tell there are water springs there! Any place with water springs is a good place!'

Yuquanying later became the dream and the hope for the villagers joining the ranks of the great migrant army of 'lifted villages'.

'Yuquanying sure is a wonderful place!' yet another person said. 'Here in Xihaigu we have a hundred 'villages full of water', if one believes their names. But I ask you, have you seen any water in any of them? There's not even a drop of urine to be found!'

'Yes, but no matter how poor and barren they are, those mountains and that yellow dirt are what our ancestors left us!' said some other people, rushing to defend their old homes and their own poverty.

From many different discussions we can see how strong the resistance to the struggle against poverty coming from within itself really is. It often places obstacles against itself, making the task at hand all the tougher. The wheels of history will, nonetheless, continue to turn forward, and that distant place, Yuquanying, will continue to attract more and more hopeful people, people who dream of one day having a prosperous life. Those people will not be discouraged by any cynicism, for all they want is to keep moving forward. So they will always say: 'Let's go! Let's go!'

And there is no one who can stop them. At the crack of the whip their horse-drawn carts get moving, also the tractors' wheels start turning, and there will also be those riding their bicycles. Tears had to be shed, for it was, after all, a departure from their homeland. Tears had to be shed because people were saying goodbye to their old homes, to their fellow villagers, and even to those mountain ridges and cliffs that they had grown used to both love and hate…

But there were bitter tears that remained bitter for a lifetime. Even though it had already been several decades since the establishment of the People's Republic of China, there was still plenty of bitterness around: There were children who could not afford school tuitions, old people who died and their families were unable to afford a coffin for their burial, women who could not buy a single new dress even after decades of being married. Those were lives with no sweetness and nothing but bitterness instead. The bitterness was that of the sweat of the people of the great mountains, the true flavour of the lives of the people of Xihaigu and Ningxia. And it was because of that bitterness that the people of Ningxia came up with this term: 'lifted village'.

The way I see it, the concept of 'lifting villages' can be seen as a leap in history as big as that from the earliest and most backward cultures to modern civilisation. Could it not be that way?

That leap cannot be expressed simply in terms of geography. It is rather a leap in culture, one both tragic and heroic and part of humanity's struggle for the improvement of living conditions. At first sight it doesn't seem to amount to much more than a simple relocation of people. But, in reality, for the actual people involved, such as for a young mountain couple in love or for a family, it could represent a change affecting the rest of their lives, a change of fate in fact. And more than that, it could represent a change affecting generations to come over centuries. How could a change affecting a whole region be otherwise?

Today when we look back at that 'lifting of villages' that took place in those years, we see that the view above is justified. But three decades ago, in the early 1990s, those peasants leaving the great mountains to start a new life faced such enormous obstacles, both concrete and within their own souls, that before them even the great Liupan Mountains would tremble and even the Yellow River could have its flow reversed…

And yet no one who has not witnessed first-hand the great challenges of those 'lifted village' migrations could really describe the suffering those people went through. Between

January of 1991 and the 15th of February of 2020 (the day when the COVID-19 epidemic started) there were more than 10,000 days and nights. During that time, I wrote this book, and China experienced many earth-shattering transformations. And yet there are, perhaps, very few people who can tell accurately the story of Ningxia's 'lifted village' migrations. I just happen to have read a piece Wang Furong wrote in *Migration Days* (*Ban Jia de Rizi*), which I found particularly touching:

One afternoon in a golden autumn, the sun shone over a mountain ridge towering above my hometown. A field of sunflowers, like young girls in their first bloom, coyly lowered their heads. The autumn breeze, like boys in love, gently caressed the girls' heads, making hearts palpitate all over the land. The breeze makes the girls of the mountains bloom with love, the mountain ridge is beautifully illuminated, and the whole season is that much more romantic.

The bees have found that ocean of flowers and are now busy gathering pollen to concoct the sweetness of life. The flowers' aroma wafts up and through the air and reach very far, spreading out that sweet fragrance of honey, which makes its way into people's hearts. The gentle breeze blows, the air is pleasantly cool, and the village looks very quiet, peaceful and auspicious. The name of this village is Wangjiadawan.

Rahman lives in this village, and today he's moving away. He's moving to a very distant village called Minning[1]. Hearsay has it that he bought a little place for himself over there, and so now in the village there are women shedding tears while they talk among themselves.

Rahman has arranged for a lorry to come for his moving, and his wife Fatima has been putting the family's belongings in order for several days already. She has already arranged the belongings several times over. In fact, they don't have anything that's worth much, but they are loath to leave anything behind. Fatima has said to herself: 'We're really moving, we're moving to that Minning village, 800 *li*[2] away from my parents' home.' It seemed that it would be then nigh impossible for her to go visit her parents. Why did they have to leave that courtyard, that house, their own families? Her heart was broken to pieces and flooded with tears.

Other villagers knew about their moving away, and so many showed up to help them load their belongings onto the lorry. A few old ladies, shakily dragging their own grandchildren by the hand, also came to Rahman's home to see them off. Those old

---

1   The name 'Minning' (闽宁) is a combination of the Chinese characters for 'Min' (闽), as a reference to Fujian, and 'Ning' (宁), as a reference to Ningxia.

2   Or 400 kilometres.

ladies also held Fatima's hands, and one of them, already 80 years old, said: 'My dear, you are moving away, why should I let you people go? After that I won't be able to see you again!' And her words caused everyone present to shed tears. Fatima could no longer hold her tears back either and started wailing loudly and with great grief. Everyone was urging her not to cry, and then that same old lady said: 'Dear, you all have a long road ahead of you, after you move, you'll live a good life. That place over there is much better than ours here.'

Fatima had been living in that village for 15 years, ever since she got married. She already had two children, both older than ten. It was hard to leave her home village, and even harder to leave her neighbours, not to mention her own relatives. All the married women in the village lived and worked together. They gathered firewood and carried water together, and whenever they had some time to rest, they sat down together to sew soles on shoes and gossip. Now they all had heard that Rahman's family was about to move away, and so were all very saddened. They all came to see them off, and once there they all put their arms around each other to form a circle and started to cry together. They all said that Fatima was a very dutiful daughter-in-law, very good to her husband's parents. They said that she was always very kind and never caused any offence. She always looked after everyone's children and was very considerate of everyone else, was also very respectful of all the village's elders, always greeting them by saying *salaam* whenever she saw them, and always helping anyone who needed helping.

'Ah, you're a really good girl! How much sadder this place will be after you're gone!' the people of the village said.

Other people from the village also came, and then this one gave them ten yuan, that other one gave eight yuan, pushing the money into Fatima's hand and into the hands of her two children. That is a custom those people have whenever seeing somebody off. They also filled two bags with boiled eggs, some fried *youxiang* cakes, and bread. Fatima gave away her used spatula to the wife of a neighbouring family, her iron fork to a neighbouring older woman, a cooking pot to her brother's wife, and whatever firewood she had left she gave also to her neighbours, saying:

'Make the children's *kang* beds plenty warm, just as a little thing to remember us for. And if I have ever offended mother or uncle or brother or sister when saying anything, please tell me now, so that, with your permission, I can make it all right now, since later we will seldom have the chance to see each other. Take care of the old ones and the children, and remember that I'll call you on the phone to say hello…'

The many exhortations were repeated over and over again.

It was a heart-wrenching departure scene, but very touching at the same time. Those were Rahman's neighbours, the very warm-hearted elders of his village.

The rafters for the construction of a new house were loaded on to the lorry. Some older man also placed shovels and shovel heads on to the lorry. 'Dear, we are peasants. We need to take our shovels with us wherever we go, because we don't have money to buy new ones,' they said. Some older ladies took a bag and a basket off Fatima's shoulders and placed them on the lorry as well. Then some younger men came with a lifter and loaded some more stuff. The last things to be loaded on to the lorry were Rahman's and Fatima's pair of wedding chests from the time when they got married. Those were mementos that she had to keep with her for all her life, and which she could not leave behind.

Rahman then visited the graves of his ancestors and lit incense for his father, his grandfather, grandmother, great-grandfather, and others. He bowed deeply saying *salaam* and then knelt down before the graves… At this moment Rahman could no longer contain the grief in his heart and started sobbing. He had seen the graves of those resting there, and remembered that, after that last goodbye, he would not be able to return often to visit the graves of his father, grandfather, grandmother, great-grandfather, and of all his other deceased relatives. Kneeling and sobbing, he told them all that he was moving away from the village. He was leaving his native village, the land where he had lived for 35 years, that loess upon which he had been born. He had to say goodbye to the souls of the departed, say goodbye also to his living relatives and to his fellow villagers, and also to the mountains and valleys and to the trees and to every single blade of grass. Rahman's heart was burning like fire inside, and deeply conflicted… His tears fell like a string of pearls just broken, tumbling down and hitting the front of his jacket, to slide further down to the ground of the cemetery. Rahman stayed there, kneeling, for a very long time, unwilling to get up.

There was, however, a strong reason for Rahman's reluctance to get up and leave. A few years earlier Rahman had intended to move to the village of Minning, and he had told his father of his intention. But his father withheld his permission, telling him: 'I know that you want to move away, because you're already grown up and can have an independent life, and because we're old. But can't this place feed you? Our ancestors have lived here for generations, and you are the only one who somehow can't make a living here. Do you think you'll starve? That this land is too poor? A son never complains that his mother's too ugly, nor does a dog complain that his house is too poor. This place is your home. Here is your land, your family, your house. A home made of mud is better than any castle made of gold and silver somewhere else. In that village of Minning there will be no father, no mother for you, you'll be a stranger without a family around, no one to rely on, and the children will have no school to attend. Will you be able to endure the mosquito bites? There's only sand there, no water. The sun there cooks people's brains, and you won't be able to take it all, my child. People from Yuquanying and Huangyangtan all say that those are no places for people to live. It's windy all year round, the wind blows from spring to winter. There are no birds in the sky, and on the ground the grass doesn't grow, for hundreds of miles on end there are no signs of people living anywhere, the wind blows and carries with it only sand and grit. It couldn't be more desolate. Son, just think about it. If that place were any good, the people of Huangyangtan would already have developed it. Do you think they're waiting for you, a child of the mountains, to come and develop it yourself?' With those words his father had been able to change his mind at the time. His father also loved his son and was afraid that his grandchildren would have to endure too many hardships. That is why he withheld his permission for his son to move away.

But several years have now passed, Rahman's father is no longer among the living, and the son is again planning to act in opposition to his father's wishes, which, for him, is the worst of all offences. That is why Rahman cried with such deep sorrow as he knelt there. He cried because he was about to betray the wishes of his late father. His heart was conflicted, full of pain and sadness.

His mother then came to pull him by the hand and said:

'Son, just go. It's your life you have to take care of. I can stay here in the village and take care of our old place. If things don't work out over there you can come back. You won't lose your old home, mother will look after it for you, mother will also look after our ancestors' graves.'

But it was Rahman who comforted his mother instead:

'Mother, it'd be difficult for you to go with me now, but once I've built the house there and am settled, I'll come back to pick you up. Your permission is all I need.'

Rahman then said *salaam* to his mother, and she wiped the tears off his face with her hand, saying:

'You go and do your best. If we can take the pain now things will be all right later.'

Rahman agreed with his mother and said *salaam* again, slowing letting go of the grip on his mother's hand. In his heart he felt like his flesh was being cut with a knife.

The lorry started to move, and everyone in the village,

men and women, young and old, started walking alongside it. Together they all wailed, a heart-wrenching wailing. They followed the lorry for a kilometre or two along the road, and then Rahman said *salaam* to his fellow villagers one by one, urging them to turn around and go back home. The villagers stood there, waving their hands and crying, and eventually the lorry disappeared among all that weeping and wailing…

Towards the end of his piece Wang Furong added also that those villagers, as they stood atop the tall ridges along the road seeing off their friends and kin, still shout out to them: 'Come home often to see us!'

Come home often?! But where would that home be? Would it be their old house and the old village they were leaving behind, or would that be their new home in that land called Yuquanying? Apparently, both were home, and neither were. But it is inevitable that whenever people leave to go somewhere very far from home, be they men or women, adults or children, there will be sadness and crying. And some will cry so much as to be unable to raise their heads off their knees. Children will cry in their mothers' arms, and women will sob on the shoulders of men as the men drive their tractors along the road.

And the men chasing after lorries or driving their own tractors will also cry. But they will not allow themselves to make a sound, or let their wives and children see them crying. Their tears are only meant to flow while facing the wind… Soon they will have before them the tall mountains, the canyons, the mountain ridges, and gradually the sand dunes will appear, and the Gobi Desert will open up before their eyes. At that moment they will no longer be able to hold it back and will let out a wail.

'We have to make a living!'

'We have to live like real people!'

'We must have a decent house!'

'Do not ask how far we still have to go, because we'll never go back!'

'We'll never go back! I pledge my life on it! Not until we have made it!'

It was only one man shouting those phrases at first. Then all the others started shouting along after him.

It was only the men shouting at first. Then the women, the children and the old all started shouting along…

Their shouting makes the earth shake, the Liupan Mountains tremble, the Yellow River seethe, and the Helan Mountains shout in reply!

In the middle of a severe winter and against the fierce winds of the open country, the tears of men and women, of the elderly and the children, still roll gently down. This time, however, the tears are not bitter, but hot, burning hot…

Chapter 4
The Story of Hongsibao

Numbers to Make the Heart Tremble

There will always be people who will say that numbers are a drab business. But for some people in Ningxia, and particularly for some people in the province's poorer mountain areas, some numbers can be equal to tears and sweat, or maybe to the blood flowing through all the pain they keep hidden within their hearts…

With many years of the great fight against poverty now already behind us, the numbers have naturally become the most cherished treasures the people of Ningxia and of the province's relatively poor mountain regions have to show off and to be proud of. The reason is that those numbers can be a representation of mostly every change, including in the fortune and in the states of mind of the people. Great changes jump out of those numbers. Numbers are also like musical notes inserted deep within a person's heart. As the numbers change, they play out a melody of the person's strengths and weaknesses, their pains and their joys, the fortunes or misfortunes they encounter in their lives. Finally, numbers are also like daemons. They can make you obsessed or overly excited, take you to extremes of action or else make you very complacent.

To the people of Hongsibao, moreover, numbers are also witnesses to their recent history.

Two hundred and ninety-nine metres, that is the figure that represents the beginning of history for Hongsibao, the revival of its land. That figure is the total height to which water is pumped by the Yellow River Water Lifting Project, the key element allowing for Hongsibao to exist at all at the place where it exists today. The barren yellow loess of its land was only able to come to life after water was pumped up over the several levels of that project's infrastructure.

The water that is finally delivered to Hongsibao is sourced from a system combining water pumping and gravity-assisted water sourcing. The water pumping is carried out at a pumping station built by the bank of the Yellow River on the Quanyan

Mountain, in the county of Zhongning. That station can pump 30 cubic metres of water per second. That water then enters the Elevated Main Canal, a widened canal that runs for 19.4 kilometres. The gravity-assisted sourcing component diverts water from the Yellow River at Zhongwei, adding another 8 cubic metres per second to the system and sending it through the Qixing Canal for 28.4 kilometres before joining the Elevated Main Canal for a combined flow of 38 cubic metres of water a second, which then goes on to its destinations. At Hongsibao, the Water Lifting Project takes that water at a rate of 25 cubic metres per second and distributes it through a system made of 104 kilometres of large canals and a further 84 kilometres of branch canals to irrigate the entire district. That distribution network counts with eight additional main pumping stations and nine auxiliary ones, divided in three sections. The maximum height water is pumped up to in this system is 299.1 metres, and the irrigated area receives a total of 304 million cubic metres of pumped water a year, with an average consumption of 405 cubic metres of water per *mu* of land. The Water Lifting Project pumps the water at a cost of 0.181 yuan per cubic metre.

Between 1996 and 1998 pumping stations numbers 1 through 4 of the Water Lifting Project were built and went through the first level of their operational testing. Then the

16th of September of 1998 became a date that, for the people of Hongsibao, was to be remembered as though engraved in great monuments. In Hongsibao even the children now know what that date represents, and some people there even regard it as the 'birthday' of Hongsibao. 'It's because it's really a very important date for Hongsibao!' a local business pioneer told me. A team of prospectors had once dug a deep well in the area of Liquan, but although that well could produce water in large quantities, the salt concentration in that water was too high, rendering it unsuitable for long-term human consumption. For that reason, immigration to and further development of the region of Hongsibao simply had to wait for the arrival of the water pumped through the Yellow River Water Lifting Project. After more than a year of hardships and challenges, on the 16th of September of 1998 the pumping station number 1 of the Water Lifting Project had its water trials officially started with a grand ceremony. As soon as the leader of the Ningxia Hui Autonomous Region pressed the button inside the engine room, dozens of giant water pumps started to rumble, and the whole earth seemed to be shaking, trembling just like the hearts of all the people present. At that moment all heard a loud humming, more like a breathing sound, coming from the open end of a huge water pipe. That humming was followed by a sort of wheezing or snoring sound, so deep it felt like it was about to swallow up the entire world. And then suddenly a powerful water stream gushed out of the open end of the pipe with a rumble, producing a vertical water column more than two metres tall, water that then flowed into the main canal.

'That water then flowed like ten thousand horse galloping, rushing on to the mountains and pouring into a land that, for a thousand years, had been nothing but a barren wasteland,' someone said. And when the people of Hongsibao mention that first wet trial of the water pumping project their faces turn red with excitement!

'To see back then that water over our dry yellow soil, that fast silver stream of water flowing towards a wide expanse of yellow land... I don't know why, but I then realised that my face was full of tears...' one of the migrants told me.

'The Yellow River's water is sweet and the Communist Party's dear to us!' some anonymous person shouted during that water trial, drinking the water and shedding tears at the same time, and prompting the officials and the rest of the people in attendance to shout back the same phrase, from deep within their hearts.

'The Yellow River's water is sweet, and the Communist Party is dear to us!' That is a phrase very often heard in Hongsibao today, and even throughout the Ningxia Hui Autonomous

Region. It expresses the unified aspirations of the many different ethnic groups of this once extremely poor province. And, in fact, had the thirsty people of Ningxia not drunk the sweet water from the Yellow River, how would they know that those other people were dear to them? And if the Communist Party were not dear and did not have their interests at heart, how would they be able to drink that sweet water?

It is, nonetheless, common knowledge that the water of the Yellow River is far from being clear and limpid. But the scientists behind the Yellow River Water Lifting Project have thought through this problem and developed a system of lateral water intake that removes the silt from the water, enabling clear water to flow on to Hongsibao.

That sweet water flows through the well-designed channels, and also through the migrants' long-suffering hearts. It flows with great urgency and with great love to thousands upon thousands of families, filling people with joy, for that is the water that irrigates the fields they grow their crops on. And for a long time now the price of that water has remained the same, 0.135 yuan per cubic metre. Careful readers will certainly remember that the cost at which the water is pumped by the Water Lifting Project has already been mentioned, and that it is 0.181 yuan per cubic metre. This means that the government subsidises the water to the common people at a rate of nearly 0.05 yuan per cubic metre. Those five cents per cubic metre may not seem like much, but if one considers that the water needs of each peasant household include also water for crop irrigation and for livestock consumption, and is therefore substantial, then those five cents per cubic metre really do add up!

A government official from the county of Tongxin once shared with me an interesting fact: In the years of 1992 and 1993, Ningxia was affected by another particularly severe drought, and the common people had to rely on water deliveries made also with lorries of the People's Liberation Army. 'Everyone had to queue up to buy a bucket of water. At the time the going rate for a bucket of drinkable water could be as high as 18 yuan.'

Isn't there a huge difference in 18 yuan for a bucket versus 0.135 yuan for a full cubic metre of water? How meaningful that difference would not be for people living in poverty?

'There's only one word for it: Sweet!' the people of Hongsibao now say.

During the first year of operation of the Water Lifting Project, the resettlement of peasant families progressed simultaneously at seven different counties, with many people from all the most impoverished counties of Xihaigu setting out for Hongsibao. The first people to settle down in Hongsibao were people from the county of Xiji. Shortly after arrived the people from the counties of Jingyuan, Longde, Tongxin, and then from the other counties.

During this process, the officials working for the Cooperation on Poverty Alleviation Between Fujian and Ningxia provided manpower and financial resources, focusing mainly on the selection of adequate locations in Hongsibao for the resettlement of the migrants. Working in coordination with the Planning Commission for the Development of Hongsibao, they took part also in the construction of the first houses and in the opening up of the first fields on former wastelands for corn production.

The undertaking of resettling all those poor migrants was a mighty struggle that had to combine forces and methods of many different kinds, through many different channels. Of all the chapters in the whole struggle against poverty in Ningxia, this resettling is probably the one that needs the most to be adequately recorded, not least because it has much to do with numbers, the resettlement of a large number of migrants in a very short period of time. In an uninhabited and particularly arid area of the Gobi Desert, where the wind is always blowing sand through the air, several hundred thousand *mu* of land were irrigated and opened up for agriculture. In 1999, the year after the completion of the Water Lifting Project, tens of thousands of people coming from the impoverished mountain regions of Ningxia were resettled there, and there they had access for the first time to clear water from the Yellow River and were to have the first good autumn harvest of their lives. He Xinhai. a poor farmer originally from a valley deep in the mountains of the county of Haiyuan, said that ever since his family of five moved to Hongsibao they have been living in a new house with three rooms, having received also ten *mu* of land to grow their crops on. They have also grown wheat for the first time in their lives, with a yield of more than 200 kilograms of wheat per *mu*. 'There was one night when I woke up three times just to catch myself laughing!' he told me. He Xinhai is just one among a million migrants, but the numbers he mentions bear witness to a great transformation that swept the land: One million migrants. Two million *mu* of newly irrigated fields. Three billion yuan invested. Six years for the whole project to be completed.

'1-2-3-6!'

Let's go Ningxia!

Defeat poverty!

That number series is like the steps of the people of Ningxia as they march forward, to a fixed rhythm, in their journey towards the eradication of poverty and the creation of a moderately prosperous society under the leadership of the Communist Party of China. That rhythm has now been reverberating over that vast stretched of land between the Liupan Mountains and the Helan Mountains!

There is still, however, another fact that needs to be mentioned: Because the government has developed Hongsibao based on proper scientific data, to this day the number of migrants allowed to be settled there has been limited to a little over 200,000. That limit is imposed by the maximum volume of water the Yellow River Water Lifting Project can provide. Even though the infrastructure does provide the water necessary for the needs of people and livestock currently there, farmers' migration must be kept within the limits of what that infrastructure allows. When I saw for myself how prosperous Hongsibao has become, I asked a local leader what kind of impact the rapid increase in the number of workers and businesspeople moving there would have on water consumption levels at Hongsibao. Or, in other words, how to keep water consumption under control as the economy of Hongsibao rapidly developed and naturally attracted more businesses and factories?

But that leader laughed it off:

'Heaven's helping us! Rainfall here used to be less than 200 millimetres a year, but now we can get more than that in a single day!'

Indeed, I remembered my first trip to Guyuan. when I passed through Hongsibao and Tongxin. It rained torrentially for a full day, and that day's rainfall was recorded at 168 millimetres.

The ancient land had changed and come to life, and that change was accompanied also by great changes in the sky above. That is today's Hongsibao.

A Home Is Made of Sweat, Heart and Blood

There is a major mountain within the limits of Hongsibao that is called Luoshan. Mount Luoshan looks like a woman's breasts pointing upwards, and it adds a certain alluring charm to an otherwise barren landscape. For that reason, throughout the centuries many have kept the mountain in their minds and thought of ways of coming near it despite the 'extraordinary wildness' of the area. But people who are too ambitious invariably turn out disappointed. Mount Luoshan remained all along like a girl forever unwilling to get married, lying lonely where she has forever been, and never revealing even the smallest scrap of that womanly charm she is sure to possess. And so, for a long time, Hongsibao was home to neither people nor beast, housing nothing but desolation and bleakness.

When that heaven-shaking rumbling was heard on that

16th of September and clear water gushed forth over the land of Hongsibao, it was like Mount Luoshan had finally awaken from her long dreaming, turned on her side to look, and then had her eyes filled with tears: I want to live! The world must know all my many beauties.

Some of those who moved to that previously uninhabited land would also eventually climb Mount Luoshan, and so its true beauty soon became known to the world. The beauty of Mount Luoshan is such as to make people get there and forget about the rest of the world.

An official posted to Xiji once told me that, on the first occasion when he was bringing migrants over to be resettled at Hongsibao as part of the Cooperation on Poverty Alleviation Between Fujian and Ningxia, there was among them a peasant family with five children. Once those children arrived at Hongsibao they discovered that the landscape around them was all very flat and made of yellow sandy soil. Looking around and not finding the mountainous landscape they were used to, they found it so strange as to be afraid of all that open country. 'What do we do when the wind comes?' one of the boys asked his father. 'When the rain comes and brings down the house what do we do?' asked a girl. The father of the children then thought about it and said: 'That's right! If the winds carry away the brats

I've raised through some much hard work who will till the land and tend the animals in the future?' The mother then added: 'If the rain really brings down the house there's nothing we women will be able to do about it! Let's go back! Back to our old house in the mountains!' And so, in secret, that family went back to their old house. 'We then had to go back several times to that family's home in the mountains and spent quite a lot of effort before we finally convinced them to come back to Hongsibao,' said the official. 'Without laying the proper foundations how can we get rid of poverty and turn the people prosperous?' he added.

Before setting up a home in a previously uncultivated land, one has first to become familiar with the properties of the soil. That's what every farmer says and what's at the top of their minds. But to get used to that yellow loess, that sandy soil, takes quite a lot of effort.

Yao Jianguo was Hongsibao's first work committee secretary and leader of the place's first management committee. Yao Jianguo and the other members of those committees spared no efforts helping migrants settle down. 'When my superiors first sent me to be head of the working committee at Hongsibao, from Zhongning also came Tian Zhiguo, and from Tongxin came Ma Kai. The three of us brought along also about a dozen other officials in total. We took up a few one-story houses in the programme's headquarters in the village of Shuangjingzi, and there we put up our desks and our beds. We also set up a tripod for our cooking pot, and that was about all we had to get started with our work,' Yao Jianguo said, adding also that, in the three years before their arrival, more than half of the officials sent to Hongsibao had gone away. And why was that? Because most of those officials had never imagined just how strong the winds at Hongsibao were, and just how much sand was lifted up in the air by the wind. They were scared away! 'I remember it very clearly that, on the 8ᵗʰ of December of 1998, the wind blew with violence and a huge and yellow sandstorm remained above our heads for a very long time. People were scared and no one dared to set foot outside their houses. I had a meeting to attend in the afternoon in Yinchuan, but I was also unable to leave the village. I stepped out of my office and walked three hundred, perhaps four hundred metres, before a sudden strong gale threw me off balance and sent me crashing down into this big rift in the ground. I hit my head somewhere and it got swollen. It hurt so much I really screamed, and tears came to my eyes. I remember thinking: I'm over fifty years old, lived more than half of my life already, am I still supposed to take things this!? But when I opened my eyes and saw those houses for the migrants dancing before my eyes, houses that were still under construction, I calmed myself down.

Because thousands upon thousands of poor people were at that moment waiting to be settled down there, and without houses how could they be settled down at Hongsibao? Therefore I had to get up, wipe away the tears from my face, and continue marching forward.'

'Better to suffer myself than to wrong those migrants in any way!' that's what Yao Jianbao told himself as he gritted his teeth and got up from that hole in the ground to confront the strong wind. Later it would become a phrase that all the people involved in the construction of Hongsibao would often say.

That was the attitude adopted by all the officials and all of those involved in the construction of Hongsibao. It was very touching for the migrants, who had also started their own hard work and who now relied on their own efforts. They were often heard shouting out a similarly inspiring formula: 'Move in the first year, be fully settled in the second, feed and dress ourselves in the third, and by the fifth shake off poverty and become prosperous!'

Those goals were as firmly established as the Liupan Mountains themselves. We are the people from Xihaigu after all, so our words must be just as solid as the great mountains, whatever is said must be considered done, and so we have to build our 'beautiful homes' upon this yellow loess. The migrants were used to hardship and were not afraid of it. Their hearts were also encouraged by the officials and the army of construction workers who had come to Hongsibao prior to their own arrival, so the determination to 'come and settle down' took hold among them. All that was left to do was to struggle against heaven and the land till they finally yielded. Tu Zhifu, a peasant of the first group of migrants who had arrived from the village of Dahe, said:

'My mother named me *Zhifu* when I was born, meaning *willing good fortune.* If this generation of ours does not get that good fortune, they we'll have let down many generations of our ancestors. I was the first to sign up to come to Hongsibao, but I didn't know the soil here would be so different from the soil back home. Back home both the yellow and the black soil can yield a good crop if there's enough rain. But here in Hongsibao it's not like that, the soil here is all full of sand, the water hits it and, before you see it, it has all drained out and it's gone, like a pit with no bottom to it. There are some parts of this soil that's so hard that if you wet it all you get is a whitish puddle, and if you want to dig a whole into it the size of a basketball, you'll have to sweat your brows for a good half an hour. Then you will pour half a bucket of water into that hole and come back after two or three hours to see that most of that water is still in there and that you can slosh it about with your hand.'

That was the situation faced by the first migrants who set up their homes in Hongsibao. On one occasion it took Tu Zhifu and his wife ten full days to plant 70 white poplars. The palms of his wife's hands were both bleeding, and tearfully she asked her husband: 'How can we make it here?' Tu Zhifu wiped off his wife's tears and answered: 'Now that I have brought you and the children to this place, I don't even think about going back to Xihaigu. On the day I must die, I will want to die in a land where there are flowers and the fragrance of wheat in the air.'

Tu Zhifu had his mind made up, and so he went ahead and planted poplar after poplar in that yellow sandy soil. Then, with the land already irrigated, he planted row after row of corn. Finally, he planted a field of day lilies, and later brought in the cattle and the sheep. He also arranged a few beautiful flower beds to the front of his house, and in the end he had made his home in a beautiful garden. He then took his wife's hand and said: 'Now I don't want to die any time soon. I want to live to a hundred years old here with you and enjoy this beautiful and blessed life in Hongsibao!'

Naturally, that was at all possible thanks to the hard work of both work and management committees of Hongsibao on wind-blown sand containment and on vegetation recovery. Moreover, policy makers and construction teams had both, from the very beginning, set a few 'iron rules' for themselves with the goal of establishing ecological 'green' zones. Specifically, they aimed for the creation of 'mountain areas with natural vegetation between crops, networks of forested areas among the irrigated fields, parks embellishing urban districts, and front yards fragrant with flowers and fruit'.

During the second half of 1999, the construction and resettlement process in Hongsibao reached its most challenging and critical moment, when it seemed like it was impossible to either reverse course or move forward. But both the migrants and the people involved with construction received then great moral support and had their faith in the whole enterprise renewed. A group of officials of the Cooperation on Poverty Alleviation Between Fujian and Ningxia arrived from Fujian with the purpose of helping the migrants settle down in Hongsibao. Those officials saw that many of the poor migrant families did not know how to cultivate the land adequately, or how to make proper use of the irrigation available for their fields, so they started working alongside those families in the fields, greatly increasing productivity. Also increased was the migrants' confidence that they could transform Hongsibao into a fine home for themselves.

Hard work will always produce joyful results. And so, in the autumn of that same year, then Premier Zhu Rongji visited Hongsibao. While on a tour of the township of Dahe, Premier Zhu asked a migrant called Ma Xiyuan a question:

'Compared with the soil back in the place where you came from, how much more productive is the soil here?'

'Back there we had mountain soil, without any irrigation,' Ma Xiyuan replied. 'In a year, with good weather, I could get about 400 *jin*[1] of grain per *mu* of land. Here at Hongsibao I managed more than 1000 *jin* per *mu*, and this in our first year here.'

'That's a huge difference!' Premier Zhu smiled, then turned to another group of migrants to question them as well:

'Do you like it here?'

'We do!' they all answered in unison.

Visiting another family, Premier Zhu asked:

'How much did it cost you to build this house?'

'A few thousand!' the owner replied.

'You borrowed that money?' the Premier asked.

'The government gave me part of it, then some friends and family lent me the rest. But I'm not worried about that debt. By the end of this year, beginning of the next, after selling my potato harvest, I'll be able to pay them back! It will be a little tough now,

---

1   Or about 200 kg

Villagers picking golden needles in the village of Liuquan, Liuquan Township, in Hongsibao

but tomorrow will be much brighter!'

Premier Zhu was very pleased to hear that, gave him a thumbs up, and said:

'Well said! Everyone's tomorrow will be very bright!'

Hongsibao's tomorrow was definitely going to be very bright.

Hongsibao's tomorrow had to be very bright, because it was one of the main battlefields of Ningxia's struggle against poverty, and even of China's struggle against poverty as a whole. So a victory there would not only be decisive but would also be of great symbolic value. Whether or not those migrants would be able to settle down and take root in that barren land was to be crucial for the ultimate success of the '1-2-3-6' project in Ningxia as a whole, and it certainly posed a brand-new challenge to the Cooperation on Poverty Alleviation Between Fujian and Ningxia.

How those more than 200,000 migrants, relocated from particularly poor mountain areas, are faring today is what I was most looking forward to seeing for myself. During my first visit to Ningxia, back in 2019, I was particularly interested in all the activity taking place in Hongsibao.

I remember that, on the 23rd of July of that year, the sun was shining with extraordinary intensity, and it also happened to be the season of harvest for one Hongsibao's specialities: golden needles[1]. I remember clearly that entrancing scene before me, day lilies everywhere… And so I proposed visiting the farmers who grew those day lilies.

The township of Liuquan is the place where the machinery of the Yellow River Water Lifting Project was first started, and where the water lifted by the project flowed for the first time. Zheng Huiling, the local township chief and also a beautiful young lady, welcomed me to her township. In a very upbeat mood, she took me to a place where the golden needles were left

---

1   Golden needles are a kind of edible lilies used in Chinese cuisine

to dry in the sun, and from where we could have a view of her 'territory'. I could see in the distance the continuous undulating profile of Mount Luoshan. In between the mountain and where we stood there were several thousand *mu* of richly green vineyards, while closer to us there were the sunning grounds where the golden needles were left to dry.

'It's so beautiful!' I exclaimed. Being my first time ever seeing such a colourfully layered landscape, I also could not help but let out a loud sigh.

'Here in Liuquan we have it all covered: beautiful flowers, beautiful wine, beautiful water, beautiful life…' the township chief laughed.

'And also beautiful people!' I quipped.

'Ha ha, mister writer is a good talker!' the township chief laughed heartily.

But I had spoken in all sincerity. The lady in front of me, the chief of the township, was indeed very beautiful. But much more important indeed were the common people there and their smiles, each more beautiful than the other, because their lives were full of good fortune and joy.

Next to the area where the golden needles were left to dry there was also a workshop to process them. At that workshop I met Xie Renyi, a 47-year-old who had migrated from Haiyuan in 1999. He told me that the new house where he now lived was a 'product' of the government's policy of 'demolishing the ramshackle and building new'. As part of that policy, the government had given him a subsidy of 30,000 yuan, which he complemented with 80,000 yuan out of his own pocket to build his house. Thus his house was unique, brand new, and built with great attention to detail. His was very clearly a very fortunate and now moderately well-off family!

'I have nine *mu* of land, all growing golden needles. Sowing is guaranteed, and so is the harvest,' Xie Renyi said. The government was now subsidising his crops of golden needles at 500 yuan per *mu*. He then harvested and processed them himself, to increase his income. 'It is also possible to leave it all for the cooperative to manage, to ensure your income in the end and to have less to worry about. But going that route means you earn much less in the end than if you do the processing of the golden needles yourself. We have people to do it in our family, so we'd rather do it ourselves.'

In fact, after the golden needles are plucked from the ground, they need to be put to dry. And once they are dry, they still need further processing before they can be sold in the food markets. Fresh golden needles can also be sold, but those fetch much lower prices.

'During busy times I hire eight people to help me pick the flowers. I get a harvest of golden needles once a year, so it is a stable income. The weather here in Hongsibao, with little rain, is very good for the golden needles after all.'

Xie Renyi picked some fresh fruit from the trees in his front yard orchard and had some watermelon cut for us. One could not but praise the taste of that watermelon.

The golden needle processing plant nearby was also very distinctive, fitted with very large and modern equipment. It was capable of processing more than ten tons of fresh golden needles a day. The owner was a local man put in charge of purchasing and processing the golden needles from several nearby villages.

Golden needles left to dry in the sun in the village of Liuquan, Liuquan Township

From there the processed golden needles are sent to all parts of the country. Xie Renyi led me into the processing plant and said:

'In the past our peasants were all very happy at seeing the luxuriant flowers grow after they had spent so much effort during sowing. But they still ended up seeing very little results for themselves. Why was that? That was because they didn't have the equipment to dry and process the golden needles themselves. So, if the weather happened to be cloudy for just a few days too many, the golden needles wouldn't fully dry up and become the "golden needles" people buy at the supermarkets!'

So that was the meaning of the phrase 'the golden needles have cooled', which I had heard before.

'Now our farmers no longer need to fear that!' the township chief said. 'This drying equipment here can take in all the fresh golden needles picked every day in many of the villages around!' she said, pointing at the massing drying equipment. She also told me that the machinery had been bought with funds obtained through the Cooperation on Poverty Alleviation Between Fujian and Ningxia.

The results of the Cooperation on Poverty Alleviation Between Fujian and Ningxia were really showing up everywhere!

There was a fresh fragrance in the air over the fields where golden needles were left to dry. It was a very unique fragrance, and it came not only from the golden needles themselves, but it was mixed also with the fragrances brought by the breeze of the nearby vineyards and orchards. It was an olfactory experience one really could get lost in.

'I'm sure you also want to take a look at our farm stay and experience it for yourselves!' the township chief told us, and it was so kind an invitation that we could hardly refuse. So we all went over to that farm stay located inside a farm in the village of Yongxin.

The owner was called Li Wenbin, and he was the owner of a truly extraordinary farm stay. It had on offer a handful of very neat and clean rooms, inside of which, to my surprise, there were computers one could use to go online. 'Our guests come from everywhere, so we must think of their needs,' Li Wenbin explained.

There were also in that farm stay, besides the rooms, two very important things: a bathroom and a kitchen. Also to my surprise the bathroom in Li Wenbin's farm stay was equipped up to the same standards as those found in city hotels, including both sitting and squatting flush toilets. The kitchen was even more surprising, as it was certified by the county's authorities as a model kitchen. 'After going through a joint assessment by the tourism departments of our township and of the Autonomous

Region, it was awarded a star certification!' the township chief told me proudly while pointing at the hygiene inspection certificate and the restaurant star certificate hanging on the wall of Li Wenbin's kitchen.

'Come on, let's take a look at the backyard,' Li Wenbin said, taking me by the hand and insisting that I should go take a look at his main 'tourist attraction'. And it did not disappoint. Twenty or thirty steps into his backyard the sight one was greeted with could only make one shout out in praise of its beauty. There was in Li Wenbin's backyard, as it turned out, a large orchard, in the middle of which, among all the trees laden with fruit that could be easily picked, there was also an open space for children to play in, featuring a large toy spacecraft.

I had to feel very happy about it all. Here was a man who knew how to run his business!

'I can have up to ten guests at a time here, and I charge 100 yuan per person per day, 120 yuan during the high season. Operating costs are about 30% of that, so that means I can make up to about 700 yuan a day. So tell me, isn't this piece of land worth a lot?' Li Wenbin asked rhetorically. Then he directed some praise also at the lady who was the chief of the township: 'She often tells me that, besides taking good care of the crops, one also must make sure one's house looks beautiful. That's the only way to have a good life. And she's right. We now have 20 families of villagers running their own farm stays. Some opened last year, some this year, but they are all doing well, and making plenty of money!'

'So, what do you think?' the township chief asked me. And, as if reading my mind, she added: 'How does this farm stay here compare to those in Jiangsu and Zhejiang? Or to other ones abroad?'

I couldn't lie about it, so I told her:

'Except for the fact that getting here is not so easy as getting to farm stays in Zhejiang or Jiangsu, I'd say that this one here is in no way inferior.'

Upon hearing that, the officials and the people of Hongsibao were all very upbeat. They said that it wouldn't be long before a high-speed rail line and an airport were built in the region, bringing visitors from all over the country to that land of golden needles and vineyards.

In my opinion, the place is definitely worth a visit.

But why are there so many vineyards in Hongsibao? And why is their productivity so high? Those were questions I was also particularly interested in finding the answers for.

When the topic is the vineyards of Hongsibao, the village of Zhongquantang must be brought into the conversation. This is because the history of grape production in this village is very representative of the history of grape production in Hongsibao at large, both in terms of the entrepreneurship involved and of its eventual success. So when I said that I wanted to see the vineyards of Hongsibao, my hosts decided to take me to the place where grape production had started in the region, the village of Zhongquantang, which is to this day the leading grape producer in Hongsibao.

In the past Hongsibao was a desert where strong winds lifted yellow sand up in the air, but now there are vineyards as far as the eyes can see. Unless one has seen it in person, it is impossible to believe in this transformation. But in the vast land of Hongsibao, man-made miracles such as that one are everywhere to be seen. Looking at it from a different perspective, it is also a testimony to how capable the Communist Party of China is of leading its own people and country in the fight against poverty and on the road towards prosperity.

Then, while we were on the road, a local official and former soldier called Wang Qingshan joined us in our car and told us that he was now the 'King of Grapes of Hongsibao'. So I asked him to tell us about the history of grape production in Hongsibao. Wang Qingshan, a very capable and experienced man, explained to us that he did farm work during his time in the

Army, and that, after returning to civilian life, he was assigned to the Forestry Bureau. Grape production, he explained, is under the jurisdiction of the Ministry of Agriculture and Forestry. So, with time, that soldier-turned-official became also the 'King of Grapes'.

In the fashion of a true king (*wang* in Chinese), Wang Qingshan had us step out of our car in the middle of a large vineyard and led us on foot along a path, about a kilometre long, through the grapevines. He went talking as we all walked. He told us that during the first edition of the Chinese Farmers' Bumper Crop Festival, in 2018, ten sites throughout China's countryside were selected to represent the country's agriculture, one of them being that long corridor of grapevines in Hongsibao we were walking along. That meant that the grapes of Hongsibao were already very famous, being even chosen as a symbol of the productivity of China's countryside.

'If grape production in Hongsibao exists at all today, that is thanks to the work of the Cooperation on Poverty Alleviation Between Fujian and Ningxia,' he said. 'When we were discussing the studies and trying to decide which crops the migrants would grow here in this arid land, and which industries they would develop, we went first to the town of Minning, in Yinchuan, to look around and learn. We saw some vineyards there that caught our eye. The grapes had been introduced there by entrepreneurs from Fujian.'

Wang Qingshan also told me that Hongsibao is located at roughly the same latitude as some of the areas in France most famous for the quality of their red grapes. But the soil in Hongsibao was actually better than the ones found in France, making the place even more suitable for the growing of red grapes for winemaking. 'The success the entrepreneurs from Fujian had in growing grapes in the region of the town of Minning was a great inspiration to us, so after we returned from there, we started making the arrangements for the introduction of vineyards in Hongsibao too,' Wang Qingshan said. 'But the peasants were a little reluctant at the beginning,' he added.

'There would be no profits to be made in the first couple of years,' he went on. 'The grapes would only be picked in the third year, and only by the fifth year would yield really start to stabilise. The peasants were used to sow and harvest in the same year, so when we attempted to get them to grow grapes, they asked us what they'd eat in the first two years.'

That was indeed a problem. No one could accuse the peasants of not thinking practically!

'Our officials had to take the lead in the planting of the grapevines, so if Zhongquantang is known today as "the first of all grape villages of Hongsibao" that is due to the pioneering work of those officials. The village chief himself planted grapevines in 20 *mu* of land, and he got a harvest on the third year. The years that followed also saw good harvests, and the revenue from the vineyards turned out to be several times what other crops were producing. The common people of the village were thus convinced and decided to follow his example, turning field after field into vineyards till they covered thousands of *mu*

Qiao Yingbo, a migrant to the village of Zhongquantang, explaining techniques of grapevine tending to peasants at a vineyard of the Luoshan Winery

of land, in the process turning the village into the largest and most profitable grape-producing area of Hongsibao. Then life in the village just started getting better and better.'

'This person here is the Party branch secretary in the village of Zhongquantang, so let's hear what he has to say,' someone said, introducing a man called Li Hu to us as the most knowledgeable person on the history of Zhongquantang's vineyards.

Li Hu told us that he was one of the original residents of Hongsibao. He spoke of a temple that exists near his house. He said that inside that temple there is an iron cast image of Buddha, an image that, with time, would have rusted and turned red. Hongsibao, which literally means 'Red Temple Village', would have taken its name from that temple and the rusted Buddha image within. In the past very few people lived in Hongsibao. The villages in the region were all connected by family ties, but if people wanted to go out to do anything, such as having a meal or staying over for the night at a relative's home, they would have to ride a donkey to get there. Li Hu said that, because of how barren the land was, the original population would never increase. On the contrary, the population would only ever decrease. His own father had to move to another village because the village where he had been born had simply died out. 'So I was born in that other village,' Li Hu said. He also said that he started working in 1993 after completing his education at a secondary-level polytechnic school where he studied agricultural machinery. Once Hongsibao began to be developed, he then became the place's first farm machinery inspector. His job was to inspect the local farm machinery and check the licences for their operation. He was also responsible for issuing such licences to the local peasants.

'For the most part I checked whether a peasant operating a particular piece of machinery was duly licenced, but sometimes it was a painful job to do. That's because if I found a peasant working with a machine without a licence, I had no option but to give him a 50 yuan fine. He'd then say that he had no money to pay the fine and would simply go back home to be without work. But him not going out to work any more meant his whole family going hungry. When things turned out that way, I really felt like the work I did was bringing pain to people and felt really bad about it. So I quit it. I went over to the township leaders and asked to take part in the place's development work instead.'

Li Hu also told the township leaders that he could drive, so they gave him a job driving a jeep to install signs and posters all around. 'Then I felt that I was doing something positive, don't you think?' Li Hu said. 'If things are getting done, then they need to be announced! If we don't announce them, how will people know what you're planning to do and what you expect them to do? Back them the posters I installed the most carried the slogan *better to suffer ourselves than to wrong the migrants!* At the time all the construction workers engaged in the development of Hongsibao worked under the spirit of that slogan. I remember that the director in charge of poverty alleviation at the time also thought the same. His family home was sixty kilometres away, but he'd never go back there. He was here working in the yellow sands of Hongsibao, and his family even got used to him not being at home. There was finally a day, a Saturday, when he got on the road and went back home. His wife, finding it very strange, asked him: "Why are you back? Did you do anything wrong so that people don't want you there any more?" At that point he didn't know whether he should laugh or cry.'

Later Li Hu would be dispatched to Zhongquantang to serve as the local Party branch secretary. 'The village had 387 households at the time, with somewhat over 1,300 people,' he said. 'All poor peasants who had been resettled here. They had all come from Guankou and from the Huolong Valley. '

'Wait! Wait!' I waved my hand and said when I heard the word *Guankou*. 'Are you talking about the people from that abandoned village back in Tongxin?'

'That's right. It is that Guankou.' Li Hu confirmed.

Ah, I had visited that abandoned village. It had been preserved by the government, and it showed very clearly how the living conditions of the original inhabitants of Hongsibao were in the past. We had also seen that, in many of those *yaodong* cave dwellings, the peasants who lived there had plastered the walls with newspapers. The earliest newspapers we saw dated from the 1970s, though most of them were from the 1980s and 1990s. Most fascinating of all was the fact that most of those newspapers were copies of the *Fujian Daily* (*Fujian Ribao*). When I announced that discovery to my Ningxia colleagues accompanying me on the tour, they all started to discuss it, and the conclusion, as someone put it, was that 'the relationship between Fujian and Ningxia has long had deep roots in the hearts of the people!'

When Li Hu heard that, he also nodded in agreement and said:

'The origins and the development of the vineyards in the village of Zhongquantang also owe much to the Cooperation on Poverty Alleviation Between Fujian and Ningxia.'

He also said that, at the beginning, the local people were not very keen on the idea of growing grapes, preferring to continue with their potato crops, just as they did back in the places where they had come from. But the income from potatoes wasn't great, and the market forces were pulling very clearly and strongly in another direction. So what was to be done? The officials had to persevere, and so they took the lead by planting the first vineyards. They also publicised the facts that the vineyards' productivity was high, and that they required relatively little water. 'That was the lesson we had learnt from our friends from Fujian and their vineyards in the township of Minning,' he said. 'And don't we have that verse by the poet Wang Han, which says *fine grape wine in a luminous glass*? So we persisted with the idea that growing grapes was the right thing to do. At the same time, I also took some of those sceptical peasants to the township of Minning, in Fujian, for them to take a look for themselves at the vineyards there. After that I invited them to have a meal at a buffet in Yinchuan and to visit the Western Xia Museum. Our peasants were all very pleased and were finally convinced that it was indeed possible to make good money from grapes. So, upon their return, they began the planting of their vineyards. But we also faced another challenge. There were now people painstakingly tending grapevines, for a first harvest only in the third year. What if those people wanted to give up on the grapes halfway through, just like they had given up on their potato crops, what should we do then? There were indeed a few people giving up, and secretly cutting down the grapevines to grow maize instead.'

'The pressure was great at the time!' Li Hu said, lettting out a sigh. The road out of poverty and towards prosperity wasn't an easy one for the peasants, and making people well-off in a barren land like that of Hongsibao was particularly difficult. There were the constraints imposed by the environment, ecological problems, and then also some mindset issues. 'As the local Party branch secretary, I had to face those problems head-on and find a way to overcome them. Thus, I spent several months without going back home even once. I was here in the village every day, keeping an eye on everyone and making sure that this grape business was being implemented well, so that it would be successful! Because of that I missed many parents' meetings at my kid's school, to the point that even my child was upset by it and cried to the teachers and to the other kids!'

To make sure that the grapevines of Zhongquantian would survive, Li Hu often tended to them himself, taking all the hard work upon himself. He endured that up to the fourth year. That year the vineyards of village chief Qiao Wensen produced a revenue of 7,500 yuan per *mu* and served as an wake up call to all the common people of the village. From that point on things got easier, as everyone now wanted to follow the example of the officials and shift all their efforts to the vineyards. It was that way that the thousands of *mu* of vineyards in the village of Zhongquantian came into being and became like a red revolutionary flag fluttering above this once barren land of yellow sands, serving as an example to other migrants.

'The thousands of *mu* of vineyards you now see all over Hongsibao started, as a trend, in the village of Zhongquantang,' Qiao Wensen told me quite proudly. A man apparently in his forties, he was the first to taste the sweetness of the grapes in Hongsibao. After him the common people of his village followed and tasted that sweetness too. 'After the first good vintage, the leaders of the village could purchase dozens of new vehicles,' he said. 'And now every family gets an annual income of a few hundred thousand yuan on average.'

'The vineyards of Hongsibao started in the village of Zhongquantang, but now vineyards cover an area of more than 100,000 *mu* all over Hongsibao. and production is no longer led by individual producers scattered here and there, but by large-scale investors who have also integrated red wine production into their businesses,' Wang Qingshan told me. 'You may not believe it, but we already have 28 wineries in operation!' After saying this the 'King of Grapes' shrugged his shoulders proudly in my general direction, meaning that people from Beijing. like myself, ought not to look down upon Hongsibao!

'Let's go visit a winery!' I smiled, patting him on the shoulder. He then took us to a winery called Jiangda.

Jiangda was owned by a man called Chang Liang, a native of Ningxia who was originally in the real estate business. In 2013 he saw that vineyards were now all the rage in Hongsibao, so he decided to leave the real estate business behind and come to Hongsibao to set up some vineyards of his own and start a winery. Chang Liang's winery is now on par with those found in France. It is a very elegant establishment, of the kind one would not be expected to find in one of the poorest 'badlands' of China. And yet there it was, a beautiful and very modern winery. Standing in the veranda of his winery, he raised his eyes to see a fragrant vineyard seemingly without end to either side. To his back stood a castle with facilities for the fermentation and storage of wine, also a museum dedicated to red wine, a restaurant, and lodgings for tourists. It was a place to make one sigh in admiration.

'My vineyards cover 7,600 *mu* of land, and the winery here produces ten different types of red wine, all of them sold to first-tier cities,' he said. 'The vineyards use 30,000 man-days of labour a year, and all the workers are locals. Here they have two sources of income. The first is their share for the renting out of their land, and the second are their actual wages. For that reason, I have a very good relationship with them, and they all call me "red boss"!'

Chang Liang, a man born in 1969, seemed very energetic while talking about his vineyards and his winery, and even a little inebriated, but without having drunk any of his red wine.

'Our wine industry here could only have enjoyed such healthy growth because of the assistance we received from the Cooperation on Poverty Alleviation Between Fujian and Ningxia!' said Yang Zhidong, members of the local Party committee of Hongsibao and head of the local publicity department. 'Once the migrants have stepped up to take part in the production of the grapes, winemaking also picked up steam. But where should we sell that wine? And at what prices? Those were very new questions to all of us,' he said.

Yes, so how did you solve those questions? I asked him only with my eyes.

'From April of 2018 to April of 2019, I was in Quanzhou, in Fujian, as an official of the Cooperation on Poverty Alleviation to do some learning there,' Yang Zhidong was very pleased to tell me. 'So let me tell you what that year there did for wine production in Hongsibao.'

He said that process of Reform and Opening-up had made very good progress in Fujian, and that, as a result, the province had now many people who could afford drinking wine. So one of his most important tasks while there was to promote the wines of Ningxia, and, in particularly, those from Hongsibao. 'With the support of the local governments there, and on a space provided by a local marketing cooperative, we created a "special-products embassy" with more than 400 square metres of area. In that "embassy" we promoted the products of Ningxia and of our Hongsibao, especially our red wines. Business was quite good. Later on our partners in Fujian offered plenty of support to us back in Ningxia, with their provincial leaders stating publicly that all the eight directives then issued by the Central Committee in favour of our partnership were to be upheld, and

New Ecological Migrants' Village Built in the Gobi Desert

that, when making purchases, labour organisations, as well as government and state organs, were to give priority to products from Ningxia. Following those announcements, sales of our red wines and of our other products increased immediately. I then set up a company in Fujian focused on the distribution of products from Hongsibao and from Ningxia at large. Within a year, Hongsibao became so popular as to be known by almost everyone in Fujian, and sales boomed. With market conditions improving, the peasants' enthusiasm for the vineyards increased, and so did the quality of our wines. And as the vineyards and the wineries expanded, they propelled forward also other industries and other crops in the region. Now the production of maize, of golden needles, and of potatoes have also all increased, alongside the quality of those crops. The soil adapted to the introduction of those crops, environmental conditions improved, and the natural vegetation also flourished. Thus, the homes of the common people living here became much more beautiful!'

That is how Hongsibao looks today. Could you even imagine now that, a little over twenty years ago, there was in this place nothing but the yellow sands and the barrenness of the Gobi Desert?

In this giant dormant land, the great strategies towards poverty alleviation and the great struggle against poverty have resulted in enormous changes coming at impressive speeds. This is a saga that maybe could only have been written in China.

In fact, it could only have been written in China.

Chapter 5

New Impressions from Xihaigu

Symbols of Ningxia – Red-Roofed Houses

Nothing can illustrate better the changes Ningxia's poor mountain region of Xihaigu went through than the new houses that were built there, because new houses are the most visible manifestation of the increasing economic well-being of peasants in China. Ever since ancient times there has been a saying in Chinese that goes *dwelling in security, working with contentment.* It means that only when people have secured a place to live they can feel at ease to dedicate their efforts to other pursuits. The people living in the great north-west of China, particularly those living in the impoverished mountain regions, had for generations been unable to shake off one of the most pressing problems they faced, namely the lack of adequate housing.

Even if people don't have much money, they can still bear children and move on to the next generation, even if they don't have land to work on, they can still beg or forage for wild fruit and vegetables in the woods, even if they have no social position, they can still retreat to their old mountains and never leave, and still have some kind of life. But if people have no place to live, they will be deprived of any little scrap of dignity they might otherwise have. They will have to live as vagrants and will end up either starving to death or freezing to death. If people have no place to live, it goes without saying that they will be unable to have a family or to do any kind of work.

Also, ever since ancient times there have been two things peasants in China always do after they make some good money: they buy land, and they build houses. Before the establishment of the People's Republic of China, when land was privately owned, a peasant could spend as much as half of his money in the purchase of the land itself, and the other half in the construction of his house. Following the establishment of the People's Republic of China land was nationalised, and so all the money peasants had left would now go towards the construction of their houses. Along the south-eastern coastal regions of China, you can still see peasants who have come into some money doing exactly that. Those peasants, once they have some money, continue to live just as frugally as they did before in every other respect, but their houses see great upgrades and become much more imposing, or at least they try to build it up so as to match the houses of their neighbours and make it even more stylish. That is the mentality of most Chinese peasants. For them the home is the place where they should feel comfortable, a 'cosy nest', but, more importantly, it represents the dignity of a family. Having or not having a house is what makes the difference between being poor and being well-off. And for peasants in particularly, it is also part of another problem that they cannot avoid, namely that having a house is a requirement for getting married and starting a family. Without a decent house, a 'cosy nest', how can one hope to take in as one's wife into one's home the daughter of another family? The first thing considered when marriage is proposed is the housing situation of the prospective husband, whether he has a house or not, and, if he does, what kind of house that is. That is the 'marriage barrier' that virtually every peasant in China has to overcome. Therefore, the importance of having a house cannot be overstated. It is more important for Chinese peasants than perhaps to any other group of people in the world.

So, naturally, when surveying the once impoverished west and checking the current living conditions in areas now lifted out of poverty, the first thing I had to turn my attention to was the housing conditions of the peasants, whether they have improved, and to what extend they have improved. Housing conditions are indeed indicative of general living conditions, but, more than that, they have in themselves very concrete and practical implications.

Without substantially improving the peasants' housing conditions, it would be impossible to say, in any meaningful sense, that they had escaped poverty. Housing is of the utmost importance to Chinese peasants, and even more so to those from the poor mountain region of Xihaigu. To understand why it was

The new look of the village of Qianzhuang, in the township of Guanzhuang, in the county of Longde

so important to them, one needs only to take a look at the places where the people of Xihaigu used to live in the past. Then one can understand what 'hardship' means. Maybe this is because I am a southerner, but I always thought that people who had to live in caves with walls covered with earth, or in mud caves, or in those traditional cave dwellings called *yaodong*, in fact lived lives no different from those of the most primitive peoples of the distant past! And I know that only twenty or thirty years ago most of the peasants living in the vast countryside of Xihaigu were in fact living in *yaodong* caves. The local people themselves referred to those places as 'caves', and their living conditions were in essence no different from those of their ancestors hundreds, or even thousands, of years ago. That also meant that, while the whole world was going through major transformations, even in the poorest lands of Africa, more than a million people in the great mountains of Xihaigu were still living in *yaodong* caves like their ancestors had lived centuries ago.

Caves! We all know that caves are the earliest form of human habitation. Primitive men lived in caves because they lacked the technical, and perhaps even the linguistic, means of living anywhere else better. They also had no concept of 'epochal changes' or of a 'clash of civilisations', and so cave dwellings are a feature of an epoch rightfully called the 'Stone Age'. During that time, all that people could expect from a dwelling was some level of protection from the elements and from predators. That could be accomplished with caves. Naturally, caves also offered primitive men some protection from the cold and some privacy for the whole business of reproducing and bringing into being the next generations.

Human beings were living in caves about ten thousand years ago. How many great changes and major historical events did not take place in those ten thousand years? There have been enough history books written to make it impossible for anyone to read as much as half of all that history in a single lifetime, and this is not accounting for the fact that, in the meantime, humanity have gone from making fire with sticks to flying into space and using technology to burrow into the bowels of Earth. And yet, at this one place, on this piece of land, people were still living in caves, with no real roof over their heads, and no proper paving under their feet!

It is possible that the people of the Loess Plateau of north-west China still think to this day of the old *yaodong* caves they used to inhabit. Naturally, we are not talking here about those fancily decorated *yaodong* caves that have been thoroughly converted into hotels for tourists, because those are not like the real *yaodong* caves people used to really live in. Those real *yaodong* can still be seen today in today's Xihaigu, in ruins but still in their original form, and those are the *yaodong* where ordinary peasants of the mountain regions used to live. Every time a villager in Ningxia turns to me and points at a half-collapsed *yaodong* dwelling on a mountainside next to their brand-new house and says 'we used to live in there', or when I hear someone who now has a doctor's degree or who's now a local government leader say that 'I was born there inside that *yaodong*', my thoughts suddenly take a much graver tone and I ask myself, not without some pain, is that really a place for anyone to live in?

Caves, or rather *yaodong,* are not really places where anyone should be living. They are dark inside, with no adequate sunlight, and they also lack proper ventilation. Despite that people still had to lit fires inside to prepare their meals or to warm up their *kang* beds in winter, and that's not to mention the fact that very often several generations of the same family living in the *yaodong* had to stay together on top of the same *kang* bed to keep warm… Was that any way to live? I really can't think of anything clever to say in the face of such reality. All I can do is to let out a deep sigh and acknowledge that those people have suffered immensely!

People who had no other option but to live in *yaodong* caves indeed suffered greatly! The smoke inside those *yaodong* blackened the lives and smothered the aspirations of otherwise very capable people. Those mud walls of the *yaodong* restrained the people who would otherwise have roused themselves to fight. They suppressed the people's wisdom and resourcefulness, and the earthen *kang* beds of the *yaodong* have cooled the natural passion of otherwise very passionate men and women...

People, once deprived of the opportunity to live up to their potential, can only revert to primitivism and confusion. This kind of primitive and confused life, however, went on uninterruptedly for thousands of years on the vast territory of Xihaigu, and even today about a third of the people there have been born and have lived some part of their lives in a *yaodong*.

This is the reason why poverty alleviation in China is said to be a fierce battle where fighters do not have the option of retreating. The victory it aims at is against a condition that has endured for thousands, if not tens of thousands of years, and that condition is poverty and backwardness.

The work towards poverty alleviation is continuous, and what the fight against poverty aims at is not merely the improvement of the material conditions of the people, but, more importantly, to strengthen the people and provide support to the realisation of their aspirations. It is true that those who visit the Loess Plateau of north-west China will often hear some of the local people talk about the 'advantages' of *yandong* cave dwellings, how they are 'cool in the summer and warm in winter', and such like. I guess those are true to some extent, but the 'advantages' of the *yaodong* are only relevant in the context of the alternative, which, for those people, was to live rough and sleep in the open in the middle of a wilderness. Could a *yaodong* cave ever be compared to a real house? Can the warm end of a *kang* bed really be better than a bed with a spring mattress and a real eiderdown? Most people, at least, would not think so.

On the Loess Plateau, including in Xihaigu, one may find some houses built in a '*yaodong* style'. They are not really caves dug into mountainsides like real *yaodong*, but are rather built on flat ground in such a style as to just resemble *yaodong* caves. For a long time their existence baffled me. Why not build a normal house instead of going through the trouble of building a fake *yaodong*? Only after reading the work *Old Houses* (*Lao Fangzi*) by my fellow writer and Ningxia native Shi Shuqing did I come to understand the mystery behind those fake *yaodong* and the sadness still present in the hearts of the people of Ningxia:

> *… the reason why we built a house like that and not one made of bricks and tiles is very simple: it is precisely because we need to use neither bricks nor tiles, nor do we*

need to cut long rafters for the ceiling, that we build them. In other words, to build a house like doesn't require much money. All one needs is some soil and some straw, then add some labour to it, and the whole thing is done. In fact, there are many types of folks with houses like that, and so in the world, besides the magnificent temples and palaces, there are also houses like that, of people who spent hardly any money at all to build them.

Anyone who has ever lived in a yaodong *cave dwelling before will be able to talk with some relish about the several advantages of that kind of dwelling, of how they are warm in winter and cool in the summer, of how soundly one can sleep in them, and so on. If the* yaodong *in question is an old one, with many years of use, then it will have some thick vegetation growing on its roof, and that vegetation will sway freely when the wind blows. Sparrows will flap their wings in there, and small wild mice will also live among that foliage, creating a very lively and charming atmosphere.*

But people will want to avoid talking about the great Haiyuan earthquake of 1920, in which 59% of the people of the county of Haiyuan lost their lives. It is said that mortality was so high precisely because most of the people at the time lived in such yaodong *cave dwellings, and so when the earthquake struck, the ceilings and walls of those caves simply collapsed inwards, like huge fists suddenly tightening up and crushing the people inside.*

And those yaodong caves have also left another deep impression in my mind. As can be seen in photographs, there is an opening above the entrance of most yaodong dwelling, an opening that villagers call 'the sentry eye'. As the name suggests, those openings were probably used for observation, but it is not clear to me why they had to be placed so high up above entrances. There was a case in our village, however, of a man who had the idea of passing a rope through that hole and use it to hang himself. A lot of people then came to his door to see him lying on his front yard. He was placed there, with a towel covering his face, but his neck still showing. And one could still see on his neck the dark purple line where the rope had strangled him, and where there still seemed to be a little blood oozing out. I still remember also that the one shoe he was wearing had no shoelace, and that the tongue of that shoe jutted out, like the tongue of a cow, lolling from side to side... From that day on, whenever I saw a yaodong dwelling and its little dark 'sentry eye' above its entrance, I had this eerie feeling going through me, and couldn't help feeling a little scared.

But what am I getting at with this talk?

I did not originally intend to talk about this. I had in fact a well-thought-out plan of what I wanted to say but ended up talking about this instead. This came to my own surprise as well.

But the fact is that I do like such yaodong *dwellings, so much so that I feel like crying whenever I see one.*

I'm not sure how I should express this feeling.

All I can say is that, when I first cried, it was inside a dwelling like that. It was inside a dwelling like that that I first sought my mother's milk, scarce as it was. And many of my best dreams, if I reflect on this now, where all dreamt in a dwelling like that.

It seems that one such a dwelling is the only testimony I have that I was once a baby and then a naughty child. It seems also that only one such a dwelling can testify that my father once had any strength to his muscles, and that my mother was once a young woman...

It is the old home where those treasures, those years of innocence and the world of dreams that I dreamt, are kept...

Now I understand why Shi Shuqing and many others who have spent at least part of their lives in Xihaigu and on the Loess Plateau speak well of those *yaodong* dwellings. It is because their lives started inside such dwellings, and because those dwellings were their companions as they grew up. Those are feelings that one cannot easily discard. Even if outsiders come and explain the disadvantages of the *yaodong*, those explanations have no real effect on the 'Shi Shuqings' of the north-west.

The only way to completely change their perspective is to have them move out of the *yaodong*, to have them completely removed from those dwellings, living in new houses and feeling for themselves just how much better they really are. But that change will probably just start for real with the next generation of Shi Shuqings, those born in new houses. Precisely because their lives will not have started in those old *yaodong* caves, they will be able to appreciate just how much better and how much warmer real houses are. Those real houses are where people should really be living, and only a life where one no longer needs to live in a cave is really a life.

One of the main goals of the Cooperation on Poverty Alleviation Between Fujian and Ningxia, and of the struggle against poverty more generally, is to enable people living in the poorest mountain regions of Ningxia to leave those mountain regions, moving out of dangerous dwellings and into new houses offering adequate protection against earthquakes and cold winters, and which meet the standards of a moderately prosperous society.

In that struggle there is no battle more arduous than this one, because it involves solving the housing problems of a large number of poor families, moving into beautiful new houses all of those still living in *yaodong* caves and in other types of precarious dwellings, and then making sure that those people will be living moderately prosperous lives without having experienced first any sort of gradual improvement in their standards of living. Just imagine how big of an undertaking it is to move all 'cave dwellers' in all corners of the country out of their precarious homes and into new homes, all of them without exception. How much money would that cost? Did any dynasty in the past even attempt it? Was any of them ever determined to do achieve this? And was any of them ever in a position to do it, to turn such a vision into reality?

Never before!

The Central Committee of the Communist Party with comrade Xi Jinping at its core has nonetheless found that determination, and so government and Party members at all levels in Ningxia, sparing no efforts, started a construction campaign in Xihaigu of a scale the region had never seen before. That construction campaign enjoyed the kindest support from the people of Fujian through the Cooperation on Poverty Alleviation Between Fujian and Ningxia.

The mountains rejoice, the great plateau sings, and villages dance.

Under Xi Jinping's leadership, the new village of Minning was built in the county of Yongning, in the southern part of the prefecture of Yinchuan, and by the foothills of the Helan Mountains. Later that village would grow and turn into the town of Minning, nowadays a thoroughly modern town that will certainly enchant any visitor with its beauty. But how was one to proceed with the task of getting all the people living in *yaodong* caves to move out of their precarious dwellings? How to carry out this task effectively? That issue was raised at a joint meeting of the Cooperation on Poverty Alleviation Between Fujian and Ningxia, and the leaders of both sides of the partnership, after careful consideration, came up with a plan that could not only be quickly implemented, but also easily replicated. All the work in all of the impoverished counties and regions was to be carried out in accordance with the model decided upon and first implemented by Secretary Xi Jinping through the creation of the village of Minning, which was to serve as a model village. All the new villages built within Xihaigu and the region at large through the partnership with cities in Fujian would be built following the standard set by the 'model village of Minning' and would be always called 'New Village of so-and-so'.

'Great! We spend the money, and with that money new houses for our dear relatives in Ningxia are built!' was said. So the provincial Party committee of Fujian and their provincial government issued an order, which was to be answered by each city and county with a partnership with another city or county in Ningxia.

'Money is very important.'

'But money is not the only important thing.'

'Public sentiment is of the essence.'

'Care for the people, serving the people, that's what most essential of all!'

'So essential as to be the ultimate purpose, that is, to move the poor people out of their precarious dwellings and into new houses.'

That was the wish of the people of Fujian, would it be fulfilled? Having Travelled through all of Ningxia, from north to south, I can bear witness to this fact: that the wish of our brothers and sisters in Fujian, through much hard work, has been almost entirely fulfilled!

Like the Liupan Mountains themselves, that wish stand lofty and high before the eyes of the people of Ningxia, nourishing their hearts like the Yellow River that runs by the foothills of the Helan Mountains…

I did not get to see with my own eyes the pain of the common people as they left their old *yaodong* homes to be relocated elsewhere. But I have heard many stories about that pain:

There was, for instance, the story of the family of an old man called Ma, who was initially unwilling to move out. But later, as he saw the neighbouring families move out of their *yaodong* one after another, he started to think that, perhaps, he should not be the only one holding out alone among several empty *yaodong*! And, to everyone's surprise, that same year there was also a very strong downpour that caused water to rush down the mountains like bolting wild horses. That not only resulted in the collapse of many of his neighbouring *yaodong*, but also nearly took Old Ma's life. He later explained that, were it not for his son arriving to rescue him just a few minutes before catastrophe hit, he would be 'long buried deep inside that yellow soil…' Old Ma now lives in a new red-roofed house, and one of his joys now is turning on his television every day to watch traditional opera. Life is going very well for him, because after his new house was built, he started working at a greenhouse growing vegetables just 100 metres away from his home, earning a monthly salary of 2,000 yuan.

In fact, moving out of a *yaodong* and into a new house amounts to much more than a simple relocation. It is tantamount to 'uprooting poverty', an action with both a material and a spiritual element. I have also seen for myself a particular characteristic of the construction of the 'Minning' new villages, something common to all of them, and which I found very touching. In every one of those new villages, Fujian also paid for the construction of a 'services centre' for the villagers. Those centres include a public square, a supermarket, bank branches, a small clinic, an events hall for Party members, a dining hall for the elderly, a space for after-school activities for children in primary school, a 'poverty-alleviation' workshop, and other such facilities, essentially covering all the needs villagers might have in their daily lives, all of them 'behind the same doorway'! Those are places where villagers can find basically anything they could wish for, all sorts of services.

I went to the village of Jimei, in the county of Jingyuan, and the first thing that caught my eye there was the very impressive public square. Around that public square there were a 'culture wall', the village's primary school, and one of those 'single doorway services centre' offering nearly 30 different services to make the lives of the villagers easier. The day I visited, the secretary of the Party committee of the county of Jingyuan happened to be on the main square on official business, and so he took the opportunity to take me to the homes of two families living nearby. He told me that, after moving into their new houses, the villagers were at a loss as to what to do with all the space they now had in their large courtyards. So the local officials of Jingyuan got together with the officials posted there from Fujian as part of the Cooperation on Poverty Alleviation to discuss the matter with them and to try to come up with a solution. They decided to draw from the experience of other communities back in Fujian, and so they helped set up in every new house an orchard and a vegetable garden.

'Look how beautiful this courtyard is now, and how productive. One can grow vegetables here, and there's also some fresh fruit…' the Party secretary said, asking our host to pick a fresh apricot from the tree and give it to me to try.

'That's delicious!' I had to exclaim after tasting it.

And indeed, fruit grown in Ningxia are among the very best in the world!

Our host was called Ma Chenghu. When he met me, he pointed at the great mountains in the distance and said:

'My family used to live in a *yaodong* in a ridge within those mountains over there. I'm more than 70 years old now, and for more than 70 years I drank muddy rainwater. Last year, because of the partnership with the Jimei district in Xiamen that gave us a few million to invest, we were able to build new villages here. My own family and 360 families from five other villages were moved out of their *yaodong* caves and from other dangerous houses and moved into those nice new houses here with red roofs. Not even in my dreams could I've imagined this. Now we not only drink sweet water from the tap, but we can also shower every day with water heated with solar energy.'

The smile on Ma's face really came from the bottom of his heart.

Entering the home of another Ma, I discover that the owner had used a space of over 30 square metres to build a shed where he now raised goldfish. It was a very elegant shed. The goldfish swam happily in the tanks while their owner sat leisurely next to them, drinking green tea and reading the newspaper. When he saw me walking in, he naturally began to talk about the great joy raising goldfish brought him.

I was curious, and so I asked him how he came up with the idea of building a shed to raise goldfish at home. He told me that he liked water ever since he was a child but had always suffered with the water scarcity where he used to live. After moving into that spacious new home, it simply occurred to him that now he could realise an old childhood dream of his, so he built his shed… Ha! This old Ma turned out to be a man of great vision and perseverance!

Besides having the orchard and the vegetable garden other houses had, his courtyard was also very uniquely and colourfully decorated, in a style that was simple, but clearly very elegant.

'Who helped you design it?' I couldn't help asking him.

'My daughter who's studying at Tsinghua University. She did it!' old Ma told me proudly.

After old Ma moved into his new house, he found only joy after joy, with his life getting better every year. His daughter had been admitted to a university of great renown, and now, if something is not great in style, then it is simply not about old Ma's family that we talk about!

Transformations such as the ones seen in both Ma families mentioned above and good lives such as the ones they started living after moving into their new red-roofed houses can now be seen everywhere in Xihaigu and throughout Ningxia. My friends in Ningxia also took me to visits to other new villages clearly named after places in Fujian, such as 'Putian', 'Anxi' and 'Quangang'. And I could not help but sigh in amazement upon seeing how modern each one of those villages was, and how blessed the lives of the villagers were. I have learnt from people employed by the Autonomous Region's Poverty Alleviation Bureau that in Xihaigu and also in other regions of Ningxia there were now hundreds of such 'Minning model new villages', built with funds from partnerships with towns and districts back in Fujian. And it was precisely because of the positive impact the construction of those new model villages had, and because of the support offered by the central government, that a unified programme was launched to rebuild precarious houses throughout the entire region. From 2018 to the end of 2019, throughout the whole region, most of the people living in precarious conditions were moved into new earthquake-resistant and winter-proof houses, houses that had an average area per inhabitant of no less than 39 square metres. Through that programme, by the end of 2020 all people living in precarious dwellings will have been moved into new homes. 'This construction programme covers an extensive area, makes substantial financial investments, and will have a profound and lasting impact. The assistance Fujian provides has been very great indeed, and the friendship they have shown towards us will be forever remembered by the people of Ningxia,' an official of Ningxia's Poverty Alleviation Bureau told me.

'Why do all those new houses have red roofs?' I asked, and it was indeed a question that had been lingering in my mind.

'The soil in Ningxia is mostly loess and sand, and so red stands out when it has that as a background,' the official explained. 'From an aesthetic point of view, red goes very well with the ground's colour, and, more than that, it enhances a general mood of happiness and prosperity. From yet another perspective, it serves also to express the gratitude the common people of Ningxia, having been lifted out of poverty, feels towards our brothers and sisters in Fujian, towards also General Secretary Xi Jinping, the Party, and the government. It expresses also the determination of that same people, urged by their feeling of gratitude, to build a new Xihaigu and a new Ningxia! In short, the choice of colour carries with it a sense of joy and celebration...'

Indeed, you, the red in the roofs of the houses, the red colour itself, the red in one's heart, how many deep and secret meanings don't you have! You give people joy and fervour, and when you call upon them, you cannot be easily forgotten.

Red houses of Xihaigu, we salute you!

Dream of the Maixiangs: From Poverty Alleviation Workshops to Global Factories

Maixiang's full name is Qin Maixiang. One may say that she is 42 years old, but she really does not look her age. If she were in a city and were to put on some make-up and a dress a little more stylish, you'd say that she looked like a young woman 'looking for a husband'. And you wouldn't say that as a joke. That's because Maixiang's skin is unblemished and beautiful, and because she is also very feminine.

'But make no mistake,' she says. 'I'm 42 this year! And soon I'll become a grandma!' She blushed a little when she heard our compliments, but we could tell that, inwardly, those made her very happy.

'What woman doesn't like a compliment!' Maixiang said.

Maixiang, who was soon to become a grandmother, was also considered a 'village beauty', a 'village flower', when she was younger. It is a pity that, back then, her family was very poor, and so was the land where she lived. Thus that 'village beauty', then planted in unsuitable soil, didn't end up being all that she could have been. Maixiang, however, says that she has no regrets and does not feel sorry for herself. Her husband may not be a genius, but he's a good person and works very hard to provide for her and for the children. He makes money in Fujian and elsewhere and supports the entire family.

Being about to become a grandmother at the age of 42, as Maixiang was about to, is not such a big deal in the region of Xihaigu. Back then in the region it was not against government policy to get married in your early twenties. She got married when she was 20 years old and her oldest daughter is now 22, and already married. Maixiang's second daughter is now 16 and her son is 12, both now attending middle school.

'I feel like I let my eldest daughter down somehow. Our family was very poor at the time, we couldn't send her to study, and so she ended up getting married early,' Maixiang said. The only thing she felt a little guilty for is having her eldest daughter marry early, but now it was thanks to her daughter's 'contribution' that Maixiang was about to become a grandmother at such a fairly young age. That now gives Maixiang that same restlessness and that same vitality and enthusiasm she had within herself as a young, recently married, woman. And that was not on account of sexual desire but was rather an enthusiasm for both life and destiny. She was building a 'blessed little heaven' for her own family. And now she wanted to buy a place in the city.

'Maixiang wants to buy a place in the city!' people were

saying. That piece of news grew wings like a bird and flew away, very fast and very high. Soon people all over the region knew about it, and that made Maixiang's heart beat a little faster. It was just an idea at first, but now she had made her decision, and so she had to buy it!

'Why can't people from the countryside buy properties in the city and live in foreign-style houses?! Why can't the people of Xihaigu go into town and buy houses for themselves to live in?! I have money, money I earned through my work back at home, and the more I work the more I earn. So what's to be feared in buying a house?! If I have earned it with my own sweat, I can buy it, and once I have bought it I can go and live in the city and be like other townsfolk, get up early and go to the park to jog, or to the square to dance, shaking my butt from side to side, that will be so nice! Ha ha!' Maixiang laughed, and the more she thought about it, the merrier she got.

Maixiang now works at a poverty alleviation workshop at the county of Jingyuan, making clothing for Ningxia Quanxiang, a maker of outdoor clothing. The workshop where she works has placed a very large and eye-catching sign on its outside that reads *Minning Poverty Alleviation Workshop*. Poverty alleviation workshops with signs such as that one, which are standardised, can now be seen in once poor villages all over Xihaigu and

Ningxia. Those workshops are also a very important part of the partnership between Fujian and Ningxia initially proposed by Xi Jinping. Those workshops are of relatively small size. They are very functional, made to suit local conditions and to solve the issue of unemployment among those people unable to move very far, but who are otherwise very capable workers. Women like Maixiang are among those who benefit the most from this programme.

One of the first measures taken in the context of the Cooperation on Poverty Alleviation Between Fujian and Ningxia consisted simply in taking poor workers from Xihaigu and other such regions to work in Fujian. That policy, initially proposed by the Fujian side, is still in place because labour remains in short supply in the coastal regions, and because it also allows the workers to receive relatively high wages. A family from those poor regions with one of their members working away from home like that will have an annual income, from that person alone, nearly enough to support the entire family. That is how labour is 'exported' from many relatively poor regions in the north-west of China. Some workers spontaneously leave the mountains where they have always lived to go find temporary work elsewhere, whereas others move away in a more organised fashion, that is, in the context of a partnership between regions aimed at poverty alleviation. The latter way of 'exporting' labour offers workers several advantages over the former, such as, for instance, job security. As long as the workers are committed to their jobs, their livelihood will be thus guaranteed. Another benefit available for workers from Ningxia who come to work in Fujian through the Cooperation on Poverty Alleviation is a subsidy, made to grant them some extra degree of comfort. Workers who work in Fujian for at least half a year will receive from the Fujian side of the Cooperation on Poverty Alleviation a monthly subsidy of 2,000 yuan, which represents a considerable addition to one's income. 'This is done to encourage the people of Xihaigu to leave the great mountains. Not only will they be given a job, but they'll also be able to learn new skills and expand their horizons, so that, when they eventually return to their places of origin, they'll be able to support happy families and prosper with their own work,' a comrade from Fujian's Poverty Alleviation Bureau told me.

And that is true!

'But later we encountered another problem...' the comrade from Fujian went on. 'Getting young people to do temporary work far away from home is relatively straightforward. You make an announcement, saying where the work is at, how much the salary is, then you buy the tickets for them, and so off to Fujian they are. But after a few years some of them will want to get married, particularly the female comrades, and once they get married, they will want to have children. Having a child means that, for a couple of years, they cannot really go anywhere. And people usually have a relatively large number of children in those rural areas of Xihaigu. After a baby is born, it usually doesn't take much more than two or three years for another one to come, and so women who get married will very rarely leave the region again to work! What can be done then? We asked ourselves whether some businesses from Fujian could come to Ningxia instead, so that the people who stayed back in Ningxia could also earn money working in the factories… And that's how the poverty alleviation workshops came into being!'

But then why are they called 'poverty alleviation workshops' and not 'poverty alleviation factories'? That was something that I, from the very beginning, could not understand.

'There is a reason for that,' said the comrade from Fujian. 'A workshop is something relatively small and simple, and it can usually be more easily moved to a new location. The number of workers in a workshop can be anything from ten or twenty to a couple of hundred. Workshops can also be separated into smaller units or else operate as a single unit. Naturally, some factories can also be said to be workshops, such as those small reworking factories.' Moreover, poverty alleviation workshops were conceived and implemented in accordance with the needs of mountain regions such as the ones found in Xihaigu, where perhaps in one village and in the few villages around combined one can find just a few dozen suitable workers for them. Those workers are usually middle-aged women or people with disabilities. Those workshops also operate relatively near to those people's homes, so that they can be back home in just a few minutes if need be. Those poverty alleviation workshops

Workers from peasant families from the town of Liupanshan, in the county of Jingyuan, busy at work at a poverty alleviation workshop operated by Quanxiang at the village of Shizi

also usually operate on a piece-rate basis, so if you leave early or arrive late that is not much of a problem, since one is paid for the work accomplished and not for the time spent at the workshop. That way people can earn an income from a job while keeping their freedom to go back to take care of one's home as necessary, as is usually the case of women with children.

Maixiang is one of the many beneficiaries of that programme. And, like her, many other women now work at poverty alleviation workshops, where they can earn between 2,000 and 3,000 yuan a month. And earning that amount by working virtually next door to home is in no way a worse deal than earning 5,000 or 6,000 yuan a month some place very far from home.

'Now every month I can take home a stable income of 3,000 yuan. That's enough money to keep my two children in school, and so the money that is left from the work my husband does away from here we can use for other important things, such as improving our house or buying things we might need in the house. And if there is no need to spend the money, then we can just save it. Then when we have enough, we just go and buy that Western-style house in the city!' Maixiang laughed.

Now everyone believes Maixiang. There are many other women in the same situation as hers, including several of them at the same poverty alleviation workshop where she works. 'If you work for a long time and save money for three, five, ten years, can't you just buy a house in the city and go live there? He he, you think that I'm joking!' Maixiang laughed, and the other women also drowned us with their laughter. And the vision they have for themselves now is in no way outdated. The things they want to do when they get themselves a place in the city are what other city people do, like roaming the markets when they have some free time, going to the cinema, dance in the public square, and, most important of all, get their children to attend good schools. It is, essentially, that. See, those are the people of today's Xihaigu, and their way of thinking is no different from that of city people!

Within only a few years the people of Xihaigu have achieved the goal of being able to work at factories just a stone-throw away from their homes. When one hears that, it may indeed sound strange, but in many remove valleys up in the Liupan Mountains I have seen for myself that this has indeed become the living reality.

On the 8th of June of 2020, Old Ma and his wife were working at the poverty alleviation workshop they usually worked at. Their job was very simple: to manually fold carton along a production line to make cardboard boxes. That day something they could never have imagined even in their dreams happened. General

Secretary Xi Jinping, whom they had often seen on television, paid a visit to their workplace, shook hands with them, and had a little chat with them about their daily lives.

Now Mrs Ma smiles when she meets new people, and once she smiles at them, she will want to tell them about that day when she chatted with the General Secretary. 'He asked me how old my husband was, if we found our work very tiring, and what had changed in our lives. I told him that now we were very happy, that we had everything we needed at home, and that we could also earn money by working very close to home. The General Secretary was very happy to hear all that and said that the good days are still to come!'

Two days after first meeting them, I got to see the poverty alleviation workshop where Old Ma and his wife worked. It was a relatively large workshop, featuring a very large yard. Inside twenty or thirty people worked on a production line making cardboard boxes. The age of those workers varied. Some were young, while others, like Old Ma and his wife, were older. But they were all from peasant families of the local village. The work they did at the workshop was simple, but it provided stable incomes to them. It was thus suitable for older people with relatively little schooling, people like Old Ma and his wife, both in their sixties and people who had never travelled very far where they lived. Normally, people like them would be working in the fields, or else be at home taking care of housework. But there was only so much to be done at home, so after the poverty alleviation workshop was opened in the village, both were asked whether they would be willing to work there, each receiving 600 yuan a month. 'And if you work a little more maybe you can take in more than a thousand!' they were told.

'I'm going! And my wife's going too!' Old Ma said, signing up not only for himself, but also managing to get a spot for his wife at the workshop as well. From that moment on it was as the saying goes, *the sesame stalks putting forth flowers higher and higher*, that is, their lives started getting better by the day. Mrs Ma is now all smiles all day long and seem even to have turned a few good years younger. After the images of the General Secretary having a chat with her at the workshop were broadcast on China Central Television's *News Simulcast* (*Xinwen Lianbo*), that smiling face of hers very quickly became the 'happy face of the people of Xihaigu'!

'Are you happy to have met the General Secretary?' I asked her.

'Yes, very happy!' she said.

'I'm going back to Beijing tomorrow. Do you have anything you want me to take back to Beijing for the General Secretary?' I teased her, seeing that big smile on her face.

'Please take this message to the General Secretary, tell him that our place here is getting better and better, and that we, the people of Xihaigu, thank him and the Party. Every day our lives here get better. And next month I have to make 300 yuan more!' she laughed.

'Ha ha!' I laughed, and all my colleagues present at the moment laughed as well.

Old Ma pulled at the front of his wife's jacket and whispered to her:

'Mind what you're saying!'

Mrs Ma took no heed, and continued to smile as she told us:

'It's 300 yuan more! The boss here at the factory said that productivity has increased!'

And indeed, that was the case! I asked the boss, and he confirmed it, and from all over the workshop came at once an outburst of joyous laughter.

There are actually quite a few people in Ningxia who, like Mrs Ma, had the luck and honour of meeting General Secretary Xi Jinping at the workshops where they worked. Since 1996, when he took charge of the Cooperation on Poverty Alleviation, Xi Jinping visited Ningxia four times. And, particularly in his last two visits, he made a point of visiting some poverty alleviation workshops and exchanging a few words with the people working there. He also talked with the entrepreneurs from Fujian and the Ningxian officials who ran the workshops to discuss topics he was concerned about, such as how to further improve the working conditions for the people of those poor areas who worked in those workshops, how to guarantee the workers' incomes, and the like. By keeping investments going year after year, in an orderly and persistent fashion, soon those poverty alleviation workshops were firmly established in formerly impoverished villages all over Xihaigu and, in fact, all over Ningxia.

Some people say that those small workshops effectively 'dragged' the people of the mountain regions of Ningxia out of their remotes valleys and homes to work in factories, taking them from a society that, for thousands of years, had depended solely on agriculture and brought them into a modern society based on manufacturing… If one thinks over this carefully, one sees that, when the masses of the people say this, their remarks are rather very apt and profound.

Poverty alleviation workshops were originally intended for those people who could not move elsewhere to find work, and were also designed to create incomes for families with available surplus labour that would be otherwise difficult to employ.

The concept is somewhat similar to work-study arrangements through which students can study while also working and earning an income. It may not seem like much, but it allows peasant families, especially those in the mountain areas, not only to transform for the better their means of subsistence, but also to transform their way of living.

The transformation of peasants into manufacturing workers and the transformation of their ways of life it entails is one of the major revolutions in humanity's march of progress. Also in the history of the development of the advanced nations of the West that transformation represented a major revolution, one that took one or two centuries, during which time herders and farmers were gradually adapted to mechanised production, to the progress of industry, and to life in modern cities. Today many city people still talk disparagingly of 'country bumpkins', meaning that they don't understand the rules and customs of city life, or that they have no care for work discipline and norms. But little do those 'city people' know that their own ancestors, before becoming 'city people' themselves, were once 'country bumpkins' as well, farmers and herders unaccustomed to punctuality and used instead to an undisciplined lifestyle. Changing their habits was, in fact, not easily accomplished. It was indeed much more complex and took much more time than simply turning a poor person into a well-to-do individual.

However, in the context of China's battle against poverty, the Communist Party, having comrade Xi Jinping as its main representative in the Cooperation on Poverty Alleviation Between Fujian and Ningxia, made use of every poverty alleviation workshop to very cleverly and successfully tackle this issue, transforming a generation of peasants into workers of modern manufacturing enterprises. That may not seem very impressive at first sight, but the process leading to that transformation did indeed require much effort and dedication.

'Once that process is completed, the result is a splendid new world,' I was told. The day I was told that I was visiting the new facilities that a company from Fujian had built in the county of Haiyuan, fully developing what they had there from a 'poverty alleviation workshop' into a 'global factory'. There are indeed 'global factories' up there in those remote valleys. To be honest, that was more than what I expected to find there, because in order to solve the unemployment problem, reduce poverty in those mountain areas, and provide basic incomes for the peasants, setting up small businesses would be quite enough. But, to my surprise, factories and businesses of the kind and scale that had begun to pop up in places like Shenzhen and other south-eastern coastal regions twenty or thirty years ago now had also begun to appear in the remote regions of China's west! That was a development of great historical significance!

Could this be the beginning of a major shift in the world's economy and in the composition of its labour force? Would that be coming as quietly and with such great impact as the drifting of huge glaciers? Could it be that the development of the western regions, constantly debated in these past few years, is about to bring monumental changes? Could it also be that a new wave of industrialisation has begun in the vast lands of China's west? All of that I have seen very clearly before my eyes and have felt for myself the great attraction of that trend.

Wang Jianhui, a native of Zhangzhou, in Fujian, was born in the 1980s. He is a handsome young man, yet very mature, and we turned out to get along well. He would tell me that an uncle of his on his mother's side of the family is a rather well-known and respected literary theorist who also happens to be employed at the same work unit as I am.

The industrial complex I had before my eyes also happened to have been built with investments brought to Xihaigu by Wang Jianhui, who acted in response to a public appeal issued by the Cooperation on Poverty Alleviation Between Fujian and Ningxia. Having come to Xihaigu on a sudden outburst of enthusiasm, Wang Jianhui never imagined that getting a business running there required more than building the facilities, recruiting the workers, and starting the machinery.

'Things are much more difficult and complex than I imagined, mainly because of the people factor,' Wang Jianhui explained to me. At first, he thought that his task would be simply to manage a poverty alleviation workshop where clothing was manufactured, and that the workers he'd be able to recruit would be mostly women. As we talked, he gave me a tour of the workshop he ran. In comparison with other poverty alleviation workshops I had seen, Wang Jianhui's clothing workshop was rather large, with an internal area of perhaps two or three hundred square metres. The place was full of female workers making clothes.

'Our products are all sold to Europe. This line here is sold in Russia. That elegant one over there is what Italians like the most. And the French prefer this one here,' Wang Jianhui explained as we went, showing to me one by one the models of clothing in European style made at his workshop as someone listing the treasures of one's family. Thus, contrary to all expectations, Xihaigu has indeed become a global manufacturing centre!

'You're right,' Wang Jianhui said. 'Twenty or thirty years ago Fujian and also Guangdong, there by the coast, became global manufacturing centres! But, as labour costs have increased in these past few years, global manufacturing centres saw some relocations, with China's west already in the process of claiming its own position among them, or already having claimed it. Ningxia today is already a part of the world's manufacturing network, and that fact is a direct result of all the work done through the Cooperation on Poverty Alleviation Between Fujian and Ningxia. Every piece of clothing we make here at this workshop is exported,' he said.

'Most people don't understand the implications of being a part of global manufacturing, and think it is just a matter of foreign businesses taking advantage of our cheap labour! But that is just one aspect of it,' Wang Jianhui continued. 'After placing an order with us, those businesspeople from the West will come over to conduct serious inspections of everything about our factory. In fact, just yesterday we saw off a delegation from Germany. Besides inspecting the quality of the clothes we make, they mainly wanted to see for themselves the standards of our facilities, particularly what facilities are available to workers. They wanted to see whether there was a changing room, if it's large or small, how many toilets we have, how clean those are, and so on. Even minor things you might not think of they will also want to inspect. At first, I also thought this was strange, but later I realised that there is good sense in that, because the final quality of products like clothes also depends on a complex combination of issues, and so conformity with the standards applied in the developed countries of the West is something they pay a lot of attention to. Those are generally requirements for being part of the global manufacturing network. Naturally conditions for the workers, both inside and outside their workplaces, must conform to common standards that are systematically implemented. But those do not necessarily match the priorities we have here at our poverty alleviation workshop! And sometimes the gap is considerable!'

Seeing the site of Wang Jianhui's business I got a totally new idea of what means to be part of global manufacturing. It turned out to be something very demanding indeed!

'When I first arrived here, there were two aspects of the work I found the most challenging,' he said. 'The first was logistics. Logistics is really a tough nut to crack! Back in Fujian our factory was in Zhangzhou, and to send goods from Zhangzhou to the port of Xiamen to be exported would cost about 30,000 yuan per truck. But from here to the export port we had to pay, at the beginning, a few hundred thousand yuan in freight fees per truck! Then the other challenge was the productivity of our labour force. I've run factories both in Fujian and in Shenzhen, and at the assembly lines in those places one worker could make as many as 15,000 buttons a day. Those factories also paid the workers on a piece-rate basis, and so each worker could make five, six, eight thousand a month, sometimes even more. But here, during our first few months of operation, a worker would be making just short of 500 buttons a day. If we paid them piece-rate, they wouldn't be making even five yuan a day.'

Such a huge difference! It turned out that the boss really had his work cut out for him. What could he do?

'Indeed, you may be asking what I could do then?' Wang Jianhui said.

And before I said anything, the young man himself smiled and answered:

'At that early stage I really couldn't come up with a solution, and so I even thought of giving it all up here and going back. But then the local leaders turned out to be of great help. Together with the officials from Fujian on temporary assignments here to manage the poverty alleviation partnership, they helped us to overcome the challenges one by one, removing all obstacles. They made it possible for my factory to be here today, and for our products to leave this place here deep in the mountains and reach the world.'

The stories Wang Jianhui had to tell seemed to be all closely interconnected, and to be forming a very exciting plot…

The first challenge he faced was a linguistic one. Without using language it would be impossible to teach the new workers how to do their jobs. So the first measure Wang Jianhui took while setting up his factory was to make sure that the workers joining the factory would be taught Standard Mandarin Chinese. Meanwhile, he and the members of his business team also studied the local dialect. That 'dialect' was by no means easy to learn, being in fact just about as difficult to master as a foreign language.

The second challenge was educating the workers about the required discipline concerning the beginning and end of shifts, and about the norms regarding the work itself. Wang Jianhui's clothing workshop uses the 'conveyor system', meaning that, along each production line, several workers have to take each a fixed position and work in coordination with the others. Therefore, not a single one of them can be missing from their post, necessitating that workers get on and off work at the same time. Wang Jianhui instructed the workers in the simplest terms possible, but at first results were not at all spectacular. The women working at the workshop simply did as they saw fit! You asked one of them if she could be at work at 8:30, and she'd say that she had to be at home to breastfeed her baby. By no means could the baby be left to cry all day long! Some others said that

8:30 was just too early, because after getting up in the morning they still had to cook and clean up the house, and then walk to the workshop. Time was not enough! So Wang Jianhui gave in and said, okay, how about we all just start working at nine? None of the workers objected. But later it turned out that about a third of the women still couldn't make it on time. And so, the other women who had arrived on time had in fact arrived early for nothing, because on a production line if some of the workers are missing there is nothing for the others to do. So how about delaying starting time again, now to 9:30? Everyone agreed. And this time finally things started smoothly. At the beginning of the working day, at 9:30, the machinery started running, everyone was at their posts, and production moved along. But a short time later a few posts were again empty. Where did the people go? After asking around, it turned out that this and that person had gone back home. What? Do what at home? Well, breastfeed the baby! The young Wang Jianhui was struck dumb when he heard that.

'No worries, no worries, we'll sort this out,' the local county officials told him. And indeed they showed up in person to sort things out, coming up with ways to reason things out with the workers and explain the rules to them. In the end, with the help of the women's association and of other departments, solutions were found for all the difficulties workers were facing at home.

Wang Jianhui could then heave a deep sigh, thinking to himself that the system was still indeed superior, and that the government was indeed very capable!

Then a third new problem came along to give him a new headache. Training the workers was taking way too long. And not only was it taking long, but it was also costing way too much! 'It would be taking as long as a couple of years to train the women to make clothes, and that training cost quite a lot in wasted materials alone,' Wang Jianhui said, raising two fingers to indicate the figures involved: in two years, nearly 20 million yuan!

'But I have no regrets. Now my workers are fully trained and capable of accomplishing all the tasks required in our production lines. Our products are well known and well received in Europe and in the United States, and orders keep growing,' Wang Jianhui said proudly.

Then a fourth difficulty came up, and it was about calculating piece-rate wages. 'At the very beginning it was simply unfeasible to calculate those wages,' he said. 'If we calculated strictly on a piece-rate basis, the workers wouldn't be making more than five or ten yuan a day. That was much lower than what they expected to earn by joining the workshop, which was perhaps thirty or fifty yuan a day. But this *is* a factory after all, and we must focus on productivity!' he said, some sadness clearly visible on his face as he reached this point in his explanation.

Conflicts arose, and quite intense ones. The workers even organised a strike. Wang Jianhui was indeed finding himself in a terrible fix.

'But don't worry, don't worry, we'll sort things out,' the local county leadership reassured him again, reappearing to do that sorting out with the same enthusiasm as before. They went to the workers one by one to listen to them and learn what was going on in their minds. Then they came back to Wang Jianhui to discuss what they had learnt. The solution proposed left Wang Jianhui quite moved. During that early period the government would provide a subsidy to make up for the wages of the workers who could not reach an agreed-upon productivity quota.

The workers smiled and resumed their work with renewed enthusiasm. Gradually they became more skilled, till they reached a point when the subsidy the government provided to their salaries was no longer necessary, since they were already earning enough through the work they accomplished!

Wang Jianhui could then 'relax', not having to worry any more about the workers' pay. He soon discovered that the workers were quickly becoming more skilled, and that the pay they were collecting, based on that piece-rate system, was continuously growing. Naturally, productivity at his business grew at the same pace.

'Pay increases! Bonuses!' he said. That young boss's manner was something extraordinary. The workers would take wad after wad of *renminbi* into their hands and would be cheering and laughing on their way back home.

'My friend Wang, I have another piece of good news for you,' the county Party secretary then showed up and told him in person.

'Thank you, secretary!' Wang Jianhui said.

Every time the county Party secretary paid a visit to his workshop Wang Jianhui knew that it meant something good. And that was no exception this time, as the Party secretary indeed had some good news to tell him. A manufacturer of electronic products from Shenzhen, Card Cube Group (Kalifang Group), was planning to set up a factory in Haiyuan. 'They wish to work together with you, and so the county leadership has decided to ask you to coordinate the creation of an industrial development park,' the secretary said.

'Me? Coordinate the creation of an industrial development park?' Wang Jianhui said with great surprise, still somewhat incredulous.

The county Party secretary smiled and nodded affirmatively:

'That's right. Our county's leaders have decided that. You still don't believe it?' he said, patting Wang Jianhui on the shoulder. 'Since it's to help develop our local economy and to benefit the people, I know you'll give your best at it. And if you encounter any problem, just bring it to us and we'll come to solve it!'

'Oh, dear!' Wang Jianhui exclaimed. A well-travelled man himself, he was touched by all the trust deposited on him. He nodded a few times in agreement. And the events that followed allowed him to see very clearly how great the changes taking place in Xihaigu were.

At first Wang Jianhui's was the only clothing manufacturing business operating at that site. Freight costs were very high at the beginning, because it was, after all, freight from the distant mountain regions of the west to export ports by the coast in the east. But soon his company was joined by the Card Cube Group (Kalifang) from Shenzhen, the chipmaker Geil, and by an embroidery company. And so, the place where he operated his business ceased to be a simple workshop and became something more like a giant industrial complex, with all the products manufactured there meant for the export market. 'That had the effect of greatly reducing our freight costs, because there were now four companies working together to coordinate shipping for their goods, which reduced to almost zero the amount of empty space in the trucks. So freight costs got much lower,' Wang Jianhui said very happily.

But there was still another issue that worried him. His and all of the other three companies in his 'coalition' were exporting companies, but there was no local bank that could offer foreign currency accounts. That caused Wang Jianhui to break out in a cold sweat again. What should he do? It meant they would do all the work, dispatch the goods, but then wouldn't be able to get the money coming in from abroad! International markets are turbulent, and exchange rates can go up and down like on a roller coaster in a matter of just a few days. How could Wang Jianhui and others who settled their transactions in foreign currencies not worry?

'We'll handle this at once! I'll come personally to sort this out!' the county Party secretary said, and so he showed up again. And his ability to sort things out was indeed very great. More importantly, Ningxia's financial system was adequate, and matters concerning the Cooperation on Poverty Alleviation Between Fujian and Ningxia were to be handled through a special regime. Moreover, the region of Xihaigu had gone through some major changes, and if the financial system could not keep up with those changes, that could only mean that we had not done our jobs right.

Thus, good things were coming Wang Jianhui's way once again!

Such 'global factories' started popping up one after another, like bamboo shoots after the rain, in the once impoverished mountains of Xihaigu. The emergence of all those new factories is what impressed me the most about Xihaigu. In terms of its historical significance, it stands by no means behind the introduction of water from the Yellow River for irrigation, or even behind the return of the land to the peasants by the Communist Party during the early stages of the Liberation. Because the emergence of 'global factories' in Xihaigu is a phenomenon involving both traditional manufacturing and high technology manufacturing, it represents a break from what was seen in Shenzhen and at other coastal regions during the early days of Reform and Opening-up. In Xihaigu two steps were taken at once, with relatively simple manufacturing arriving at the same as the manufacturing of advanced technology products. There we can now find not only companies like Wang Jianhui's, which manufactures clothes, but also microchip manufacturers like Card Cube (Kalifang), whose products I've seen for myself, and which can be so advanced as to be very rarely seen in China's more inland cities. Located now in the west of China, a region with great availability of labour and of natural resources, and also with a good natural environment, those businesses and factories enjoy a large competitive edge over the eastern regions of China, and even over many countries in Southeast Asia.

This is a turn of events one ought to be very happy about. It has also made us understand why General Secretary Xi Jinping and the Party's Central Committee do their utmost in the battle against poverty and to promote the development of western China. That is a strategy the significance of which is much more complex and goes far beyond what we could have imagined! Those are indeed some glorious verses in a glorious epic about the rise of a great nation!

But what I want my dear readers to note is this: If the poorest and most backward regions of China like Xihaigu were able to emerge as 'global factories', it was thanks mostly to a humble beginning of little 'poverty alleviation workshops', which, though they did not look like much at first, were able to captivate western audiences! This is something that no western classical economist can fully understand, and which also sees little discussion in the works of the many famous economists within China. This is the same 'secret' that enabled the uniquely Chinese strategy of 'grain plus rifles' to defeat an imperialism armed to the teeth, the special talent of China's communists. At its core this 'secret' consists of having solid roots in the reality of Chinese society, searching for truth in facts, and following a path of service to the people and of seeking to benefit those people at the lowest strata of society.

Poverty alleviation workshops were initially conceived to be a rather simple solution. The idea was to pull in owners of small and medium enterprises in Fujian and have them bring their equipment and manufacturing techniques to Xihaigu and, more broadly, to Ningxia, while also providing them with financial support from the Cooperation on Poverty Alleviation Between Fujian and Ningxia. The workshops were meant to act as sparks for development in regions with an abundance of labour but without the conditions usually associated with industrial development. It was like planting a red flag in every village, in fact a workshop with anything from a few dozen to a few hundred square metres of area. That was to be followed by the recruitment of local peasants, mostly women, but, depending on the specific requirements of the work to be done, also older people in their sixties and seventies. Work was to consist of simple manufacturing tasks to be fully accomplished by hand, usually along assembly lines. That model was very well received by the locals. The first reason for that was that they were now able to work and earn a salary near to where they lived. For the people of those places, it felt as lucky as tripping and falling into a vat full of honey… In fact, the new kind of life open to them and that mode of production allowed those people to feel dignity for the first time in their lives. The second reason was that it represented a departure from an undisciplined state of affairs regarding work. Peasants were turned into workers who now had to mind time, mind efficiency, mind regulations, and who now also had to be self-aware. The third reason was that they came to understand labour's worth and acquired also a sense of the purpose of life itself. And what they felt most deeply was that, in taking part in the process of production, they were now learning new ways of getting along with each other, and even came to understand what the 'outside world' is like. They also learnt how to project their own 'selves' into the future.

As the people who had their lives changed themselves said, whenever they walked out of the poverty alleviation workshops, they worked at what they took with them was not only the wages they earned, but also a certain frame of mind, a hope, and a new kind of knowledge. It was a new kind of life they were just starting to understand.

At another complex of poverty alleviation workshops, Huang Shuihai, another business owner (and, like Wang Jianhui, also born in the 1980s), told me that the workers' wages were paid daily. He pointed at the data scrolling on a computer screen and explained to me that each worker can check his or her task-completion rate in real time. That rate is the data point that will later determine his pay. Also taken into account were the quality of the products and other essential factors pertaining to the work, such as personal clothing, work discipline, and so on. All of that was entered into the calculation to determine a worker's actual pay.

'This style of management actually makes the relationship between workers and managers very transparent, and it is also a way of allowing workers to "self-manage", Huang Shuihai said. 'Another advantage of this method is that, through the data available to them, workers can better hone their skills, thus growing into more mature individuals who are always making progress and who are also better suited to the company's requirements.' Huang Shuihai also told me that, under that system, a peasant from the mountain regions who has never seen a piece of machinery before can become, within a year, a very 'modernised' and highly skilled worker, capable of quick thinking and of demanding progress from himself.

Isn't that an amazing transformation? Could that not be another transformation that 'changes the world'? Strange it would be indeed if Xihaigu had not changed as a result!

And, with so many changes going on, is the Xihaigu of old still to be seen anywhere?

Humanity's greatest revolution in history, the Industrial Revolution, has driven the progress of humanity for the past three centuries, producing changes a hundred times faster than during any period of the previous 4,000 years of slave and feudal societies. In those small poverty alleviation workshops we can also see the changes it brought to the people of those impoverished regions, changes that once more confirm the correctness of the path in the fight against poverty the Communist Party of China has decided to take.

The distinction between a 'poverty alleviation workshop' and a 'global factory' is not a very clear-cut one. There is, in fact, a large grey area between those two concepts. That is because, although many of those workshops are, individually, very small, when an entrepreneur from Fujian sets up ten or more of them together, a spark is then ignited that soon becomes a 'large fire'. The workshops link up together, enjoying convergences both in terms of production processes and in terms of the products they make, to the point that they become one huge 'global factory', 'global' because most of their products are then exported to the world. The poverty alleviation workshops run by entrepreneurs like Wang Jianhui, themselves founders of large businesses, are examples of such 'global factories'. The products they make are often cutting-edge technology products aimed at customers in the most developed regions of the world.

In the industrial development zone of Longde, I saw one of those factories that is, in a true sense, a global factory. Its full name is *Ningxia Longde Artificial Flower Craft Company Ltd.* It was built in 2013 with an initial investment of 100 million yuan, and it was the first business set up in Guyuan to be aimed at the export market, making all sorts of artificial flowers designed for the taste of European customers. I can myself be considered a worldly and well-travelled person, and so were many of my Ningxia colleagues in our group. And still, the moment we stepped into that 'world of flowers', we found ourselves laughing like fools. That was because of how attractive the flowers were, because of how fast a 'flower' you created in your imagination could be simply manufactured, and because of how many of the 'flowers' there were of kinds you'd only expect to find in fairy tales or in science fiction… If they were not right before one's eyes, no one would ever believe that such a fantastic 'flower world' could be hidden away back in a deep valley of those great distant mountains.

The owner was, as expected, a businessman from Fujian. His name was Pan Wenxian, and he had already become well known in the region for his 'stylish generosity'. He is, after all, one of the businessmen who have dared to invest a very considerable sum in the mountain areas of Ningxia through the Cooperation on Poverty Alleviation. Pan Wenxian said that he was very confident about Xihaigu from the moment he set his eyes on the region, and so he fully committed to it. Now he has even brought his grandson over to Longde. 'The idea is to put down roots here in this land,' he explained.

The day we visited Pan Wenxian took us on a tour of the workshop where the flowers were made and explained all his products to us. He explained that, at his workshop, they could produce both the most ancient 'flowers', and also 'flowers' that people had never seen in the real world before. Moreover, as required, they could also produce 'flowers' with designs customers provided. 'The workers here are locals, and so are everyone at middle management and below,' he said as we walked into a room fitted with 3D printing equipment. 'Among our designers we have foreigners, and also locals with college degrees. The machinery we use here is also among the most advanced in the world.'

But most entrancing of all was those 'flowers' we saw arranged together in what was called a 'Flower Season Exhibition Hall', a space filled with hundreds of different designs of artificial flowers. Those included *ikebana* arrangements, flower baskets, flower archways and corridors, flower screens and hanging flowers. In short, any kind of flower and flower arrangement you could, or could not, think of, they had it there. Prices were, moreover, very reasonable, as low as a few yuan. More sophisticated and luxurious arrangements were, naturally, more expensive, going up to the hundreds of thousands of yuan.

Pan Wenxian's artificial flower business amazed me and my fellow travellers, and there was no way we could praise it enough. Because his flowers are both beautiful and elegant, and because you can take them in your hands and make flower arrangements as if building with blocks of all shapes and colours, they are particularly useful both as tools for children to develop their intelligence and creativity, and also to add beauty to a family's everyday life!

'This type here is already very popular in primary and middle schools abroad,' Pan Wenxian smiled. 'And if we also make it into the market of China's primary and middle schools, then this place of ours here will really become the flower capital of the world! It isn't a wild dream to say that our sales can grow to billions of yuan!'

See, do you believe now that this is a 'global factory'? There I met another 'Maixiang', who also told me her personal story:

'I'm very happy at this factory! For us making 40 or 50 thousand a year here is definitely a possibility, since three people in my family now work here. My husband does field work for the factory, my mother-in-law works making flowers. Each person in the family makes nearly ten thousand a month. We already have a small car, and our next goal is to purchase an apartment in the city… That is not a dream! Next year it will come true!'

When I asked her what was the greatest change she had seen in her own life and the lives of the people in her family in those past few years with the poverty alleviation programme, that 'Maixiang' told me that 'before escaping poverty, we the women counted as practically nothing in the eyes of the head of the family, even though our full names were in the *hukou* registry. Now that we're no longer poor, our names are written on the first line of the *hukou* booklet. That is because, with our work at the factory, we also earned the money to buy our houses. Now the baby's daddy has to let us be head of the household too, ha ha…'

When this 'Maixiang' finished telling her story, she pursed up her lips and smiled, a smile that added even more charm and beauty to her face.

Oh, indeed! Xihaigu, that poverty, shabbiness, backwardness, and even that benightedness you were once known for has long now disappeared, left behind in the dust of history. And now a new, beautiful, and modern Xihaigu has emerged before our eyes. This is a new Xihaigu made not only of the beautiful 'Maixiangs', their children and their husbands, but also of strong and brisk horses, towering mountain ridges, a vast blue sky, green grasslands and wide roads, an open country and a vast and beautiful landscape…

And if today Xihaigu has a constellation of 'global factories' scattered all over its territory, that is to say, if the great waves of industrialisation have risen over this ancient land, still what impressed me the most during the time I spent there was that, despite all the progress, one doesn't hear the loud rumbling of engines, nor sees the least trace of pollution. The factories there do not require plenty of labour to run. They are rather like nature, like the flowers and the tree trunks and the limpid water flowing, also like the drifting reeds, the soaring birds, and the fragrant fruit on the trees. And that is undoubtedly the most exciting of all, what makes one most enthusiastic, confident, and filled with a deep sense of meaning.

Indeed, that is today's Xihaigu, a land constantly making progress, from 'poverty alleviation workshops' to 'global factories', and again to 'green global factories'.

And there is still something else I learned about Xihaigu, something I learnt from a conversation I had during dinner with Zhang Zhu, then secretary of the Party committee of the prefecture of Guyuan.

'Guyuan's development is no longer simply a repetition of the development we've seen in the coastal regions and in the areas a little further inland,' Zhang Zhu told me. 'We need to find models of development suitable for the unique characteristics of the mountain regions, which also work hand-in-hand with the protection of the environment, and which are compatible with an idea of civilisation that is both industrial and ecologically conscious. That means that we need to bring ecological construction and the fight against poverty close together, and win on both fronts, of keeping the mountains green while also making the people prosper, since what is good for the environment and what makes people prosper can be indeed one and the same. I have asked the officials of Guyuan to keep those two things well balanced, and not to favour one at the expense of the other, which means that both are necessary, both the modernisation of our industry and then the environmental protection of our rivers and mountains…

'And so, in 2017, under the leadership of the Party committee and the government of Guyuan, the "four-ones" programme for the environment and industry was started in the prefecture. It included the "one fruit tree" initiative, which planted fruit-bearing orchards over large areas to bring prosperity to the peasants; the "one seedling" initiative, which involved setting up tree nurseries over large areas for the cultivation of trees with good market potential, while also being well-adapted to the climatic characteristics of the Liupan Mountains; the "one flower" initiative, the construction of landscaped flower gardens scattered over large areas to beautify the countryside; and the "one stalk of grass" initiative, which promoted the planting, also over large areas, of plants of both economic and ornamental value, on lands that can be used both as pastures for the raising of livestock and as areas dedicated to tourism. The model of a "store at front, production at back plus base plus farmers" implemented in the experimental demonstration plantations of the "four-ones" in Guyuan encourages farmers to pool their land and labour together and contributes to the creation of a vast "green poverty alleviation workshop" over the territory of the Liupan Mountains.

'During the implementation of the "four-ones" programme, the prefecture of Guyuan made ample use of and further promoted the experiences provided by the Cooperation on Poverty Alleviation Between Fujian and Ningxia, cooperating also with several academic institutions, such as the Fujian Agriculture and Forestry University, the Fujian Academy of

Agricultural Sciences, the Northwest Agriculture and Forestry University, and the Ningxia Academy of Agricultural and Forestry Sciences, to form groups of experts, experts on the ecological engineering involved in the "four-ones" programme, to provide technical training to local officials, cooperative managers, and villagers, thus solving this capability bottleneck. That way we'll also have more people capable of generating prosperity and of making prosperity-generating green industries take root among the farmers and in the countryside as a whole. And, in accordance with the chosen guiding principles, such as the scientific apportioning of the areas, diversification, and species suitability, each county, town or village will develop their own green economy, the one that best suits their own unique characteristics. The dwarf apple variety introduced in the town of Touying, in the district of Yuanzhou, has a very high survival rate, and some of the trees have already begun to bear fruit. Agronomists went over to the apple orchards of Ma Jun, whose household had been lifted out of poverty, to explain techniques to the farmworkers there. Ma Jun said that the productivity of his apple trees used to be quite low, with the trees suffering regular damage from insect pests, and the taste and texture of the apples were also quite unsatisfactory, so much so that he couldn't sell them at any reasonable price. After the introduction of a dwarf apple variety, however, work at the orchards got much easier, because trees were now shorter, which meant a great reduction in labour costs during harvest. The proportion of the area that could be used productively, meanwhile, also increased, alongside the productivity per area. Quality also improved, capital input requirements were reduced, and the apples can now even be sold prior to being ripe for picking. The dwarf apple trees also bear fruit sooner than the taller varieties, taking only two to four years after first planting, and entering their high yield phase in four to five years. After reaching full maturity, those dwarf apple trees can easily yield three tons of apples per *mu* of land a year, and as much as four to six tons if particularly well managed. If we calculate using the local market rate of four yuan per kilogram, farmers can make nearly as much as 30,000 yuan per *mu*. Other fruit varieties, such as Dangshan crisp pears, red plum apricots, and crown pears, are also grown in the region now. In Mugou, located in town of Piancheng, in the county of Xiji, other tree varieties such as hazelnut and cherry trees were introduced into an experimental domestication orchard. In the town of Baiyang, in the county of Pengyang, the *da hong pao* prickly ash was introduced in experimental plots that cover a total area of almost 1,000 *mu*. In the county of Jingyuan, black chokeberries and box elder maple trees were also introduced. Because of the colder climate of Xihaigu, which makes flowering season longer and also the seasons themselves different from those in the south, those different varieties of trees and plants cultivated as "poverty alleviation workshops" are themselves foundations for businesses that have allowed local peasants to find prosperity. Chinese roses, for example, will wilt away after five months elsewhere, but in Guyuan they will be in bloom for seven or eight months. Thus, varieties such as that one, which are of great economic significance, are very well received in markets everywhere across China. Due to their being very resistant to cold and easy to care for, the seedlings grown in the tree nurseries of the Liupan Mountains gradually made a good name for themselves across the entire north-west. The "four-ones" programme in Guyuan thus resulted in brand new landscapes and industries and generated also great wealth.'

The emerge of green solutions is an unstoppable trend. In the meantime, poverty alleviation mechanisms have played an extremely important role in reducing poverty. Those mechanisms have solved problems involving labour, land, and capital through measures such as subsidised interest rates, land transfers, the tying up of investment projects with poverty alleviation programmes, and also direct financial incentives to investments. Such very concrete measures have contributed to the multiplication of such 'green poverty alleviation workshops', and to the expansion of existing ones. Since the beginning of experimentation with new plant varieties, Guyuan has seen the creation of 39 experimental cultivation areas, covering a total area of 21,000 *mu*, and introducing and conducting domestication experimentation on 149 species of trees and 269 varieties, with survival rates of 95% and above. In 2019 the viability of further 86 varieties was to be demonstrated and 1,636,000 *mu* of land was to be developed with trees and other economically significant species of plants. Those 'poverty alleviation workshops on the fields' are bringing more and more prosperity to the region every day. The seedlings grow strong, and the demonstration fields make clear their economic viability. Many different species originally cultivated only in those demonstration fields are already to be found all over the vast territories of the Liupan Mountains. Barren mountain ridges have turned green, with the total area of the prefecture covered by forests reaching 28.4%, or 73% if grasses and other types of vegetation are also included. Guyuan's territory, including both its urban and rural parts, has become much more beautiful, and complete infrastructure for tourists has been created, attracting visitors from many different places to come and enjoy the great sights. What a great transformation that was! One must not forget that this is Xihaigu, the place the mere thought of once made us shrink back, the 'most barren place in the world' that once instilled so much fear.

From a 'beautiful environment' to a 'beautiful economy', Guyuan has composed to us an inspiring victory song. That song has been recorded also in a work by Wang Yongwei, a native of Guyuan, titled *Climbing Over the Last Great Mountain – Records from Guyuan's Battle to Escape Poverty*, a book that has now now become Xihaigu's new *Records of the Grand Historian*.

Chapter 6

Affection Is as Precious as Gold and Poetry Is the Soul of the Land

In Saying My Dear, Tears Are Hard to Hold Back

On a certain day 24 years ago, in 1996, Lin Yuechan, an official from Fujian's Poverty Alleviation Bureau, entered in a hurry the office of the then deputy secretary of the provincial Party committee Xi Jinping. She had a document folder under her arm and a very important suggestion she had to bring to the attention of her boss.

Prior to going into Xi Jinping's office, Lin Yuechan had asked the staff at the Poverty Alleviation Bureau to compile for her some material on the situation of the disabled, of women's health, and of school absenteeism in Ningxia. Once that material had reached her hands, she found herself unable to keep still, because she saw that the people of Ningxia were suffering! They suffered because the children lacked education, mothers had poor access to healthcare both while pregnant and after giving birth, and because many people acquired some form of disability!

That wouldn't do! If the assistance provided to Ningxia did not get the children into school, if it did not improve the health of mothers and conditions for the disabled, then the poverty alleviation work being carried out, as it was, was obviously inadequate! For that reason, Lin Yuechan had to do something. 'I am a woman, so I was all the more concerned about the issues affecting women, children, and the disabled there,' she said. 'So I brought my concerns to Secretary Xi Jinping's attention, and the suggestion I had was that the poverty alleviation work of the cooperation between Fujian and Ningxia should also include mechanisms for cooperation on the areas of health and education.'

When I interview Lin Yuechan she also told me rather proudly that 'this was my "invention", which secretary Xi immediately approved of, following up with personal calls to the people in charge at the provincial bureaus of health and education, to have them come up with plans for cooperation on those areas. After that, groups of officials started being dispatched to Ningxia every year to offer assistance. They were accompanied by supporting doctors and teachers. At the same time Ningxia also dispatched their own doctors and teachers to Fujian to hold temporary positions and undergo further training...'

As a result, the cooperation between the provinces on health and education, including care for the disabled, really took off.

There's hardly anything parents care more about than getting their children into school. But when a family is poor and lives in an economically backward region, going to school may often be considered 'pointless'. So how to convince parents and their children to be happy to 'waste time' at school?

Without education, the only asset men have for their survival is their physical strength. It is thus like a return to a most primitive era, when all one could do was to sell one's own manual labour. If you had the strength to work, then you had 'become a man', and could now get a wife for yourself to beget the next generation. That was all there was to life.

The maturing process of girls into women would also revert to its most primitive form: your mother would give birth to you, and when the time came, you'd bear and raise your own children to carry on the family line. There would be no need for education in any of this, because you'd be, in essence, no more than an 'instrument'. You do the housework and bear children for your husband. Sure enough, in your free time, you'd still go out to the fields to dig out potatoes and herbs, and to feed the cows and the horses...

Without education and culture life is equally drab for both men and women.

Without education there is also no hope that one's own hometown and the economic conditions of one's own family will ever improve. For that reason, young people, both men and women, have abandoned the great mountains to find work elsewhere, saying farewell to their hometowns and setting off on a long journey... For young people in such poor areas, that was perhaps the best course of action they could take.

But again, without education, even if they left their hometowns to work elsewhere, the only work they could do was still the simplest and most arduous kinds of manual labour, for which they were paid the lowest possible wages. Things being that way, those young people would still be forced to return to their hometowns in order to get married and have children. Their children would then follow the same life path as their parents. And that would go on for generation after generation, as the children further divided among themselves an already very barren and poor land.

Year by year, the poor were becoming poorer, and the barren land was getting even more barren, till getting even as little as a *yaodong* cave dwelling and a simple *kang* bed to get married became impossible. Because of that, families even stopped including the girls and the women in their households' official tallies. 'But girls were the key to change a family's situation, because the money a family had to get their son a wife often depended on the amount they'd get as betrothal gifts when marrying their own daughters away,' I was told by a local.

Because many families could not afford to have their children go to school, and because many felt that studying was pointless, their sons often ended up unable to afford getting married to a girl of another family. That situation led to an increase in consanguineous marriages, which in turn led to an increase in the number of children with mental disabilities and other birth defects.

Even if a family was relatively well-off, to the point of being able to afford a car, without education they often ended up developing an arrogant attitude and going about driving dangerously, with no consideration for the safety of themselves and others. Thus, if they did not end up crashing into other people and injuring them, then they'd get off the road and plunge down a ravine with their own cars… That way the number of maimed people, people missing arms or legs, only increased in the region.

It also came to my attention that, in a particular county with a population of somewhat over a hundred thousand, the proportion of people with either mental or physical disabilities was as high as one in ten! How could it be possible to escape poverty that way?! It is by no means a matter of Heaven not helping. Heaven was certainly in great pain. But what could be done, after all, about such places of such immense poverty, those miserable mountain backwaters? Indeed, Heaven had already screamed itself hoarse, and even the rivers wailed in lamentation.

'I hope that you, the officials in charge of the partnership on poverty alleviation, will keep one more thing in mind, and that is the issue of education with the goal of poverty alleviation, an issue secretary Xi Jinping is also very concerned about,' Lin Yuechan thus told the first few groups of officials being dispatched to Ningxia to be temporarily assigned there. And there is no doubt that those officials then kept the issue of education in Ningxia at the very top of their minds. Huang Shuiyuan, sent to the county of Tongxin by the city of Shishi, was one such official dispatched and especially instructed to focus on education during the course of his poverty alleviation work.

In April of 1997, Huang Shuiyuan was appointed as deputy county chief of the county of Tongxin. Also in that same month, Xi Jinping, then the person in charge of the Cooperation on Poverty Alleviation from the Fujian side, visited Ningxia for the first time and inspected the village of Jianxin, in the township of Hexi, in the county of Tongxin. Huang Shuiyuan was present at the occasion and listened to the important instructions Xi Jinping had to give on the issue of education in Ningxia. 'Those carrying out poverty alleviation work should not neglect the assistance impoverished families need to get their children into school,' Xi Jinping said. The concern contained in that admonition, amounting to a mission to him entrusted, would later become Huang Shuiyuan's top priority during the two years of his temporary assignment to Ningxia.

The county of Tongxin is an old base area of the Revolution, and when the Red Army passed through during the Long March, they established there the first revolutionary government of the Hui ethnicity. But a considerable portion of the county is made of remote mountain valleys, where schools had always been few and far between, resulting in very high dropout rates for children in those areas. To get an idea of the situation of education throughout the whole county, Huang Shuiyang visited village after village, school after school. Some primary schools deep in the mountains were so simple as to have only one teacher and a handful of students, and the students often had to walk long distances to get to it. A jeep was specially assigned to Huang Shuiyuan's use by the county government, and as the vehicle made its way at crawling speeds along steep mountain roads, it and its passengers often saw themselves in rather precarious situations. Because the roads were indeed very dangerous, some even urged Huang Shuiyuan to stay behind at the county seat, arguing that it was not necessary for everyone to go, and that there were some points along the roads that not even the locals would dare to cross. But Huang Shuiyuan just smiled those concerns away:

'If I don't go, I simply won't know how the situation really is,' he said.

During the summer holiday of 1998, Huang Shuiyuan's wife, herself a teacher, came to Tongxin with their daughter for a visit. At first, she was curious and said she wanted to go to the countryside to see the schools up in the mountains for herself. Their car then left the local county seat and started following a rather rough mountain road along a very steep precipice, shuddering and jolting from side to side over the very uneven surface. A moment of inattention by the driver could indeed send the vehicle plunging down the cliff.

'Go back! Let's go back!' Huang Shuiyuan's wife exclaimed, one hand holding tightly her daughter's hand and the other grabbing her husband.

'But we've just set off! Why should we go back?' Huang Shuiyuan said.

'Do you take dangerous roads like this every day?' his wife asked.

'Well, not every day, but most days!' Huang Shuiyuan replied calmly.

'You're really here to help? You are going to get me and your daughter killed!' his wife exclaimed, while also reaching for the driver and the steering wheel. 'You're going back home with us!' she said to her husband.

But Huang Shuiyuan replied to her:

'The time of my assignment here is not over yet. There are many schools up in those poor areas that still need to be built...'

'Tell me, how many schools still have to be built? I can donate all the family's money, and if that's still not enough you can think of another way… But you have to go back with us! Do you hear me?' his wife sobbed. And then their daughter was also so scared that she too started crying.

Huang Shuiyuan's eyes suddenly filled up with tears too. He tried to comfort his wife and daughter, and once they had calmed down a little, he said:

'I know that you worry about me. But think of this. I have already come here and seen the children of this place, who can't go to school or who can't stay in school, and so even if I go back to Fujian, I won't be at peace! Give me some time and I promise I will not waste it. I will do all I can to help Tongxin build more and better schools, to make sure that the children who dropped out return to the classroom. That way I will be at peace when I go back...'

And having thus set his mind to staying in Tongxin, he stayed on his journey across the mountains, on the 'path of poverty alleviation through education'. Two years later, when the time of his temporary assignment to Ningxia came to an end, the official 'list of accomplishments' of his time there recorded the following accomplishments: 'During the time of Huang Shuiyuan's temporary assignment the new town of Shishi and the new migrant village of Huangshi were built. In Shishi a vocational secondary school and seven primary schools were also built, all named after towns and villages in the prefecture of Shishi, in Fujian. Several Hope Elementary Schools were renovated and received support, while dozens of planned initiatives were carried out, initiatives that brought over a thousand dropout children back in school.'

That 'list of accomplishments' has now been included in the *County Annals of Tongxin (Tongxin Xian Zhi)*. And other such 'lists of accomplishments', of other temporarily assigned officials from Fujian, can be found in the local annals of virtually every locality in Ningxia. And after Huang Shuiyuan concluded his own temporary assignment, the city of Shishi in Fujian sent other groups of officials, also on temporary assignments, to conduct work within the scope of the mutual assistance programme. Among them there was one such official who, arriving one day at Tongxin county's Middle School No. 2, was very touched by what he saw, and so decided to write the following testimony:

The school director took me to a classroom for me to see the present situation at the school. The moment I walked into that classroom I could not help but feel shocked. The place was overflowing with students. There were basically three of them squeezed against each desk, which were very ordinary school desks. The students had to sit very tightly together and seemed almost as if glued together as a unity whenever they had to reach forward to write something down. Many students also sat sideways in relation to the desks, crowding the aisles between them. If the teacher wanted to walk around his classroom, he would have to go around squeezing sideways through the crowded aisles. Once the class was over, I was told that the class I had just been watching was class number seven of the first year of middle school, and that there was a total of 91 students in it. That was still, however, not the most crowded class at the school, as the most crowded one had no less than 110 students. I was shocked. Where would all those students find seats?

Behind the school building there was an open space, paved with nothing but the local loess of the bare ground, very uneven, and with a pile of rubbish to the side. Whenever the wind blew a little stronger, little clouds of dust and some scraps of paper would dance about in the air. Were it not for a couple very old-fashioned basketball stands and the sports logos painted on the wall of an adjacent old house yet to be demolished there would be no way for us to tell that we stood on the sports ground of Middle School No. 2. There was no real basketball court, no ping pong table, and whatever little scrap of athletic equipment one could find there was clearly very inadequate for the purpose. For their physical education classes students basically had to make do with playing whatever game on an area, this one paved with cement bricks, between the school's three buildings.

I asked the school's physical education teacher how he could keep his classes going under such conditions. The teacher just shook his head helplessly. There was nothing he could do about the conditions! He also told us that the school grounds had in fact already been expanded to include that other space we had seen, since originally only the area enclosed by the three buildings were part of the school.

Many of the students of Tongxin's Middle School No. 2 are from the countryside. Some parents come to the county's seat to work and then also bring their children along with them. But because Middle School No. 2 does not have a students' dormitory, it is unable to provide any accommodation to the students who need it. Those often have to rent nearby houses. One such house I've seen, a small single-storey house, is crowded with students. It has only very simple beds for them to sleep on and some quilts, and it seemed like everyone goes cold in there. The house does have a heating stove that burns coal. But whenever coal is burning the fumes fill the air inside the house, lifting also some solid particles that are inhaled and make people feel sick. Those students usually go back home *once a week, and when they come back, they bring with them some dry food from home. That dry food is called* momo. *They're like wheat pancakes, but very dry and hard, and there is no way to ever get used to eating them. There are some students who go back home even less often than others, and so it is their families who send them the dry food every once in a while. Those who live with their parents can have a little more variety in their diets, eating also noodles, dumplings and cooked millet. But, for those who stay by themselves at the county seat in order to attend school, meals consist mostly of* momo, *with the occasional splurge on a quick meal sold by the school's entrance for one yuan (a food bag containing some rice topped with some chilli sauce and radish or cabbage). And although there is running water at the county seat, that is only available at some workplaces, guest houses, and at a few relatively large communities, so many people still have to rely on water stored in their water collection pits. I boiled water from the tap, and after the water had boiled a white residue remained at the bottom of the pot, like little pellets. That's how I managed to make it tasteless. And if that's how even tap water is there, there's no need to mention the quality of the water kept in those collection pits.*

Jin Chan is one of the students of class number seven who comes from the countryside. According to her teacher, hers is not the financially worst-off family in her class, but because her home is in the village of Zhangjiatan, in the township of Dingtang, thus relatively close to the county seat, I made a plan to pay a visit to her family. Being mindful of the cultural differences between different ethnic group, I first obtained permission from Jin Chan and then asked her to call her parents to ask them as well if they'd agree to my visit. Jia Chen's family does not have a phone line, so she had to call some relatives living in the same village and asked them to convey the message to her parents. Once Jin Chan's parents had agreed to our visit, I set off from the school with my team and with Jin Chan.

We waited for quite a long time for the only bus that drove to their village. The ticket was quite cheap, only 1.50 yuan per person, but the bus jolted for nearly two hours on the uneven dirt road before it arrived at the village of Zhangjiatan. We all alighted from the bus and walked for a while along another road before we finally reached the home of Jin Chan's family. Their house was inside a quite large yard surrounded by a low mud wall along the four sides. There was no gate, so we entered the yard through a gap left in that low wall. As our host shouted out his enthusiastic welcome greetings at us, I had the chance to size the place up. A single-storey house with two rooms stood not very far from the yard's entrance. There was a level difference between the yard and the house itself, overcome by two broad steps. It seemed evident also that our host had been preparing for our arrival, as the open area of yellow earth next to the house had been swept clean. To the right side of the yard, just outside the entrance, there was the hole to store the water the family relied on, their 'water pit'. There was also a pile of corn cobs nearby, which the family burned in their coal stove or otherwise in their kang *beds to keep them warm. Around the water collection pit there was no pavement or finish of either cement or brick, and so one can just imagine how the water inside was like. There were also several piles of dried corn stalks in the yard, and one dead tree of a kind I couldn't identify was lying between a pile of corn stalks and the water collection pit, its exposed roots making it clear that there was no hope of life ever returning to it. To the left side of the yard there was also an outside toilet, and right next to that toilet stood the sheep pen.*

From inside that pen a few sheep looked back at us, reciprocating our curiosity.

And so, under the enthusiastic welcome greetings of our host, we entered the house.

The house was very modestly furnished inside. There were a kang *bed, a kitchen top with a stove, and two tables. We sat on the* kang *bed, and our host, very politely, brought some fruit and some* momo *pancakes for us and entreated us to eat some. A moment later a steaming-hot large bowl of* jiumian *noodle flakes was placed before us. It was clear indeed that our host had long been preparing to welcome us. Thinking about it now, I feel really sorry, because we had already had lunch not much earlier, and so we ate only some of the* momo *pancakes they offered us and did not touch the* jiumian *noodles at all.*

But by chatting with Jin Chan's father, we learnt a lot more about the family. Jin Chan's parents had six children, one boy and five girls. The elder brother had not yet returned home, as he was taking supplementary classes at a senior middle school, while the five girls were all at either junior middle school or at primary school. The whole family's only source of income was the work their father did over in Inner Mongolia, which consisted of picking Chinese wolfberries in the summer, and then, in the autumn and winter, going there to gather fat choy to bring back and sell it. He had just returned that same day from Inner Mongolia, where he had been gathering fat choy for over half a month. Jin Chan's father showed us the fat choy he had brought back. It was in a cloth bag and weighed something like four or five jin[1]. He told me he could sell that amount for four or five hundred yuan. Standing next to him, his sister-in-law told me that he had got seriously ill this last time while in Inner Mongolia, and almost didn't make it back to his family. Upon hearing this, a feeling of unspeakable sadness spread throughout my whole body.

The dire situation of education in the mountain areas of Ningxia and the many hardships the children there were facing to attend school left a great number of people back in Fujian deeply moved.

'I will go to Ningxia,' one said.

'I will sign up too,' said another

'I'll stay here now,' then said the first.

'I can't leave either. My students are here,' said the other.

---

1   Two to two and a half kilograms.

'The sick people here need me. How could I just shrug my shoulder and do nothing?' yet another said.

And so group after group of the best sons and daughters of Fujian left behind their beautiful and pleasant home towns, the prosperous home towns they were so familiar with, left also very fine and comfortable jobs, perhaps even when on the verge of a promotion, and, of course, left also their loved ones behind, their own parents and children, and went to that distant place they had only heard of before — Ningxia.

'You were sent there to help, and you answered a call from the Party and from your country, to work with the people there for the elimination of poverty, for the construction of a moderately prosperous society,' they were told. 'That is a place facing plenty of hardships, and so we're sending you over there, the best sons and daughters of Fujian. You shall represent Fujian, the youth of Fujian, the teachers of Fujian... In sum, this is a mission of historical significance that's being entrusted to you, and this mission is to defeat poverty. So you have to be prepared to face hardships yourselves!'

Prior to their departure, the trust deposited on then by their leaders, the exhortations of their loved ones, and the tears and hopes of their children, were all tightly woven into the hearts of those teachers, medical experts, and of the other members of the poverty alleviation team, who were now all going to that 'distant place'.

The pledge they made before departing had already stirred up great waves on the Min River and also along the promontories on the coast. And the roaring of those waves now reverberated over the vastness of the Helan and the Liupan Mountains...

Yingzi is one of the many teachers dispatched from Fujian to Ningxia. Her story reached also the ears of the leaders of the Ningxia Hui Autonomous Region. But Yingzi herself knows that stories such as hers are not unique among her own colleagues. 'Mine is just the most ordinary among them,' she said humbly.

However, though very ordinary, it is also a very valuable story. An ordinary story may very well still have the power to move great rivers and mountains, because within its commonness lies something precious like gold, a kind of radiant nobility.

Back at home Yingzi had been just a rather 'pampered girl' who had never travelled very far. Now a little under thirty years old, she was born during a time when parents had to observe very strict family-planning regulations. For that reason, she was her family's only child. After completing her teacher's training at a normal university, she completed also a postgraduate programme while working at a junior middle school. There she gradually rose till she became one of the school's core teachers. She then signed up to work for the Cooperation on Poverty Alleviation Between Fujian and Ningxia, and, as a core teacher at her school, she naturally received a recommendation from the prefectural education bureau. All teachers sent to Ningxia to assist with education had to be classed as a 'core teacher'[1] back in Fujian. 'We wanted to make sure we were sending the best teachers to help with the education of the children in those impoverished mountain areas. That requirement was in fact put in place by General Secretary Xi Jinping during his tenure in Fujian,' said the leader of Fujian's Education Department.

And so Yingzi went to Guyuan, to a place called Xiji, an impoverished county up in the mountains. Upon arrival, Yingzi requested to be assigned to teach at a middle school up in the mountains. 'Now that I'm here, please arrange for me to be sent to the most challenging place,' she said then. Yingzi's enthusiasm and determination touched the leaders of Xiji's department of education, but after taking all into consideration, they opted for sending her to a junior middle school facing challenges they had classified as 'average-level'.

But what would 'average-level challenges' mean in practice? For Yingzi in particular it would mean a junior middle school

---

1   *Gugan Jiaoshi*

and a class with thirty or forty students who boarded at the school. Those were students whose homes were tens of kilometres away, and who therefore couldn't commute to and from school every day. Prior to 2010, the prefecture of Guyuan was still rather far from a decisive victory in the struggle against poverty, as poverty alleviation and poverty elimination are actually two different stages in that struggle. The former involves addressing issues concerning the most basic living necessities, whereas the latter aims at creating moderately prosperous standards of living. When Yingzi first arrived in Guyuan, the region was still mostly poor, and the construction of the main road leading into the mountains had not yet begun. Since the only available roads at the time were dirt roads, travelling to and from the villages up in the mountains was still very difficult. So, if Yingzi wanted to go down to the county seat for any reason, that would be a challenge. Thus, in the first three months after her arrival at the school she was to teach, she did not get to leave the village even once. But after three months she felt she had to go down to the county seat at any cost, the reason being that she had spent those three months without taking a single shower. So she felt that if she did not go at once to take a shower somewhere at the county seat, she would never be able to return to her home in Fujian again... She felt like there was too much of 'that thing' on her body, but out of sheer embarrassment she would not spell out what 'that thing' would be. It was not really a disease, but rather something that she could smell, a very distinctively fishy smell. And once a woman gets that kind smell, she can't help but feel repulsed by herself.

Yingzi had been used to live in a beautiful city by the sea, and where there is the sea there is water. It is usually said that women are made of water, and women who live by the sea even more so, never being apart from water since the day they were born. And indeed, Yingzi had loved water ever since she was a child. Very early on it was about the fun she had with the little bucket her mother used to bathe her as a child. Later, once she had grown up, she'd go to the beach with the boys to swim. The satisfying feeling Yingzi got from wrestling with the waves instilled in her a boldness of spirit — she did not fear the water, she liked the water very much, and could not bear to be apart from it.

During both middle school and university, she was a member of amateur swimming teams. Later, after she had started to work and after she got married, she would remain inseparable from water. Every day before leaving the house, no matter what, she would take a hot shower. Her mother had also taught her as she grew up that 'girls must wash often, especially "down there", once in the morning and then once again in the evening…' That 'down there' required women to pay special attention to their personal hygiene. Yingzi's mother was, indeed, right, and that was something women from the south and from the coastal regions of China all understood very well. Women from the cities understood it, and so did countryside women. Women in areas where water was scarce in fact also understood it, but there was nothing they could do about it. And after there being nothing they could do about it for a while, gradually there would be women who do *not* understand it. And it is rather tragic for women not to understand it, because it means they will often get sick, and even the children they give birth to can be affected… In the mountain areas where water was scarce, there would be a much higher proportion of women suffering from gynaecological diseases, and that is due to the simple fact that, without water, there is no way for women to wash themselves.

So where was water to be found? After waking up in the first morning after her arrival at the school in the mountains, Yingzi pushed aside the quilt she had been sleeping in and went to the toilet. After going to the toilet the first thing she wanted to do was to wash her face and brush her teeth. 'But where's the water?' was the question she wanted to ask but did not dare. That was because the evening before the school director had instructed a student to take a bottle of hot water and give it to the newly-arrived Yingzi. Before going to sleep, Yingzi tried to have some of that water, but almost puked her guts out. What kind of water was that? It smelled very foul. Yingzi thought that the student had made a mistake, so later, without attracting much attention, she asked some female students where that water had come from. One student pointed to a covered water collection pit by the school entrance and said that the water had been taken from there.

'And where does the water in that pit come from?' Yingzi asked.

The student pointed up at the sky:

'We get it when it rains.'

'And when will Heaven send any rain?' Yingzi asked.

The students looked up at the sky.

'Hard to tell,' one of them said. 'Sometimes we go for several months without a drop.'

'And when it doesn't rain like that, what do you drink?' Yingzi insisted.

The students were silent for a while, then one of them said:

'We have to go to a place very far to get some and carry it back.'

Yingzi asked no more questions. On the first day of class

Yingzi was very energised and focused on the students' thirst for knowledge. The children up in the mountain areas were very eager to learn, and as she made use of the experience she had acquired in Fujian to teach them, they were all very curious, motivated, and earnestly focused. By the end of the day her throat was so dry she felt like it was about to burst into flames. But when a student handed her a cup of water and she had a sip of it, again it made her so nauseous as to almost vomit her guts out.

In the evening, once she had returned to her room, and tired from the long day, she felt like it was about time to take a bath. That had been her habit ever since childhood, and it was almost as if it had a connection with her biological clock. It was her body telling her: 'Time to bathe!'

'I have to take a bath!' Yingzi thought aloud to herself.

'Teacher, the water is here…' the female student who brought the water said, placing a basin only half-full of a muddy yellow water in front of her and then gently closing the door as she left.

Yingzi stood stunned in front of that basin. How could she bathe with so little water? How could she bathe with *that* muddy water? Would there be any other water there? She felt anxiety creeping in and started searching about the things in her room. But there was no other water. In fact, there wasn't much of anything else. The only things there were were a few bags of instant noodles she had brought over from Fujian. But instant noodles also need to be soaked in hot water before being eaten.

And that water in the basin was suitable neither for making instant noodles nor for bathing. All she could do with it was… moisten her face perhaps? But upon coming in contact with that muddy water, the delicate skin on her face felt like it was being rubbed with sand.

It felt more comfortable not to wash her face at all then to wipe it using any that water. That was then the first time in Yingzi's life that she tucked herself under a quilt to sleep without either bathing or washing her face. And so that turned out to be a very uncomfortable night. And nights up in the mountains were eerily quiet, so quiet indeed that the sound of a dog suddenly barking far in the distance came in as frighteningly loud thunder striking from nowhere…

During the second day of classes, Yingzi felt the discomfort on her body from head to toe. It felt like tiny bugs were crawling all over her skin. But there were, in fact, no tiny bugs. It was just the constant reactions of her body, a body very much used to water.

That day she swore to herself that she was going to wash her body, no matter what. But by evening it seemed like the students had already fallen in love with their new teacher from Fujian. After dinner, several female students came to her room to 'consult with' her. Faced with students that were so eager to learn, Yingzi did not hesitate and started 'doing overtime' with them. That 'extra class' went on till after ten o'clock. By the end the students were tired, and Yingzi even more so.

She was tired and in need of a shower, but ended up falling asleep on the warmer end of her *kang* bed… She woke by daybreak the next morning, and once again she wished she could have bathed. But there was nothing she could do about it, and so that was the second time in her life that she had gone to bed without bathing.

On the third day her body started to react even more strongly, to the point of making it hard for her to continue teaching her class… The discomfort was all over her body, and every now and then she found herself scratching it here and there, which made her feel extremely embarrassed.

In the evening of that day she once again swore to herself that she was going to bathe even if it turned out to be a busy evening again… And indeed she did start to clean herself. She took the clean towel she had brought over from Fujian and put it in the water so that she could rub her body down with it. But when she took the towel from the water her hands froze in midair, and for several minutes she couldn't bring them down. And why was that? Because she couldn't understand how a towel that just a moment ago was spotlessly white and clean now looked like a dirty rag. Could she even rub her body down with that water? She started to cry. That night Yingzi got under the quilt in tears… It was another sleepless night, as her body felt like it was being bitten by insects everywhere. At the crack of dawn the pain in her body was suddenly gone. She found it a strange and took a closer look at herself. And, by Heaven, her entire body had swollen up. It was red and swollen!

'That's allergy! Your skin is having an allergic reaction!' said another female teacher, who quickly found some allergy medicine and applied it on Yingzi.

By the fourth or fifth day, Yingzi had lost all hope that she'd be able to bathe any time soon, and even lost her desire to do it. The key factor in that was her conviction that she would never dare to touch that muddy water. She knew that sometimes she'd be so thirsty that she would have to purse her lips and take a few sips of that pit water. But she would be doing that in order to 'survive' and so to continue teaching her students. Bathing, on the other hand, didn't seem so crucial to her role as a teacher any more. But still, for Yingzi being unable to take a bath felt worse than being in prison.

In any case, once Yingzi had arrived in Xihaigu to take part in the efforts of the education component of the Cooperation on Poverty Alleviation, for her bathing became a sort of aspirational luxury. And what a luxury it was! For a southerner like herself, having a proper bath meant, of course, having access to clean water, and then having a virtually unlimited supply of it, so that one could bathe to one's heart's content.

With the allergy medicine applied on her skin, Yingzi felt another kind of reaction from her body, a sort of numbness that gradually made her less sensitive to the wind-borne sand and the dryness of the air. And she found it very strange.

Do you normally bathe? Don't you feel uncomfortable sometimes? Don't you bathe if you feel some smell on you? As discreetly as she could Yingzi asked her female students all of those questions, and others like them. Some students were clearly embarrassed by the questioning, others shook their heads, while others simply stood there, as if in a daze, wondering why their teacher was asking them those questions.

But gradually Yingzi understood it, and came to a realisation on her own: Because the girls there went for very long periods without bathing, their bodies had become rougher and much less sensitive…

Oh dear! I cannot become like this! Yingzi thought. And

when she thought that she shed tears in secret. After the second week of classes there was a day off. The students were to go back home to fetch food and whatever other items they might need, while teachers could also take the day off to do as they pleased.

For that day Yingzi made a decision. She would go down to the county seat, find a bathing and recreation centre, and take a very thorough bath there. And so, in the morning of that day she asked about for any of the student's parents who could be going to the county seat. Finding some people who were going there to sell livestock, she caught a ride with them.

At the county seat, Yingzi spent a long time looking for a bathing and recreation centre, but could not find nothing like it. She then began to panic. How terrible the situation was! Back in her hometown the streets were full of places like that. How come she could not find a single one in that town? She asked about everywhere, only hitting dead ends. At long last someone told her that there was one hotel in town where she could take a bath. After struggling for some time to find that hotel, she was told there that the stand-alone bathing facilities had long been out of service!

'But is it still possible for me to take a bath here?' Yingzi asked.

The hotel employee looked her up and down for a while,

noticing also that hers wasn't a local accent. Upon learning that Yingzi was a teacher from Fujian there to support local education, the employee turned much more friendly and said:

'If you want to take a bath, you can stay for a night in our hotel. The better rooms have solar water heating, but...'

'But what?' Yingzi asked.

'But you'll need to formally register as a guest...' the employee answered with some embarrassment.

Yingzi then produced her identity card and some money.

She had now spent 150 yuan to take a bath, but she never returned there to take a second one, because, just as she was washing herself up with soap, the solar-powered water unit cut the water. Finding herself in quite a fix, Yingzi then 'fled' the hotel.

Riding on the tractor, Yingzi went crying along the whole way back to the school. 'What's wrong sister? Who gave you a hard time?' the parents who were giving her a ride asked her again and again. But she could only cry and did not answer them.

The next day Yingzi taught her lessons as usual, but somewhat gone from her face were that smile and that enthusiasm she had when she had just arrived...

That smile and enthusiasm were, however, to make a return. The diligence and the commitment of her students, as well as the cool breeze of the mountains, made sure that, gradually, she would adapt to life there, including to the habit of not bathing. Her body's reactions also started to become more 'Ningxia-like', as she said in a letter she wrote to her family: 'I've already become a person of the mountains…'

The Tang poet Tan Han wrote a poem Yingzi read aloud in her class:

> *He rode his horse to strike with the long sword, travelling to the Xiao Pass.*
>
> *He took his time in Wuyuan, that forever overlooks the Guanhe River.*
>
> *Among three hundred thousand northern prisoners, one always draws the bow.*
>
> *The citadel of Qin covers all the world, the Han Emperor rules with his banners.*

In that reading, sounding loud and clear over the north-western plateau, was indeed the now somewhat changed voice of Yingzi, the teacher, but also her forever unchanging heart dedicated to the children and to Ningxia. Time now seemed to go by many times faster than when she had just arrived. And just as her thoughts, her habits regarding food and drink, and in fact her whole body were finally fully adapted to life in the mountains, the time of her group's temporary assignment was over. The few dozen teachers of her group were then to be all picked up by the leaders of Fujian's Education Department. It was agreed that all teachers in the district of Guyuan would go to the city proper of Guyuan one day in advance, then travel by car to Yinchuan, from where they would all take the same plane back to Fujian.

And now that she was about to leave behind those mountains and those students who had grown close to her, Yingzi once again felt unwell. What was going on?

The night prior to her departure she was again unable to fall asleep. That discomfort all over her body had made a comeback, but Yingzi knew that it wasn't because she hadn't bathed. It was something psychological, or else it was the land itself telling her body *do not leave the children, do not leave Ningxia...* The next moment her tears soaked her quilt.

The next morning distant cockcrows woke her up. She got out of bed, took her luggage, and started the walk down the mountain road. The school she had been teaching at sat atop a hillock on the way, and there was still a long way to go to the bus station. The students knew that their teacher was leaving, and so, from very early in the morning, they stood on the hillock to see her off.

The girls started to cry. Yingzi didn't dare to look back, keeping her gaze fixed on the tip of her shoes as she walked. She wanted to walk faster, and so quickened her pace a little. But much to her surprise, the faster she walked, the more she heard footsteps coming up behind her and quickly catching up with her. Then she couldn't help it any more and had to turn back to look… Yingzi's legs froze on the spot when she saw it. Heaven! There were about a dozen girls, crying and shouting, and running towards her as if they had gone mad. Then she saw herself surrounded by them.

'Teacher…' one said.

'Teacher, don't go…' said another.

'Don't go…' said yet another.

Some of them were hugging her legs, others knelt on the ground, others still buried their faces in their arms to hide their tears.

'My students… you… don't do like that… I… I…' Yingzi mumbled. Confronted with that scene, she really did not know what to say to her students. In the end she couldn't help but cry together with her students.

Yingzi and her students hugged each other and sobbed convulsively. At long last Yingzi wiped away her tears, waved her hands, and let out a loud sigh up to the sky, exclaiming:

'Ay! I'm bond by fate to Ningxia!'

Then, turning to her students, she said:

'Don't worry! I'll stay and continue to teach you!'

'Ah! Long live the teacher!' the students shouted. 'Long live the teacher!'

Teachers are indeed great, because they teach and influence us, generation after generation, with their noble sense of mission and with their values, building our character and nurturing our abilities so that we can constantly advance and grow. They are like the sunshine that illuminates all things on earth, like a caring mother who dearly loves her children. Their selflessness and dedication cause all of those whom they benefit to hold them in great esteem. And every teacher working for the Cooperation on Poverty Alleviation Between Fujian and Ningxia has bestowed a gift warm like sunshine and the spring upon the children of those poor families in the poor mountain areas of Ningxia. It is a kind of warm gift that makes any dried-up heart, or any dried-up young sprout, to be revived and to grow up in health.

'Long live the teacher!' the students exclaimed. And all over the Liupan and the Helan Mountains that rallying cry was heard. I have heard it several times, and every time I heard it my heart would tremble…

Li Dan is a young teacher originally from the city of Fuzhou, where she taught at the city's Middle School No. 18. In 2006 she came to the county of Longde to teach at that county's Middle School No. 2. Over the years after she moved there, her body went through a number of small changes she would simply take no notice of. Li Dan took no notice of those changes on her body because, at first, she believed that her body would not adapt to her new environment. Nonetheless, as she went on with her routine of hard work, teaching her classes at the school during the day, and in the evenings providing guidance to and helping those more hard-working students with their assignments in her dormitory room.

'Teacher, don't you get yourself too tired! Have some rest! We can ask you this question again tomorrow…' a student said. It was another evening of tutoring, and the students had witnessed Li Dan bring her hand over to her chest and have a coughing fit seemingly without end. She looked pale, and so the students rushed to give her some boiled water and then to allow her to have her rest a little earlier than usual.

'It's nothing, it's nothing,' she insisted. 'You'll have your final examination the day after tomorrow, so I'll revise with you one more time tonight…'

When Li Dan took a sip of the hot water, she felt suffocated, and her face turned red. After some panting and puffing trying to recover her breath, she leant her body forward again and resumed her tutoring.

Then the day finally came when the other teachers and the students of Longde's Middle School No. 2 had to say goodbye to Li Dan, that young teacher who looked so slim and fragile… Some time after her departure from the school, a piece of very sad news came back to them about their teacher. Not long after returning to Fuzhou, Li Dan had been diagnosed with leukaemia.

'She was only 27 years old, an age when one is still just a big child in the eyes of one's parents… But, for our children… Now she's just gone like that…' said Xu Zhimou, the director of Longde's Middle School No. 2, unable to hold back his tears. 'During the year she spent with us, she not only taught her classes and offered guidance to the students, but also visited students' families in the mountains dozens of times, and even offered financial assistance to six poor students. Even after returning to Fujian she kept very busy raising money to cover the living expenses of quite a number of poor students…'

'Don't waste more money on me. Take what is left assigned to medical costs and donate it to the children of Ningxia,' said Li Dan shortly before passing, wishing to make a last gift to the cause of education and to the children of distant Ningxia…

'Teacher Li Dan…' someone said.

'Teacher Li Dan is here again…'

One Li Dan left, and another one, in fact another group of 'Li Dans' arrived… Each one of them was different in their own way, but they all seemed to be the same person when it came to their love for and dedication to Ningxia and its people.

Yang Ming, an English teacher from the Putian Strait Vocational Middle School, is another volunteering teacher like Yingzi and Li Dan. Yang Ming said that she was particularly grateful to the programme to support education in Ningxia because the five years she spent as a supporting teacher there gave her 'an unbreakable emotional connection' with Ningxia.

'Women of our age, whose children have already grown up, and for whom both family life and work are already peaceful like the water on the surface of lake, usually no longer have those outbursts of fervour and enthusiasm they once had when they were younger,' Yang Ming said. 'But after arriving in Ningxia and spending time together with the children and the teachers there, I felt that my fervour was reignited.'

At first Yang Ming worked as a teacher at Xiji's Middle School. That is one of the largest middle schools in the region of Guyuan, with four or five thousand students. It did not, however, have a single English teacher at the time. The lack of English teachers was due to a few teachers being pregnant with their 'second children', and thus having time off from teaching. Because of that Yang Ming ended up being in charge of classes that three different teachers used to teach.

'I teach first and second grades of senior middle school, two grades in a row…' Yang Ming said. She seemed to be a fairly strong woman, with a personality not prone to shedding tears. 'When my son was still at university, I went to Xinjiang to work as a supporting teacher there too. After he graduated I then came over to Ningxia… Volunteering as a teacher seems to have become the most inspiring thing for me to do, especially when it means joining the efforts of the Cooperation on Poverty Alleviation Between Fujian and Ningxia. I think it has raised my self-worth to new heights, making me very enthusiastic about the work I do, even to the point of often losing myself in it.'

It is not like straight-talking Yang Ming has not encountered her share of difficulties, but all those difficulties were overcome with the help of the passion and the enthusiasm she had for working for Ningxia, and for the children of Ningxia.

'I spent five years in Ningxia as a supporting teacher,' Yang Ming said, confessing to me also that, back home in Fujian, everything about her daily life was taken care of by other people. 'But once in Ningxia, I in fact had more time for myself, despite the many classes I had to teach. Thus, shopping for food and cooking meals became a part of my life. And I also learnt how to give a taste of Fujian to the ingredients I could find in Ningxia, claiming several "patent rights" on the dishes I invented!' she joked. 'Both teachers and students liked my food a lot!' And Yang Ming was indeed a very lively and upbeat teacher, certainly bringing much sunshine to her students!

Wang Nana is a girl very much eager to learn and very dedicated. Her family, however, was very poor, and could not afford to let her continue her studies. So, on the second year of senior middle school, she had to drop out and return home to do farm work on her family's land. When Yang Ming heard about it she was so anxious that, despite being an outsider and thus unfamiliar with the region, she walked several kilometres to the Wang Nana's home, lodged with them for a while doing farm work for her parents, and, once all the work that needed to be done was done, dragged Wang Nana back to the school with her…

'If I lose one student it reduces the value of the work I do here,' Yang Ming said. 'When I left my hometown to come here, I told the leaders that I was a real supporting teacher, and that in Ningxia I would set a personal record I could be proud of. That meant spending a long time supporting education there, teaching a large number of students, and teaching them to the highest possible standards.' And, by putting pressure on herself, she kept that promise.

Later Wang Nana became Yang Ming's 'adopted daughter', in a customary sense.

'I wanted the children there to call me "mum", so that I would be loving them and caring for them for a lifetime…' Yang Ming said. And her generosity and motherly feelings touched many people. She said also that she was the most grateful for the support her family and the people back at her original work unit gave her, which made it possible for her to forge 'an unbreakable emotional connection' with that land called Ningxia.

Because of the Cooperation on Poverty Alleviation Between Fujian and Ningxia, and because of their experiences as supporting teachers, countless teachers like Yingzi, Li Dan and Yang Ming were able to form such an 'unbreakable emotional connection' with Ningxia. This is in fact true of virtually every teacher who came from Fujian to take part in the efforts to support education in Ningxia. The challenges they had to overcome during the time they spent in Ningxia can hardly be expressed in words. I have heard from many male teachers, too many to be counted, that the differences in temperatures between Fujian and Ningxia alone were enough to toughen up anyone and get them used to any sort of harsh discipline.

'In my hometown temperatures usually never drop below 16°C or 15°C,' said a teacher surnamed Chen, also from Fujian. 'But, around the same time of the year in Ningxia, temperatures can go as low as minus 15°C or minus 16°C. That's a 30-degrees difference. It isn't something you learn how to endure through empty talk. It's impossible to adapt to it at once, but you have to adapt, because you have work to do. While working to support education in such impoverished areas, you're going to be confronted with some difficulties you could never have imagined before.'

Teacher Chen urged me repeatedly, out of humbleness, not to include his full name in this book. His reasoning was that, as a man, his determination may sometimes not have been as strong as that of Yang Ming, Yingzi, Li Dan, and other such female teachers. He told me that, after his arrival in Xihaigu, he at times felt lonely and helpless. 'Some difficulties of everyday life that you wouldn't think much about back in Fujian, there would come to perplex you,' he said.

Then teacher Chen told me the following recollection:

'It was around the year 2000 when we all left Fujian to go to Ningxia. At the time poverty alleviation work in Ningxia was still at its early stages, so the rural schools, and even the middle schools at county seats, were all in very bad conditions. So there is no need to mention that classrooms were in poor conditions too, but living conditions in general were worlds apart from how it was back in Fujian, where many years of Reform and Opening-up had already brought about plenty of development. And if we leave all the rest aside and focus on food only, back in Fujian we were used to eat seafood and to have rather thin soups. But in Ningxia most of the food consisted of potatoes and maize, and those make you feel very stuffed, and once you're stuffed like that… you just cannot poop! This sort of predicament is not only unpleasant to talk about, it was also very uncomfortable and embarrassing, especially when it affected you during class! You may laugh, but I don't know how many times I made a fool of myself because of it in the first few months there only! I'd be standing before class teaching when I'd suddenly feel my belly distend and get very bloated. I'd then run to the toilet, only to be unable to get it out. Then, as soon as I had returned and gone on with my class, I'd feel the urge to rush back to the toilet again… I could have to go back and forth like this three or four times during a single class. Now don't you think that that was both very uncomfortable and very embarrassing?'

That 'predicament' teacher Chen found himself in is for sure no laughing matter. That was the result of a southern suddenly changing his diet and starting to eat potatoes too often. It was indeed quite a torment. I believe that all the teachers and doctors and other comrades who left Fujian to help supporting education and health care in Ningxia experienced at some point some kind of predicament that they wouldn't be too comfortable talking about.

Teacher Chen mentioned this predicament of his to one of his 'predecessors' in Ningxia, and that teacher told him that, if he wanted to go 'there' the right way, he would have to 'fix' himself some beer. At first Chen didn't understand very well what his colleague meant. He explained to him that he never drank much, so there was no point! That other teacher smiled at him and then told him the 'secret', and it was that, if you drink the water there, you'll certainly have intestinal problems for the first few months, whereas if you drink beer, you won't.

'Later all teachers there used this trick,' Chen said. 'But a few years later the water problem was solved, and that kind of embarrassment we went through stopped being a thing there.'

Those awkward moments in life were, nonetheless, 'small problems'. Teacher Chen said that among the greatest challenges supporting teachers faced was that of figuring out how to use one's own teaching experience to be of help to the people in the mountain areas. That was the crucial point and what was foundational for everything they did. 'That was what every teacher from Fujian on that battle front of education was most concerned about,' Chen said. 'After arriving in Ningxia, everyone kept this one maxim in mind: Better to go through countless hardships than to be sloppy in one's work.' Teacher Chen indeed expressed the thoughts and feelings of every teacher from Fujian who joined the efforts to support education in Ningxia.

'For more than 20 years every teacher who has come to Ningxia to support education has been fully committed like this,' the leader in charge of education in Ningxia told me. 'Every single one of them! As far as supporting teachers of the Cooperation on Poverty Alleviation are concerned, they're all outstanding teachers chosen by the Fujian's Education Department among all the schools over there. Once they found themselves at a different place, where conditions were much more backward than what they were used to, they all brushed aside any personal difficulties they might be facing and dedicated themselves wholeheartedly to the cause of education here, and to teaching the children to the very best of their abilities…' the local leader sighed. 'Every time I went down to the ground to check on them, I returned with loads of amazing stories. That I found very moving!'

That leader said that he once witnessed a teacher of the education support programme collapsing from exhaustion during an examination at a middle school, and then being carried away to a hospital. He said also that he once went to inspect a primary school building in the countryside and saw there a teacher from Fujian carrying a student on his back. That teacher, staggering along the mountain road, was taking the student back home, and the sight of those two bodies nearly glued together, like a shadowed image on a screen, and almost touching the ground, remained deeply engraved in his mind.

'But in fact I know,' said that leader, who is also from a mountain village in Guyuan. 'That if you look at the primary and middle schools in Ningxia today, you'll see how much modern they've become, both in terms of teaching staff and in terms of their buildings and facilities. A change like this is just like a huge leap through time, a leap that was made possible thanks to the selfless generosity of the people and the teachers of Fujian working through the Cooperation on Poverty Alleviation. The help they provided will forever remain in the memory of this vast land, my homeland, as though carved on the rocks.'

Indeed, had I not seen it with my own eyes, I would not have believed that, in both rural and urban schools throughout Ningxia, the surroundings, the playgrounds, the classrooms, the libraries, the computer network rooms and the students' dormitories are now, beyond any doubt, more complete, more advanced, and more beautifully arranged than their counterparts in the schools of relatively well-developed regions. That indeed is a fact, or at least that is the impression I got from the at least ten schools I entered and the dozens of others I've seen from the outside in the course of my travels. And the schools located deep in the mountains were indeed the ones that impressed me the most for how much they had improved. Almost all the schools I visited had a network link connecting them directly with famous schools back in Fujian, a link that enables children in the mountain regions of Ningxia to learn with the famous teachers of those famous schools thousands of kilometres away, in real time and together with the students of those other schools, and without ever leaving their villages. Another thing that one could never have imagined is that those schools in once very impoverished areas now all have garden areas for studying, and also exhibition areas for the works created by the students. Both kinds of area are marked by the special characteristics of each ethnic groups that made and use them, those groups' intangible cultural heritage. Those are areas where the students can be particularly productive and focused, because they are spaces made as extensions of their own inner traits, and made also of the things they love and are keenly interested in. That gives each school its own characteristics and flavour, creating a culture made of the customs and culture of Ningxia and of the lands beyond the Great Wall, and creating also a future those children can look forward to.

'One can say that none of that would be a reality today without the help and continuous support from the teachers and from the Education Department of Fujian,' said Ji Zhilin, the director of the Vocational Secondary School of Pengyang County. 'It was their sincere feelings that thoroughly transformed our school and brought about all these improvements, producing in particular a great leap in our teaching philosophy and direction.'

The day when I walked into the new campus of the Vocational Secondary School of Pengyang County, director Ji was very thrilled to tell me that, in the past ten years or so, his vocational school had gone from a campus with 13 *mu* of area to one with 30 *mu*, and then to a new one with 100 *mu*. Three great leaps, all made possible by the Cooperation on Poverty Alleviation Between Fujian and Ningxia. In the few years since he took office, director Ji has taken many groups of his teachers and students to visit their counterpart school in the partnership, the Jinjiang Vocational School, to 'confer with the family' and to 'learn the directions'. He explained:

'Confer with the family' meant that they already saw each other as family, as 'people on the same side', helping each other with their learning experiences. 'Most important thing is to draw from the learning experiences of that family of ours,' director Ji said. As he sees it, the Jinjiang Vocational School being a very well-reputed school back in Fujian, their administrative experience could also serve as guidance to his own school for the ten or twenty years to come. 'The region of Jinjiang was already known throughout the country for its fast economic development back in the 1980s, and many of the industries located there are now famous even globally. The Jinjiang Vocational School has developed in tandem with Jinjiang's economy and society. Forty years of development of the local society in Jinjiang has provided plenty of opportunities there to foster middle-level vocational talent, and so tapping from their experience is, for us, the equivalent of taking a shortcut, one that provides the skills necessary not only to escape poverty today, but also to the rapid development of Pengyang in the future. Being able to take such a shortcut is, for us, an immense help!'

As director Ji talked about his school's partnership with the Jinjiang Vocational School, there was a big smile of happiness on his face. 'You see, in terms of both "software" and "hardware", we're now in no way behind the secondary schools of Beijing or Shanghai!' he said. 'And I can tell you in all honesty that, if we run into any problem here, our "family" in the Jinjiang

Vocational School will send us a "prescription" to help us keep things moving. That is because of their strength, being among the best vocational schools in the country. And so, in a few years, we will be deficient in nothing here, either in terms of teaching standards, or with regard to the disciplines we offer. In the past, for instance, the disciplines we offered were not keeping up with the needs imposed by the pace of economic and social development, resulting in constant adjustments that led in fact to much disorganisation. But then our "relatives" from Jinjiang came by to assess the situation. They recreated some disciplines, while also reorganising, together with us, some others. Results were seen very fast. In the past we had issues recruiting new students, and then finding a job after graduation could also be an issue for the students we had. But now we're expanding admissions every year, and the employment rate of our graduates is basically at 100%. And what makes us the happiest is that, in the past few years, 576 of our graduates went to work in Fujian, while all the ones remaining in Pengyang are now employed as skilled technicians in many different sectors!'

A vocational school that shines from the inside and from the outside, and which trains experts in many fields, now rises among the great peaks of the Liupan Mountains. That is indeed an achievement to be cherished and to be proud of!

'Maybe you don't have to write about our school, but you must absolutely write about the gratitude we feel towards our dear family back in Fujian,' said Qi Juan, the young female director of Longde County's Primary School No. 2. Seeing that I was about to leave in a hurry to conduct another interview, she grabbed me by the hand to keep me there a little longer and to make sure that I would hear her story about her 'dear family back in Fujian'.

'Now it is like director Lin and me are real sisters,' Qi Juan said. 'Lin is from Minhou, in Fujian, and if a week goes by without us talking on the phone, we'll really worry about each other! The help she and her school gave me, in particular, and also to our school here is something like the sea. It could be described also as coming from heaven, because it was indeed a lot of help! Just this last winter, she and the teachers of her school organised a "keeping warm in winter action" especially for us, because she knew how cold winters can be here. With money and material donations they made sure that the children of our poor families here had warm quilts to sleep in and new warm clothes to wear. A few years ago, director Lin visited us with her team and saw that there were many children here whose parents had gone away to work in other regions, so that their children had no one to look after them in the afternoon after school. Because of that, they brought to us the experience they had in Fujian with community-organised "four-thirty classes", to address the worries parents had about their children, our students, being left on their own…'

Ha! Now I understand why, as I made my way through villages and community streets to conduct my interviews, I often came across community gathering sites with signs advertising '4:30 classes'. It turned out those were also a product of the Cooperation on Poverty Alleviation Between Fujian and Ningxia!

'Our dear family in Fujian is always very concerned about everything that matters to our children and to our school,' school director Qi Juan said. 'In order to give our children here from the mountains an opportunity to travel and see the world, every year director Lin arranges funds for us to organise a tour called "leaving the mountains to go see the ocean". The happiness of the children taking part in those tours is indescribable, because for each one of them it is the first time they take a plane, the first time they go out on a long trip of any sort, and the first time they set their eyes on the sea. And the children seem to go crazy the moment they see the ocean. They jump around and cry and laugh. That is an experience that becomes engraved in their young minds, to be forever remembered,' said director Qi Juan, her eyes brimming with tears as she spoke.

'After returning from a trip to see the ocean, one of the girls composed an essay and recited it during the flag-raising ceremony at the school,' Qi Juan went on. 'After that, all the children on our sports ground started shouting "We also want to go see the sea!" and "We also want to fly like the sea gulls!" Is it possible not to shed tears just by thinking of such a scene?! It was so moving! It really touches the heart! How would it be possible for me and for the children here not to be grateful to our dear family in Fujian?'

Indeed, there is in the world no greater love than the love forged between friends living far away from each other, but friends who nonetheless become, for life, like caring and sincere relatives, so that one can no longer do without the other. That is the most important legacy left by the Cooperation on Poverty Alleviation Between Fujian and Ningxia, a cooperation initially proposed and supported in the long term by General Secretary Xi Jinping. And a very special part of that legacy is the deep-rooted friendship created between the youth of the two provinces.

Love Between Mountain and Sea, the Yellow River Roils

As I write this book, happy stories made possible by the

Cooperation on Poverty Alleviation Between Fujian and Ningxia continue to take place, one after the other. But, of course, what made the people of all ethnicities in Ningxia the happiest was that, after four years, General Secretary Xi Jinping once again paid a visit to Ningxia to see for himself the progress made by the Cooperation on Poverty Alleviation, a programme that, from the very beginning, has been close to his heart.

On the 8th of June of 2020, which happened to be the day I also arrived in Ningxia, General Secretary Xi Jinping once again set foot in the land known as the 'Jiangnan north of the Great Wall', a place with which he has a deep emotional connection, and which always returns to his mind from time to time. In the three days following his arrival, the General Secretary hit the road to inspect the agricultural areas now irrigated with water from the Yellow River. He visited also the people in Hongsibao who had been lifted out of poverty and some poverty alleviation workshops. During those few days I followed the track of the General Secretary, visiting the places he had visited, seeing and hearing what he had seen and heard. Everywhere over the vast land of Ningxia one could feel a glow of happiness. A particular phrase was then being repeated often, and it came from the bottom of people's hearts: *We're very happy that the General Secretary has come to see us.*

Indeed, for the people of Ningxia who had been lifted out of poverty, and for those countless officials who had gone to great lengths and made great personal sacrifices to make that victory possible, there was no greater happiness than to achieve that comprehensive victory while having also by their side the General Secretary, who fully supported them!

The kind of affection the people of Ningxia feel for General Secretary Xi Jinping is not easy for people from other places to fully appreciate, because at the origin of that affection is Xi Jinping's own initiative, 24 years ago, to kickstart the Cooperation on Poverty Alleviation Between Fujian and Ningxia, and also to support that programme over all of those years. It was precisely because of that programme and of that sincere friendship between the two provinces over nearly a quarter of a century that today this 'love between mountains and sea' has emerged so spectacularly, and with such great fervour.

> *More than 2,000 kilometres apart,*
> *Ningxia and Fujian,*
> *We were once so far,*
> *and now are so close,*
> *Thanks to 24 years of care and help,*
> *over mountains and sea...*

Indeed, were it not for the opening up of this great era, were it not for the total commitment of the members of the Communist Party of China, and were it not for the uninterrupted dedication of General Secretary Xi Jinping over those 24 years, would there be today such a strong bond of love, such beautiful long-distance harmony between the 'mountain' and the 'sea'?

And indeed, were it not for the great generosity of that 'sea', would the 'mountain' be so green and luxuriant as it is today? Were it not for the great energy and the great waves of that 'sea', would the 'mountain' be opening up to the world today and looking up at the sky with new ideas and convictions? If the 'sea' had not persisted in sending its warm breeze, how could the 'mountain' stretch out its giant arms today to embrace the 'sea'?

The 'mountain' and the 'sea' were, from the very beginning, like siblings. When the 'mountain' and the 'sea' help each other, Heaven and Earth benefit together. And when the 'sea' surges and lifts the 'mountain', that glorifies the whole Universe. And the reason why the Cooperation on Poverty Alleviation Between Fujian and Ningxia can today be seen as a model of cooperation between regions is that neither of the 'two siblings' in that partnership were a 'heavyweight' but were in fact just two siblings among many other siblings, two inconspicuous partners joining hands. And yet, over those 24 years of real affection and mutual love between them, a true poetic saga of great significance for the history of human development was written.

But how could the 'mountain' and the 'sea' come to be related that way? Maybe that is a question sociologists will have to spend lots of time investigating and analysing. But a personal inkling I have is that this classic cooperation between the 'mountain' and the 'sea' was possible because, among other things, of something very high, namely, *feeling*. Or, to put it in other words, because of the feeling that exists between country and people, leaders and people, and among the people themselves.

Everyone needs to have feeling. Someone who has no feeling will leave nothing behind in this world, no matter how high that person's status, or how rich or physically attractive that person was. Even that person's 'symbol' in this world, that is, his or her name, will be quickly forgotten.

But people who have feeling are already counted among the most noble. Even if they are poor or illiterate, their spirit and their virtue will stand tall and be revered. People with feeling will bequeath to others, to the weak, to their country, to their family and friends, and also to future generations, things that are precious and admirable. Even if all that a person does is to fetch a stick of firewood for someone else, that stick will still burn and provide warmth with its flame. If that person is an intellectual or a scientist, then they will light up the torch of thought or the engine of human progress. If that person is an official or a politician, then they will usher in a bright era of light and happiness to a group or to an entire nation...

Human feelings are like poetry, they *are* poetry.

In this journey that is the fight against poverty, strategic decisions, policy measures and programmes, plans and action are all indispensable. However, from among all of that, the feeling of the decision-makers, of the leaders, of the administrators, and of all the people taking part in that battle, is the most important of all, the most fundamental, and the most valuable.

In China's struggle to defeat poverty and to build a moderately prosperous society 'no one can be excluded' and, of the country's 56 nationalities, 'not a single one can be left behind'. That is the feeling of General Secretary Xi Jinping, and the feeling also of the members of the Communist Party of China today.

The Cooperation on Poverty Alleviation Between Fujian and Ningxia, imbued with the faith and the determination never to give up, has 'accelerated as much as possible the lifting out of poverty of the impoverished regions of Ningxia and promoted the quick, sustained, and healthy economic and social development of both Fujian and Ningxia.' That is the feeling that exists between the 'mountain' and the 'sea', a feeling formed by the masses of officials and people of both Ningxia and Fujian working over more than 20 years under the guidance of General Secretary Xi Jinping. That feeling is like the waters of the Yellow River, coming from very far and flowing over long distances. It also stands tall and lofty like the Wuyi Mountains[1], placed as they are on their eternal seat in the east.

That feeling is the boundless feeling of poetry.

Fujian and Ningxia are separated by a great physical distance. But as the times brought together the historic mission of a political party and the feeling of General Secretary Xi Jinping, those two places, separated by such a great distance as they are, came together as the 'mountain' and the 'sea' to take part in a mighty saga that transcends time and space and ethnic boundaries. Today, over the vast territory of Ningxia, from north to south and from east to west, and from the Liupan to the Helan Mountains, we see the presence and the influence of the Min people, that is, of the people of Fujian. Some say that there are as many as 100,000 businesspeople from Fujian currently in Ningxia, and some say that there are also in Ningxia today more than 10,000 factories or other businesses bearing the character

---

1   A mountain range in Fujian

for 'Min' in their names, a character that, in an abbreviated fashion, represents the land and the people of Fujian. And there are also some people who say that, if asked who they would choose as another member of their own family beyond their own blood ties, nine out of ten people in Ningxia would answer: someone from Fujian. 'The people of Fujian are like family to us,' I often hear officials from Ningxia say. And I have also heard the common people from the poorest regions of Ningxia say this with even more feeling to it. Then, as expected, when asked about that 'other family of theirs', people from Ningxia who have worked in Fujian, or who still work there, will have countless extremely moving stories to tell.

As I see it, the only other kind of relationship that is comparable to that, in the sense that people regard as their own family those who are not necessarily related to them by blood, is the relationship between the masses and the People's Liberation Army. The Cooperation on Poverty Alleviation was indeed capable of forging such deep links of affection between people, and that is a very heart-warming and uniquely bright part of the history of poverty alleviation in China. Perhaps that is a development of even greater significance than common people leaving the mountains and escaping poverty by adding a few head of cattle and ten more *mu* of land to their homesteads.

Friendship is priceless, and from that all that is meaningful is derived.

While conducting my interviews in Fujian, I came across an official named Dong Chengbi, who though originally from Xiji, in Ningxia, was now stationed in Fujian. He told me that, back in the day, when he was working under the supervision of officials from Fujian temporarily assigned to Ningxia, he conducted a first group of 97 young women from Xiji to 'labour services station agents' in Fujian. Dong Chengbi's official position was one that he had effectively conferred upon himself.

'The girls of that first group leaving Xihaigu were, for the most part, 17 or 18 years old, with the oldest being no older than 25,' Dong Chengbi said. 'I was myself only 20 at the time and had just become employed by the county's newly established poverty alleviation bureau. I was chosen to lead the team at that time because I had just graduated from school, and because I could speak standard Mandarin. Now I've been in charge of the region for more than 20 years…'

There indeed is no one better equipped than Dong Chengbi to fully appreciate the profound practical meaning of that 'love between the mountain and the sea'. He told me that he had already taken between 60,000 and 70,000 people from his native region over to Fujian to work.

'I can also tell you the names of more than 170 of my "sons-in-law". About 200 girls ended up getting married in Putian… I remember their names, the names of their husbands too, and even of some of their children!' Dong Chengbi said, and that was perhaps what made him the proudest.

Standing by the sea in Putian, Dong Chengbi let out a very long sigh and said:

'Back in those days when I was bringing people over here to Fujian, we had to travel for seven days and seven nights, because there were still no motorways at the time... The girls who had just arrived worked during the day, and at night they would cry alone in their beds, firstly because they missed home, and secondly because they couldn't speak standard Mandarin. I was always on the move during that time, helping solve a problem here, another one there, so that in the first month alone I lost 12 *jin*[1]… Truth be told, I can't say I haven't thought of giving up. But after seeing our girls receive their first thousand-yuan salaries, I… I never again thought of turning back. I realised that that was what I wanted to do in this life, to make it possible for those kids from up there in those poor valleys to make always more and more money, to make it possible for them to see and swim in the ocean, to go and eat at McDonald's, or to eat some sea food, and

---

1   Six kilograms

have hot water to shower everyday...'

Dong Chengbi was already in tears as he reached this point in his account.

'Later I realised that I just had to stay here...' he said. 'Because it was not just the case that people from over there like myself could come here to earn a living, but also that, after we'd been here for a few months or a few years, the girls got more and more beautiful, and the boys more and more intelligent. That surprised me and made me very happy! It turned out that we, the people from the mountains of Ningxia, were not stupid at all! Just like the people of the coast, we could also live good lives and get very far in life!'

The more Dong Chengbi spoke, the more animated he got:

'You know? It's not only me who's in Fujian now,' he went on. 'My brothers have also all moved here. Like me, there are now several thousand people from Ningxia living here with their whole families...'

'Do you think it's possible that you'll return to Ningxia?' I asked Dong Chengbi.

'Me? I haven't thought about it...' he said, seemingly taken by surprise.

'Why?' I asked.

'I know that my homeland has improved a lot, but people

here still need me. Because of the Cooperation on Poverty Alleviation, many more people have now left Ningxia to come here to work. Right now in Putian alone there are thousands of them. I am in charge of the people who offer support to those workers, so everyone still needs me here,' Dong Chengbi added with a smile. 'But formally my affiliation is still in Xiji, and my salary still comes from there!'

In fact, there are many more than just a couple of individuals who, like Dong Chengbi, live 'between the mountain and the sea'. And the feeling for that special connection between mountain and sea is particularly strong in those people. Such a feeling can often coalesce into concrete action and greater ideals, and thus allow two regions separated by great distances to join hands and prosper together. And so, we once again feel that the 'love between the mountain and the sea', brought to life by the Cooperation on Poverty Alleviation, has in fact already condensed into a mighty feeling as strong and solid as the Great Wall.

Feelings can give people the power to transcend, to be forever remembered, and they can also provide the courage people need to march forward without hesitating and without stopping, to keep achieving greater and greater things...

Of all the people I know, Huang Tianjin, the current

president of the Ningxia-Fujian Chamber of Commerce and of a company called Ningxia Myfun Food Ltd., is perhaps one of the most typical and most representative examples of that 'mountain and sea' feeling that now exists between Fujian and Ningxia.

Born in the 1970s, Huang Tianjin is now about to turn 50 years old. But he was only 18 when, 32 years ago, he first arrived in Yinchuan with only 3,000 yuan in his pocket. At the time, he did not understand poetry, he did not even know what kind of thing poetry is. He had then only one thing in his mind, and that was the dream to leave his poor mountain district, go somewhere far where he could forget all about his own origins, and find some kind of work through which he could make a name for himself!

That was in fact the 'poetry' of Huang Tianjin, a young man from Fujian with little education. At that time his 'poetry' was sad and anguished, without even the slightest hint of romance. It consisted only of the bitter tears he was forced to swallow.

'At the time the mountain areas of Fujian were not very developed either, but we had skills, we knew how to make pastries,' Huang Tianjin said. 'So I thought, we certainly can't surpass the people in places where the market is already developed, so we'll just go to a place where that market is less developed than our own, and that place was Ningxia... When

I first arrived here, I didn't think I'd be here for 32 years, that I, a "sea" person from over there, would become a "mountain" person here.' Huang Tianjin's emotional reminiscences today are, in a very real sense, a manifestation of the poetic nature of the connection between the 'sea' and the 'mountain'.

When he first came to Yinchuan, aged 18 and having no one he could rely on, Huang Tianjin noticed that the common people of the place very rarely ate rice pastries, and also that mung-bean pastry and the *lügadun* 'donkey rolls' people from the inland regions liked to eat were simply not available in the state-owned food stores. So Huang Tianjin rented a small building next to Yinchuan's train station, a space that combined a production floor area and a dormitory, and there he began to put into practice the pastry-making techniques he had learnt while in Hunan. That made him the first pastry-making entrepreneur in Yinchuan during that period, and, of course, also the first small business owner from Fujian active in the food industry there. But despite that, the early days of doing business there were by no means easy. He would be making about a hundred yuan or so a day pushing his cart through the train station while hawking his pastries. After rent and other production costs were deducted, there was not much left for him. The deepest impression left in Huang Tianjin's memory from that time, however, was rather how difficult it was for a southerner like him to adapt to the extreme dryness of the climate of the regions beyond the Great Wall. Nosebleeds and constipations were the most unpleasant effects of that dryness Huang Tianjin suffered from almost every day. 'Eventually a very kind local gentleman helped me get rid of the nosebleeds and the digestive problems with some of his own remedy recipes,' Huang Tianjin said. 'That's how I managed to remain in Yinchuan.'

Huang Tianjin told me also that, over the 32 years he had already spent in Ningxia, many were the occasions when some kind local helped him. There was even one occasion when he fell suddenly ill and was rushed to a hospital. After taking him to the hospital, the stranger who had helped him even returned to bring him some fruit and milk tea.

'If Ningxia is dear to me, that's because, first and foremost, the people of Ningxia are dear to me,' he said. Despite not having much formal education, pastry-maker Huang Tianjin is capable of speaking with great eloquence about Ningxia and its people. 'Those people are the real thing. They treat you like a member of their own family, and so you have to treat them as family as well,' he went on. 'After some time, you just feel like you belong to this land. And although you're here doing business, you have to always be honest and to always think about how to best serve the people, to make sweeter the life of every customer of yours, who's in fact also like family to you.

'Myfun' is the brand name under which Huang Tianjin does business. It is now a very well-known brand in Ningxia. 'To sell with cheerfulness, with joy, that's the meaning of the brand name I chose for my food products,' he explained. 'And it really reflects how I feel about being in the food business in Ningxia…'

Because of the people of Ningxia, Huang Tianjin 'sells his products with joy', and so his business keeps doing better and getting bigger. In 2006 Huang Tianjin's Myfun company opened in Yinchuan its first store selling western-style pastries and cakes. In the years that followed what was initially a single store became a chain with more than 40 locations, and implementing a model that combines centralised production and distribution with the local baking of the pastry and cake products. In 2013, Huang Tianjin saw a business opportunity and invested 130 million yuan in the construction of a modern food processing plant at the Desheng Industrial Park in Yinchuan. It is now formally a first-class production facility at a national level, making moon cakes, *zongzi* dumplings, *tangyuan* dumplings, bread, and other such food products, to a total of nearly 200 different products that combined generate more than 100 million yuan a year in revenue. This means that that poor guy who once arrived in

Ningxia coming from a poor mountain area in Fujian and with only 3,000 yuan in his pocket is now a multimillionaire. Then, in 2015, Huang Tianjin became the president of the Ningxia-Fujian Chamber of Commerce and started to offer guidance to businesspeople from Fujian coming to invest in Ningxia through the Cooperation on Poverty Alleviation Between Fujian and Ningxia.

'The Ningxia-Fujian Chamber of Commerce has grown from the 50 members it had at the beginning to more than 1,800 today, representing more than 5,000 businesses and 80,000 individual businesspeople,' he said. 'In only five years it has managed to channel more than 2 billion yuan in investments to Ningxia. For all of us doing business here, Ningxia is now our home, so that we work for our local people. Because of that our enthusiasm only grows, and the friendship between us only gets stronger.'

I know that, thirty years ago, in 1990, Huang Tianjin moved his family to Yinchuan. At the time people from his hometown in Fujian asked him why he was doing such a thing. Huang Tianjin's reply was that people in Ningxia had treated him as family, and since that was the case, he just had to move there permanently. All three of his children were later to be born in Yinchuan, and so Huang Tianjin then simply changed his own and his children's *hukou* household registration to Yinchuan. Much later, once his three children had already graduated from university, they all had the option of going to work in Fujian or in other places near the coast. But Huang Tianjin urged them to return to Ningxia:

'Ningxia is your home,' he told them. 'Now that you have completed your studies, you have to make your contribution to the place that is your home, a place that is now striving to become moderately prosperous.' Huang Tianjin's two daughters are now both married, and their husbands are both Ningxia locals.

Thirty-two years ago, a poor boy from Fujian came to Ningxia on his own. Now four generations of his family, about a dozen people, live with him here, having become true Ningxia natives. Huang Tianjin's life epitomises in countless different ways that 'love between the mountain and the sea'. The feeling he has for Ningxia already runs in his veins and through his family, and nothing can change it now. This is what we call *poetry*, written with feeling:

> *The clouds up on the mountain are the waves in the sea.*
> *And the billowing of the sea is the wind on the mountain.*
> *The mountain restrains the sea, and so the sea is*

boundless.

The sea surrounds the mountain, to glorify the mountain.

I travel over mountain and sea,

as if rolling over ripples of happiness.

I first heard about Lin Xiaohui when I was at Lin Yuechan's home interviewing her. Lin Yuechan had answered a call on her mobile phone, and I saw that she brightened up all of a sudden, talking very animatedly with the person on the other end of the line. That naturally made me very curious.

'Lin Xiaohui is a good entrepreneur,' Lin Yuechan said. 'He has invested all of his and his family's wealth in Ningxia. You should also interview him… I'll ask him to come over!'

When Lin Yuechan talked about Lin Xiaohui, it was clear by her manner of speaking that this person wasn't just anybody. It wasn't like she spoke haltingly out of nervousness or such like, but, clearly, he was someone she thought about with some gravity. And then, not much later, Lin Xiaohui was sitting right in front of me. As luck would have it, he had just returned from Ningxia to take care of business in Fujian while I also happened to be in Fujian, creating the opportunity for me to interview him.

'You should come to see me at the Minning Industrial Park

in Longde to have a look around,' Lin Xiaohui told me. He was a businessman, but not the stereotypical one. He wasn't given to much talk and had a very simple and good-natured disposition.

I accepted his kind invitation, and so, one year later, during my trip through Ningxia in early June of 2020, I met him at the Minning Industrial Park, in Longde. What I saw there was a scene more lively and deeper in meaning than I had anticipated from my conversation with him back at Lin Yuechan's home in Fuzhou. It struck one as something almost unreal, because, on that piece of flat ground in a very remote valley among tall mountains, stood a brand new and very tidy factory building and also some adjacent housing blocks. There were also broad roads with plenty of motor vehicle traffic. It was, overall, a very busy scene.

'This is our office building,' Lin Xiaohui said as he led me into a four-storeyed building. From an exhibition area on the first floor all the way up to the main office area on the fourth floor, the power and might of Lin Xiaohui's 'Loess Kingdom' was in full display for everyone to see. 'I've invested and built here, in the Minning Industrial Park, with the support of the county of Longde,' he said. 'The foundation-laying ceremony was on the 21st of August of 2012. Right now we have just completed the fourth stage of construction, so that our facilities now cover an area of 3,000 *mu* of land, including more than 200,000 square metres of factory floor. More than 600 million yuan were invested in the site so far, from a total of 51 companies that have taken up a location here. About a third of those companies are registered in Fujian, six of which are very large businesses. In total, the park produces an industrial output worth 500 million yuan a year. And we estimate that in the next two or three years the park's total output will reach between three and five billion yuan a year, not least because we've already managed to get China's pharma giant Shanghai Pharmaceuticals to set up shop in the park, and they alone are expected to produce an output worth as much as 2 billion yuan next year,' Lin Xiaohui said with much animation, while also pointing through his office's window at a new factory building not very far off.

'At first, when the officials from Fujian temporarily assigned here to Ningxia first contacted me to urge me to invest in Ningxia, I wasn't so sure about the idea,' Lin Xiaohui had told me during my first interview with him back in Fuzhou. 'But after visiting a couple of times and seeing for myself how things stood on the ground, I changed my mind. I was convinced of both heart and soul.' He also told me that he had spent 2 million yuan beforehand to get some expert opinions on the proposal, to determine whether an industrial park in Longde would be indeed viable. The conclusion he took from the appraisals he got was that a small investment could pay off, but not a large one. However, Lin Xiaohui then told me:

'Once I had started investing, I simply could not turn back...'

'Why not?' I asked him with a smile.

'Because I grew fond of the place,' he said. 'In these past few years, I have invested between 500 and 600 million yuan here in this land.'

'Do you regret it?' I asked him.

'Not at all!' Liu Xiaohui exclaimed without hesitation. 'I have invested basically all I have here... And you must certainly ask why I did it. Well, it's very simple. I fell in love with this place! My home and my work, now they're both here!'

'You see, when I first arrived here in 2012, this place was a wasteland, you couldn't spot a single house,' he went on. 'Now we can produce an output worth hundreds of millions, even billions of yuan, here. More than 2,000 locals now work here, and I'm sure that, in a not very distant future, output from this industrial park will be measured in the tens of billions, and we'll have as many as 50,000 workers here. That's about as many as half the current population of Longde's county seat!' Lin Xiaohui raised his voice with pride.

'Is this your *Huangtudi*, your "Loess Land" dream?' I asked, remembering the name of his company.

'Yes. I named my company "Huangtudi" back then precisely because I took a liking to this piece of land, and also because I wanted to transform it into a rich land that could generate great wealth,' he explained. 'That is my dream. It's quite poetic, isn't it?' His words gave me the impression that he was indeed a romantic at heart.

But I know also that that romanticism of his came about through much hard work and sweat.

'I was a little over thirty years old when I first arrived here, and had already a fortune of hundreds of millions,' he went on. 'But when I looked at the people around my age here, I realised that they couldn't even find partners for themselves and get married because they were too poor! So I decided that I had to do something to help them, something that'd allow them to find a partner, start a family, have a career... Then I remembered that, within the Cooperation on Poverty Alleviation Between Fujian and Ningxia, there were already some concrete initiatives bringing prosperity to the people of this land. My idea was building an industrial park, and with that idea in mind I brought over my own money plus 70 or 80 people from Fujian, taking them up to the valleys. And here we are today...'

So once this entrepreneur from Putian, in Fujian, had set

his feet firmly on the soil of Ningxia, he brought into play that knack people from Fujian have for taking care of practical affairs with the utmost attention to detail, and also their vast wisdom for business. He then threw himself wholeheartedly into the construction of his industrial park.

'We are a poor mountain region, so any help you can give us is welcome' and 'Huangtudi has not picked up steam yet, that's for sure, but it exists and it's solid, so come and we'll give you a quotation…' Lin Xiaohui said that those were the two sentences he spoke the most during those early few years when he was either attempting to attract investment to the industrial park, or else attempting to sell the goods his own company made. They may sound a little pathetic now, but the determination in his heart was firm. 'Even if, through all my efforts, I had managed to help only one family of the mountains escape poverty, I would nonetheless still be grateful to all of those who came to invest in the industrial park, and to all of those who ever bought the products made here.'

That was the Lin Xiaohui I got to know, and the 'road of prosperity creation' between Fujian and Ningxia he decided to follow is in fact a poem. His industrial park is actually a piece of poetry 'published' on the land itself. That piece of poetry is already extremely beautiful today and will be even more beautiful in the future.

As I travelled through Ningxia to conduct my interviews, I visited a large number of schools and poverty alleviation workshops, and also some support centres focusing on helping the disabled start and run their own businesses. In the course of those visits I have often heard that Lin Xiaohui was either subsidising or else had donated money to many of those institutions. That made me respect even more his deep affection for Ningxia. When I asked him to tell me about some of the 'good deeds' he had done for Ningxia during those years, he just narrated to me the following in his simple and straightforward manner:

'There's nothing I've done that needs any praising. It is the work of those officials who were temporarily assigned to Ningxia that deserves to get publicity. Were it not for their hard work, we would never have had the chance to come to this land, or to bring our businesses here and move here with our entire families! To speak plainly, I was just a businessman before, and so there were many things I didn't understand. But, over the years I spent running the industrial park and being engaged in poverty alleviation work, I came to understand my own value as a person and saw that it was in fact something higher and more precious than merely earning money. That is why I ended up being willing to invest all I have here...'

I spent a long time reflecting on Lin Xiaohui's words. He was a very rich man, who nonetheless did not mind moving to some remote mountain region very far away so as to be able to give poor people the chance of a better life. For the sake of those people, he was happy to 'lose' a few hundred million, or even a few billion. Could that not be due to some unique feeling within him that surpassed a mere business perspective of things? And I know that there are already in Ningxia nearly 100,000 entrepreneurs from Fujian like Lin Xiaohui. And that a considerable number of those have already started to see themselves as 'entrepreneurs from Ningxia' rather than 'from Fujian'. We see now among the children born to those entrepreneurs many who were given the name 'Minning', a combination of the Chinese characters for 'Fujian' (Min) and 'Ningxia' (Ning). How could that not be poetry? Isn't this poetry about the love between the mountain and the sea?

Indeed it is poetry, the most beautiful poetry of our time.

And if the 'love between the mountain and the sea' could create this kind of poetry, we cannot but pay our respects, in particular, to the officials temporarily assigned to Ningxia, who 'put ink on paper' and wrote that poetry. It is precisely because of those 'Role Models of the Times', travelling constantly 'between the mountain and the sea' to support the work of the Cooperation on Poverty Alleviation Between Fujian and Ningxia over those 24 years that we can see today great changes taking place in Ningxia, earth-shaking and beautiful like art. And it is also thanks to them that the people of Ningxia can enjoy much better lives today.

On the 3rd of July of 2020, the Publicity Department of the Central Committee made the following announcement to the whole country: Those who helped Ningxia by taking part in the Cooperation on Poverty Alleviation Between Fujian and Ningxia would be collectively conferred the title of 'Role Models of the Times'. The conferring of that honour on them formally took place during the celebrations of the 99th anniversary of the foundation of the Communist Party of China, with the country being already at the last stage of construction of a moderately prosperous society in all respects and fighting the last decisive battles in the war against poverty. The conferring of that title was very meaningful in a few different ways, including in terms of its timing and in terms of the number of people honoured. It was also meaningful in terms of its ordinal numbering. To wit, prior to this occasion, the Publicity Department had conferred the title of 'Role Model of the Times' to exactly 100 individuals or groups. The 101st would be, collectively, the people who aided Ningxia through the Cooperation on Poverty Alleviation. That meant that this programme, a programme looked after and personally supported by General Secretary Xi Jinping over 24 years, would now receive a place of honour in the history of China's fight against poverty. A news outlet, announcing the conferring of the title, thus wrote:

'Since 1996, the people helping Ningxia through the Cooperation on Poverty Alleviation have abided by the principles of "seeking complementarity in personal strengths, maintaining reciprocity, cooperating for the long-term, and promoting common development", and they have, of their own volition, carried on their shoulders the historic mission of defeating poverty in Ningxia through assistance partnerships. More than 180 officials from Fujian were temporarily assigned to Ningxia as members of 11 successive groups. More than 2000 doctors, teachers, industrial and agricultural support specialists, academic experts, and other such volunteers made what was at first a one-way assistance programme expand into a deep cooperation between the two provinces addressing both economic and social construction at all levels, and on a broad spectrum of domains. They worked together with

the people of Ningxia to create, through great intelligence and much sweat, the "Fujian-Ningxia Model" of mutual cooperation between eastern and western regions for the assistance of the poor, tying up for good the daemon of poverty.'

And so, in terms of both the total number of individual 'role models' honoured and of the scope and reach of the contributions they made, what the 'Fujian-Ningxia experience' brought about was something unlike anything else seen in any of the previous 100 occasions when the title of 'Role Model of the Times' was conferred. In fact, those honoured by the Central Committee with that title on that 101st occasion were not limited to the 180 plus officials from Fujian temporarily assigned to Ningxia and the over 2,000 volunteer doctors, teachers and support workers, but included also thousands of entrepreneurs like Lin Xiaohui, Yan Guosheng, Lin Shuiying, Chen Deqi, and Huang Tianjin. It was thanks to their unrelenting efforts and selfless sacrifices over 24 years that the historic changes seen in Ningxia were possible. Since the 18th National Congress of the Communist Party of China, the total number of people in poverty in Ningxia has been reduced by 937,000, and the overall poverty rate has fallen from 22.9% in 2012 to 0.47% in 2019. The average disposable income per capita in the poorer rural areas also grew from 4,856 yuan in 2012 to 10,415 yuan in 2019, and the perception of personal achievement and personal satisfaction kept getting stronger and stronger among people of all ethnic groups in Ningxia.

Perhaps there is nothing in itself special about the number 101. But, for the people of Ningxia, it came to represent the men and women from Fujian who composed that epic poem that is the 'Fujian-Ningxia experience'. They call that way those who carried out that special mission, and who 'made sincere contributions over long periods of meritorious service'. And those men and women are so remembered also because they were 'the staunch supporters who implemented on the ground the Cooperation on Poverty Alleviation that General Secretary Xi Jinping has personally set in motion', and because they were also 'the fighters who continued the cooperation on poverty alleviation between eastern and western regions, the forerunners and pioneers of the development of socialist poverty alleviation, and active explorers of the wisdom in China's governance for the reduction of poverty worldwide.'

'Staunch supporters', 'fighters', 'pioneers' and 'explorers'. Ah, the '101' Role Models of the Times, you do live up to that title of honour! It was you who, with a lofty and firm sense of mission, have persisted over 24 years with that great undertaking initiated by General Secretary Xi Jinping himself, never deviating from the set path till the mission had reached its perfect conclusion. With a selfless spirit of sacrifice and dedication to others, you kept passing on the baton until that final and decisive dash. You have overcome obstacles as they arose, building bridges that were made of willpower and wisdom, and you have been worthy warriors in the great struggle against poverty, producing countless wonders. You are practitioners of China's wisdom, explorers and champions. The mountains already have your names engraved on their peaks, and the ocean has already surrounded the monuments to you with the crests of every surging wave...

But, in any case, I still take the time to write down in this book the deeds of some of those among them. Even though the ones I mentioned here are only but a few among countless others, they are, I believe, the 'scattered musical notes' that I managed to pick up along the way. Those 'scattered notes', I believe, are sufficient to make that epochal concerto emerge with all its majestic momentum.

Lin Yuechan's name already shines like gold upon the land of Ningxia. And now I have to talk about another 'Old Ma', that is, Ma Guolin, Lin Yuechan's successor as the chief of Fujian's

Poverty Alleviation Bureau. When I interviewed Ma Guolin he had already been retired for over three years. He told me, however, that he was still busy with 'certain issues' concerning the Cooperation on Poverty Alleviation. 'As a matter of fact, none of them can be said to be a major contribution,' he said. 'They're all small matters, things we've been working on for a long time. Because focusing on small matters over time is the way to achieve great things.'

In 1999, after the first group of temporarily assigned officials concluded the period of their assignment to Ningxia, Ma Guolin, then acting as representative of Fujian's Poverty Alleviation Bureau chief Lin Yuechan, was given the task of picking up a group of eight officials on their way back to Fujian. 'At the time the group we had dispatched to Ningxia lacked a group leader, so the Organisation Department of the Fujian Party committee, together with their counterparts in Ningxia, expressed their wish that the second group of officials to be dispatched had a leader, in order to better coordinate and nurture the officials' enthusiasm,' Ma Guolin said. 'It turned out that, when the time came for a group leader to be selected, I ended up being chosen. That established my connection with Ningxia, and so in the next twenty years or so I travelled from Fujian to Ningxia and back more than a hundred times. Lin Yuechan said once that she was like a bird flying between the mountain and the sea. And I can add to what she said that I later became another such bird, building upon her work…'

Later Ma Guolin would serve as deputy agriculture and poverty alleviation commissioner of Guyuan. He told me his impressions of his first trip to the countryside there:

'That day myself and a few other officials walked for a very long time along a mountain road, and we all grew extremely thirsty. As we reached a village, we saw that halfway up a hill there was a house. We walked in and asked the family living there for a bowl of water. I was brought a bowl of water, but when I looked into it, I was stunned. The water was muddy, and it had a foul smell… If we were in Fujian, we'd say that they were trying to do us harm. But in the mountain areas of Ningxia, giving you a bowl of water like that was the greatest courtesy they could treat you with!' Ma Guolin would drink that water, and as he did so his eyes filled with tears. 'One thing was that the water itself really tasted awful, and the other was that you felt really disgusted by it in your mind,' he went on. 'At the time in Fujian even peasants were already drinking mineral water, but back in the mountain regions of Ningxia people still drank that filthy and foul-smelling water. And not only were they drinking it, but it was to them something like a treasure, something they couldn't afford to waste. Wouldn't you feel terribly sorry for them?' Ma Guolin asked me.

That distressing experience led Ma Guolin to try to think of solutions for the problem of lack of drinking water the common people of the mountain regions of Ningxia and of the Gobi Desert faced. 'From that moment on I found myself rushing back and forth between the mountain and the sea,' he said. 'And every time I was back in Fujian, I would entreat people by saying "please, please help me get some clean water for my relatives!" I spoke like that and explained it, and everyone understood that I was raising money to drill wells for the common people of the mountain regions of Ningxia who had no access to clean drinking water. So almost everyone I spoke to would contribute,' he said with pride.

The decision to drill wells was made at a joint meeting of the Cooperation on Poverty Alleviation. 'I remember very clearly that in that meeting secretary Xi Jinping emphasised to us that things like drilling wells for the people were to take priority. Such things were to be done quickly and thoroughly,' Ma Guolin said. And he was then put in charge of carrying out those instructions.

After Chinese New Year in the year 2000, while there was still snow atop the Liupan Mountains, the battle to dig a deep well in the township of Gancheng was now underway, and the loud roaring of the well drill was shaking people across the entire valley. People surrounded Ma Guolin and the drilling station that had been set up, staring blankly at the ground as they waited for sweet water to come out. Despite its name (*gan* meaning 'sweet' in Chinese), the township of Gansheng and the people living there had never in their lives seen any such a thing as 'sweet water'.

More than 80 days later, on the 26th of June, limpid sweet water spurted out of the well and rose several metres up in the air.

'Sweet water!' someone exclaimed.

'Gancheng now has sweet water!' exclaimed another.

Ma Guolin told me that, the moment the water emerged from the well, it was a scene like he had never seen before.

'It caused great commotion throughout the entire township, and even from the county seat people came over to see the water,' he said. 'There was an old gentleman, of the Hui ethnicity, who drank some of the water and immediately started to shed tears. Still crying, he clasped my hand with both of his own trembling hands and said with vehemence: "Thank you, Communist Party! Thank you, good officials!" I had no words to say in reply at that moment. I just grabbed the old man's hands and cried alongside him for a very long time.'

After that the number of tasks Ma Guolin had to take care of kept increasing. That group of officials temporarily assigned to Ningxia and the two other groups that followed helped with the digging of 15,000 wells or water collection pits, and also with the implementation of more than 100,000 *mu* of area of 'contour farming', which was meant to help preserve water, soil, and the fertility of the land, while also improving environmental conditions, thus ensuring the peasants' incomes.

'But thinking back now, what gives me the most joy about it all is the fact that, through my work, more than 30,000 contract workers from Xihaigu were sent to Fujian to work in industry and learn new skills,' Ma Guolin said. 'Some of them then remained in Fujian, while others returned to Xihaigu to start businesses, becoming pioneers in the struggle against poverty and in the building of prosperity… You see, I have my mobile phone full of the contact details of those people, hundreds of them. And even now people still get in touch with me every day. In the past, when people got in touch with me, they, for the most part, wanted me to help them solve some problem they had run into. But now they call me to tell me about the good things happening in their lives. That makes me, as an old-timer of the "love between the mountain and the sea", very very happy!' Sixty-years-old Ma Guolin then fetched a large pile of letters and newspaper clippings from his 'poverty alleviation volunteering home office' and began to read to me all about those unforgettable old 'Fujian-Ningxia exploits' he and other officials on temporary assignments in Ningxia got into. 'We kept passing on the baton of our work without a break for all those 24 years. Some of us didn't even make it back...' he choked with emotion.

'So many of them were like Lei Feng and Jiao Yulu, wholly devoted to the people and to the fight against poverty, that, in the eyes of the people, they became like dear family members and examples of Communist Party members,' Ma Guolin said. 'The governments of many counties and prefectures in Ningxia got together to compile a work titled *Records of the Cooperation Between Fujian and Ningxia on Poverty Alleviation*[1], to serve as a historical record of the partnership on poverty alleviation between Fujian and Ningxia over those 24 years. It includes detailed accounts of every topic within the Cooperation, and the most touching detail of all in that work is that the names of every Fujian official who was temporarily assigned to Ningxia, as well as of those supporting teachers and doctors and agricultural experts and volunteers, are all registered under the heading "List of Heroes". That makes all of us who worked in that 'Fujian-

---

1   *Min-Ning Fu Pin Xiezuo Jishi*

Ningxia experience' feel very highly honoured.'

But I know for a fact that there are today even more names engraved on the vast land of Ningxia. One needs only travel around Ningxia a little to find out that there are there many places named after other places in Fujian. Those include villages, market towns, schools and hospitals throughout Ningxia. From the county of Tongxin alone I can list a few from memory, such as the town of Shishi, the Shishi Vocational Secondary School, the 'new village' of Hui'an, the Hui'an Hospital Building, the Nan'an Experimental Primary School, the village of Nan'an, the neighbourhood of Nan'an, the Anxi Middle School, and the Anxi Nursing Home, all named after places under the jurisdiction of the prefecture of Quanzhou, in Fujian. After doing some inquiries, I discovered that those places and institutions had all been built with funds provided by the prefecture of Quanzhou in the context of their partnership with the county of Tongxin. Many counties and districts in Yinchuan, Guyuan, Wuzhong, and Zhongwei now all have new towns and villages, new schools and hospitals, and new neighbourhoods, all named after places in Fujian. Those names are all a result of the Cooperation on Poverty Alleviation Between Fujian and Ningxia. More than that, they are a manifestation of that 'love between the mountain and the sea', because behind each one of them there is also a very touching story. For instance, during the construction of the town of Shishi, in the county of Tongxin, there were, besides the many mutual consultations between the leaders of Ningxia and Fujian, also countless assistance exchanges and round trips between the prefecture of Shishi, in Fujian, and the county of Tongxin to handle concrete matters. I heard also that there were 'some contacts' and 'handshakes' between, on the Shishi side, Huang Yuanshui, then deputy secretary of the local Party committee, and Huang Shuiyuan, a local Party committee member temporarily assigned to Tongxin, and, on the Tongxin side, Wang Youcai the county Party secretary.

Later, the Shishi side dispatched, one after the other, He Jingxi and Lin Tianhu as temporary assignments to Tongxin. Those two officials, while taking full advantage of the strengths of their hometown of Shishi, worked hard for the sake of improving Tongxin, assisting in the construction of several public buildings, including a Hope primary school, a hospital, administrative buildings, a peasants' support centre, and a workers' training centre. The people of Tongxin were extremely touched by their efforts and, unable to fully express their gratitude in words, they decided to name place after place in Tongxin as 'Shishi', so that the name can now be found everywhere in the county. That is the best side note one can take from that story of 'love between the mountain and the sea' that is the Cooperation on Poverty Alleviation Between Fujian and Ningxia. Despite the relevant departments having later ceased to encourage the practice, the large number of such 'Fujian names' now present in Ningxia are enough to keep strong the ties of affection and blood between the peoples of Ningxia and Fujian for generations to come.

And indeed, once the feelings of affection and friendship have evolved into blood relations, they become that much more intense, and thus unbreakable. What are knit together in those feelings are precisely the emotions and actions of very real people, and what drives those emotions and actions are that kind of energy coming out of people's hearts after concrete experiences.

Among the groups honoured by the Publicity Department for their role in assisting Ningxia through the Cooperation on Poverty Alleviation were the volunteers who went to Ningxia to support the efforts there on education, health care, and agriculture. Their lofty spirits have a much stronger and enduring presence in the hearts of the people of Ningxia than any tall monument.

Below is a passage written by a teacher called Fu Wenchao:

The time I spent as a volunteer teacher went by very fast, and on the day of my return to Fujian the tears on the faces of my students, who had spontaneously gone to the train station to see me off, flooded my own heart. Their sobbing and shouting have remained engraved in my mind over all those years, very deeply and clear, and impossible to erase. The way I see it, there is nothing in this world that can be compared to those students' sincere feelings. Those feelings are for me a great treasure I could not exhaust in a lifetime, and something that no other honour can match. The way they honoured me is for me a confirmation that what pulled me twice to set foot in Ningxia and to come to Tongxin to work as a supporting teacher were those brilliant pairs of eyes, full of thirst for knowledge, and full of that joy that comes from receiving an education while also being able to watch the sun rising in the mornings and hear the cicadas singing in the evenings, holding fast to that same dream of education, that forever immutable infatuation with the cause of education...

Volunteers like Fu Wenchao, who left Fujian to go to Ningxia for a second time, were certainly much more than a handful.

Some of them even went for a third or fourth stay in Ningxia. There were in fact hundreds, if not thousands, of them, some going and staying for a full year, or two years, and some even wishing they could stay in Ningxia forever… And why was that? When I asked some of them this question, they told me very plainly and with deep emotion that it was because they had fallen in love with Ningxia, because Ningxia had become a new home for them.

After receiving an answer like that you feel even embarrassed to ask any further questions. All you can do is to praise them and offer them your respect.

Shepherd at a sheep farm driving *Tan* sheep to exercise around a purpose-built track

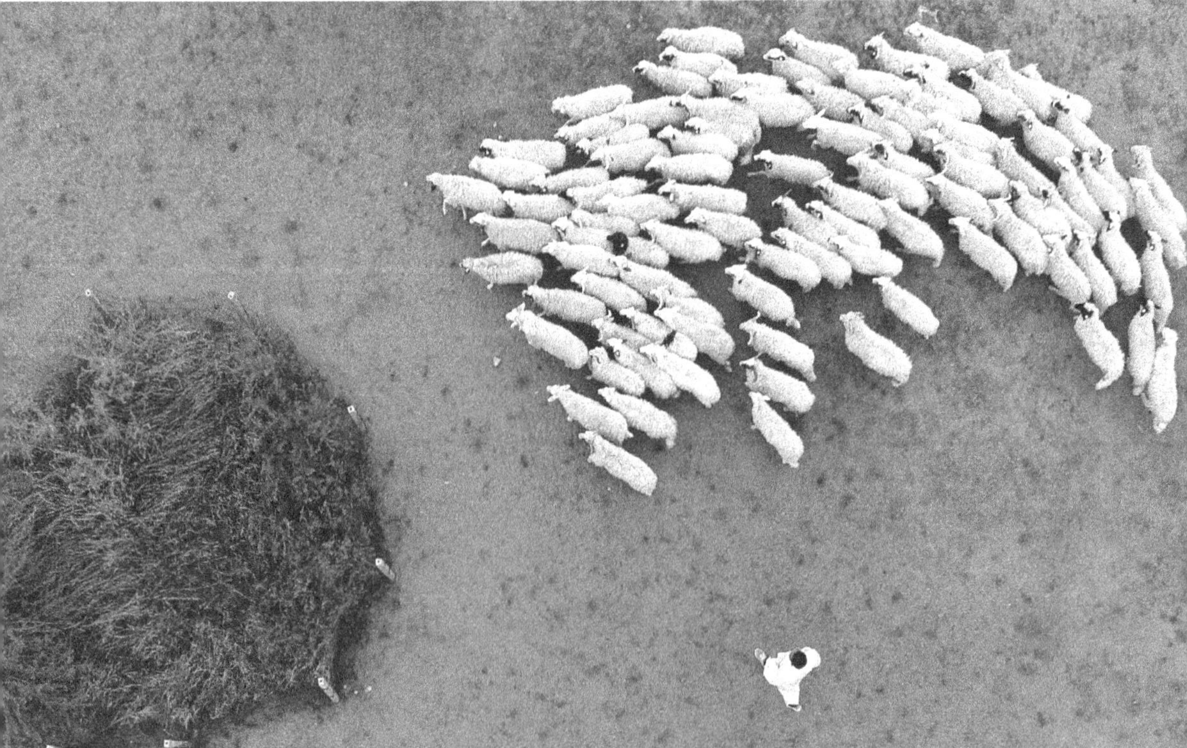

Ma Guolin also told me that, among all the local products of Ningxia, three are especially valued: potatoes, wolfberries, and *Tan* mutton. Those 'three treasures' were widely known in the past but are not so well-known now in China's domestic market, and there are even some people in the country who think that those are products from Gansu or from Shaanxi! 'But ever since our temporarily assigned officials started working on it, in the past few years the fame of those "three treasures of Ningxia" began to spread far and wide across the country. Didn't you notice it?' Ma Guolin asked me.

And it was true. His words did remind me that speciality products from Ningxia had indeed become very popular in the markets of Beijing in the past few years.

'*Tan* mutton from Yanchi is simply the finest!' I was told when I went to Yanchi to conduct my interviews, being offered a meal with real *Tan* mutton. And when I tried it, I was sold. I had never been a great fan of mutton, but that meal did change my point of view. Then, at the home of a common Tongxin resident, I was served a cup of wolfberry tea that bewitched me. 'That's tea worth of the gods!' I said.

I learnt that the price of *Tan* sheep from Yanchi had soared from two or three hundred yuan per head in the past to three or four thousand. That is a sky-rocketing increase in price that went hand-in-hand with the increase in popularity of *Tan* mutton. And that increase in popularity could not but be related to the relentless 'loud advertising' done by the temporarily assigned officials from Fujian. The people of Yanchi still remember very clearly today the names of several 'county chiefs from Fujian', such as Gao Guofu and Zhang Xueyong, and they remember how those 'county chiefs' took them to places like Beijing, Shanghai and Shenzhen to promote their *Tan* mutton. It was seen once on a street corner of Xiamen a restaurant selling *Tan* mutton in front of which customers had to queue up for as long as three hours to be served. 'People do not resent having to wait for good food, because you'll be thankful to the gods after you eat it,' Ma Guolin said. The fact that *Tan* mutton is now so highly regarded by the people of Xiamen is, to a great extent, due to the efforts of those officials I have mentioned.

As a matter of fact, in Ningxia *Tan* mutton is not produced only in Yanchi. *Tan* mutton from Tongxin, for instance, is in no way inferior to that of Yanchi. Having heard the *Tan* mutton of Yanchi being so often praised, county chief Ding from Tongxin was eager to have me try some of the *Tan* mutton produced in his own county. For that purpose, he took me to a few family-owned sheep farms in the county. 'Take a look at the grass on that pasture and at the water the sheep drink. Those are lambs that grow eating the best herbs and drinking the cleanest spring water in a pure and natural environment, free from pollution,' he said. 'And the land here is Gobi Desert land at an altitude of about 1,500 metres. That's what makes "*Tan* mutton from Tongxin, the finest in the world!"' County chief Ding happily explained to me that he was not the one who had come up with that marketing phrase, but rather a comrade from Fujian.

Among the officials from Fujian temporarily assigned to Tongxin was He Jingxi, who went to Ningxia together with Ma Guolin. Then later came Lin Tianhu, Yang Shuqing, Cai Rongqing, Fu Ziping, Xue Jianmin, Chen Jianbin, Lin Yuwei, and others… Although they all occupied different posts back in their hometowns, once in Tongxin for their temporary assignments those officials all took upon themselves the responsibility of promoting both the *Tan* mutton of Tongxin and the wolfberries of Tongxin. They spared no efforts in carrying out that responsibility, travelling back and forth 'between the mountain and the sea', and travelling also to several other places across the whole country.

'To speak the truth, our own local officials used to be a little like oxen ploughing the fields, that is to say, rather slow-tempered,' chief Ding said. 'But with the arrival of the officials from Fujian and with us working with them as a single team, those officials' style of doing things fast and decisively had an effect on us and pushed us forward, changing the way of doing things for our own officials here.'

When county chief Ding invited me to go to the countryside with him to have a meal, a few other village and township officials of the county of Tongxin also came along, and when the topic of working styles was mentioned, those officials turned out to have quite an array of different feelings about it. 'Before, when we heard that development in the coastal regions was fast, we thought that it was because they had access to good transportation infrastructure and good access to information, and that we were lagging behind because here it was the opposite. But after working with the officials from Fujian, we discovered that the differences between us and the officials from coastal areas were that, besides being still unable to cope with philosophical and ideological changes as they could, we were also very obviously at a great disadvantage when it came to working attitude and enthusiasm,' chief Ding said. 'For them, whatever task could be done in one day would never drag on for two or three, and even things planned for a later day would often be done ahead of time. We, on the other hand, were not like that. There was no one to put pressure on us, no urgent matter to take care of, so things were always postponed. We were always waiting for the moment of a real emergency, when everyone would then panic. But now we are no longer like that, because by our side we have our comrades from Fujian to serve us as role models. Hanging above our heads are the targets to be met in our fight against poverty, so we had to change our mentality, change our way of doing things, and make sure that we were wholeheartedly dedicated to the cause.

Hua Zhimin is the current county Party secretary of Yanchi. This local official is a native of Tongxin who comes from a family of little education from one of the most distressed parts of Ningxia. Nonetheless, of the eight children in his family, only his elder brother did not attend school, while most of them became officials after growing up. Hua Zhimin graduated from Guyuan Teachers' College, where he studied Chinese language and literature. After graduating, however, he went to work at the county's finance department.

'Because the county doesn't have many income sources of its own, half of the work of managing the finances of such a poor mountain region is about managing the affairs of the poor villages and villagers with money sent over from the central government,' Hua Zhimin explained. 'So I've been involved with poverty alleviation work ever since I started working at that department. I've also spent some years in Hongsibao, helping develop that place. After that I became the department chief of the prefectural finance department of Wuzhong, and after that I came to Yanchi to serve as county chief. A year and a half later, in 2015, I became local Party secretary. That's the summary of my participation in the war against poverty. I have also learnt quite a lot in the past few years, and one of the things I learnt, also from the officials of Fujian and from the practical work of poverty alleviation carried out in Yanchi, is that we have to make the common people truly change their concept of what it means to escape poverty and become prosperous, and emphasise the importance of the people's spiritual power in the elimination of poverty. In other words, it means making sure that our officials and the people in Yanchi follow their own motivations and go on to escape poverty through their own abilities.'

Hua Zhimin is a man of the countryside, so he is very well acquainted with agriculture, and naturally also has an emotional connection with the peasants. As such he was able of coming up with many different experiments in Yanchi in the context of the battle against poverty. He devised, in particular, some green initiatives at the county level, and promoted poverty alleviation through industry, experiments that turned out to be very clearly effective.

'But there is no job more important than finding the right

people, that is, nothing more important than finding talented people and honing their abilities to even higher standards!' Hua Zhimin said. He is, as a matter of fact, very uniquely talented in the art of discovering talents, while also having very strong leadership skills. If the *Tan* sheep of Yanchi enjoy a very good reputation today, and if they now account for more than 80% of the increase in the local peasants' incomes, that is because Hua Zhimin has taken the lead in opening up new channels for the sale of sheep products and has formulated also 27 new technical norms for the standardisation of production, with the effect of integrating the 'entry points' of *Tan* sheep products in the markets and stabilising prices. For that reason, the local people, having escaped poverty, now call him 'Secretary Tan Sheep', an affectionate and seemingly well-deserved moniker.

In 2017, South Africa, together with a few other African countries, organised a visit by some of their graduate students to a model village in Yanchi to study and investigate poverty alleviation measures. That visit was originally planned to last a week, but after the end of the first day those students said they just had to leave. When asked why they were leaving so soon, they said:

'We cannot copy your methods. Your socialism with Chinese characteristics is a unique wonder the Communist Party of

China has created. The capabilities, concepts, and ideas of people operating under a socialist system are things that cannot be realised under the systems we currently have in our African countries.'

'In fact, the important legacy of our experience of poverty elimination in Yanchi is the spirit the temporarily assigned officials from Fujian brought with them, a spirit that insists on freeing one's mind, opening up one's way of thinking, and having the courage to create,' Hua Zhimin said. He told me that he said to the comrades on the Fujian side of the Cooperation on Poverty Alleviation that they no longer needed to say how much money they were giving, and that what he really wished was for them to keep training his officials, and to train them some more. 'That's what makes me and the people of Yanchi the happiest,' he told them. That was, to borrow Hua Zhimin's own expression, a 'craving' for learning and spiritual vigour. And so Yanchi dispatched to Fujian group after group of officials, entrepreneurs, and any other such people who were eager to develop industries, to learn, and to be trained. Once they had completed their training, they all joined the fronts on the war against poverty, becoming leaders in the creation of prosperity. One of those officials is Zhu Yuguo, a representative at the 19th National Congress of the Communist Party of China and hailing from the Zengjipan village in the Wanglejing township, Yanchi county.

On my first visit to the village of Zengjipan I sat down with Zhu Yuguo to hear from him what he had to say about the situation in his village. Nearly one hour later, our conversation turned out to be a full 'Party lecture'. Zhu Yuguo's gift of the gab can indeed be counted among the 'treasures of Ningxia', because, for a peasant like himself, to talk so easily as he does, and with such great fluency, is something one really ought to admire.

Zhu Yuguo's village was officially removed from the roll of poor villages in 2016. To achieve that he implemented experiments he came up with by learning from the officials sent from Fujian, and, in particular, from Fujian's experience of using popular financing to lift the countryside out of poverty. The results were quick to appear and easy to see, meaning that he had managed to open a brand-new road to the elimination of poverty and the creation of prosperity. 'I often ask the villagers, what is a dream?' he said. 'A dream means that every one of us has an objective, something to strive for, a goal, that's what a dream is! A little more to the point, the dream that comes to us peasants is for everyone to have a goal to pursue, a desire for prosperity, and a way to become prosperous and pursue one's goals. Our poverty alleviation work used to be, for the most part, like blood transfusions. Sure enough, for those who are very week and vulnerable, that can be effective. But for young people and for our village's long-term development it was of little use, and even led some people to become lazy. As part of the Cooperation on Poverty Alleviation, officials from Fujian were temporarily assigned to our county, and our county also sent group after group of our own officials to Fujian to study and to be trained. Gradually we came to understand that, for people to be able to become truly prosperous, everyone needs to have a goal, an aspiration, an objective to pursue. Then minds will be quick and many solutions will appear. And when solutions are many, so are the opportunities for success!'

Of the 741 households in the village of Zengjipan, nearly a third were once formally classified as 'extremely poor'. In Zhu Yuguo's words, it was 'a poor and backward village difficult to reach and without any source of clean drinking water, suffering with severe droughts every three years, and where no one had any money in their pockets.' But, in 2007, with the help of the officials from Fujian and of the local county's finance department, Zhu Yuguo opened up a road for poverty alleviation based on 'credit building, production, and financial support'. That included establishing financial endowments for productive initiatives geared towards poverty alleviation, endowments that would support every household that had entrepreneurial ambition and a business project. It included also support for villagers through credit to their existing production and businesses, those based on the village's four major industries, namely *Tan* sheep products, traditional Chinese medicine products, grain, and pasturage. All of that was to be accomplished through credit organisations set up in the villagers' mutual-aid cooperatives. Those credit organisations were to be established by and composed of Party members and core Party figures working under the leadership of the local Party branch. Through mechanisms such as credit ratings, those mutual-aid cooperatives would then encourage entrepreneurs to work hard to increase returns on investments and thus improve general creditworthiness. As a result, businesses and production in the village kept increasing and getting stronger, with an ever-increasing number of families escaping poverty completely and setting foot on the road to prosperity. Living standards improved, and the general sense of happiness of the entire population of Zengjipan increased. The village's overall appearance also saw a quick transformation.

'The better the creditworthiness, the stronger was production growth,' Zhu Yuguo said with confidence. 'And the more production grew, the greater the financial support that creditworthiness could bring, thus spurring production to ever higher levels, which meant that improvements to the village kept coming, and that the villagers lived happier and happier lives. That is the model of poverty alleviation and prosperity building that we adopted here in our village of Zengjipan.'

Today Zhu Yuguo is not only the Party branch secretary of Zengjipan. He is also a widely known promoter of the 'Yanchi model of poverty-elimination', and every week he receives several groups of officials who come to him to learn from the model he created. 'Ten years ago, I had three dreams,' he said. 'The first dream I had was to find a solution for the problem of lack of health care in our village. So when the mutual-aid cooperative's financial endowment reached 3 million yuan, the village was allowed to take part of that money to purchase health insurance for the villagers. This was to keep them from sliding back into poverty or to suffer stigmatisation due to illness. The second dream was being able to provide care for the elderly. So when the cooperative's financial endowment reached 6 million yuan, the village purchased old-age insurance for all the villagers. And the third dream was education. Thus, when the cooperative's financial endowment reached 8 million yuan, the village gave to each poor student who had been admitted to university a sum of money as an incentive, to make sure that financial issues would not hinder their studies. And in the past ten years all three of my dreams were fully realised. That was made possible by a change of mindset.'

Today Zengjipan is already well-known in the region for the prosperity it achieved. At the beautiful site of the village's Party committee, Zhu Yuguo showed me not records of the village's 'poor households', but rather file after file of the village's now 'prosperous peasants'.

'One particular piece of data can illustrate very well the change that took place in our village,' he said very proudly. 'There used to be only *one* motor vehicle registered in our village, and an old one at that. Now there are more than 300 new vehicles!'

As he stood in front of me, layer upon layer of billowing wheat fields rolled behind him, tempestuous like great waves on the high seas. They made me feel as if I stood by the sea on the island of Gulangyu[1]… It was a kind of very intense and greatly optimistic feeling, happy and powerful. And it came about because that billowing wheat and the great waves of the ocean seemed to become one and the same thing, just like in that 'love between the mountain and the sea' created by the Cooperation on Poverty Alleviation Between Fujian and Ningxia. Their interaction, their intertwining, and their enormous energy were

---

1 An island in Fujian. It is a tourist attraction in its own right, and famous for being pedestrian-only.

in fact the great current of the times, carrying two provinces towards common prosperity and a glorious shared future.

> *Waves crash against the shore,*
> *a thousand layers of snow surge.*
> *The snow thaws over the great land,*
> *and early spring spreads over rivers and mountains*

'The officials of Ningxia all have their own self-worth to take into consideration. They all have feelings of their own, and they all want to contribute to the improvement of their native land, so as to provide better lives to the common people who live by their side,' said in his speech Zhang Zhu, at the time the secretary of Guyuan's Party committee. 'And so, precisely because of that, the arrival of officials from Fujian and the assistance they gave us make our own officials feel at the same time pressured and motivated, filled also with a determination to make the best of their time and work vigorously for the cause, so as not to let their people down. That is one of the reasons why very poor areas of Ningxia such as Xihaigu can succeed in the struggle against poverty, delivering both in terms of quantity and quality, and meeting the demands of the General Secretary.'

After concluding his speech that evening, Zhang Zhu told

me, not without a touch of emotion, that in the past two years several officials who worked with him in the struggle against poverty became sick from overwork. The chairman of Guyuan's Standing Committee had a bypass surgery, the secretary of the prefecture's Party committee developed myocarditis, important leaders from the counties of Xiji and Jingyuan collapsed on country roads and could not be saved, and there were also a few other local officials who had now forever left us…

It rained heavily that evening when Zhang Zhu told me all of this. And as I listened to his touching stories from the war against poverty, my own feelings weighed down on me. But I was, at the same time, exceptionally inspired by what I heard.

'It was the joint character of the struggle of our local officials and the officials from Fujian that touched even the heavens today to send down this rain and soak the land…' he mused.

But it is a fact that Ningxia, and Xihaigu in particular, are completely changed today.

'With this COVID-19 epidemic we're going through, we could never have imagined that there would be now more than 10,000 people from Hubei working in Xihaigu!' he said. 'Despite increasing the amount of work to be done in epidemic containment, their presence is, on the other hand, a development that rather lifts our spirits, because it means that our Guyuan, our Xihaigu, is now attracting people from other places as well!' And Secretary Zhang's joy was indeed justified.

'With the easing of the epidemic, many parts of the country started facing labour shortages,' he said. 'When we heard that there were some businesses in Fujian in need of workers, we promptly chartered 11 planes to send to Fujian thousands of our workers. That kind of thing was simply inconceivable just a few years ago, but it is now not at all surprising for us here in Ningxia!' As he said that, Secretary Zhang Zhu was nearly choking with emotion. But what he had to say after was even more touching. 'It used to be the case that people here, myself included, could not wrap their heads around what it really meant to escape poverty. But in these last few years, General Secretary Xi Jinping has visited us time and time again to encourage us and give us instructions. The central government's and the autonomous region's policies kept becoming more and more effective, and in addition to that there was also the unrelenting and loving support we received from our comrades in Fujian. Thus, the more we worked, the more enthusiastic we got, and the greater became our hopes, because light was just ahead of us, tomorrow was nearly here. It was at that moment that every one of our officials started to really believe that the completion of this great project of poverty-elimination and prosperity could be in their hands. And it had to be completed to perfection, and in the most splendid manner!'

Ah! That is the feeling we all wanted! The feeling of a great era of achievements! There is nothing that encourages and drives people's strengths and potential more than a feeling such as this one! And there is also nothing more prodigal in creating man-made miracles than a feeling like that! The mountain is already laughing, and the sea leaps with joy. That shared joy coming from the mountain and the sea working together is indeed a harbinger of the great rejuvenation of the Chinese nation and of China's splendid re-emergence in the world stage. That is exactly as General Secretary Xi Jinping has said:

> *'This town of Minning has opened up for us a bright new road...'*

And could it be any different? The experience of Fujian and Ningxia, the '*Minning* experience', was started 24 years ago as one of Xi Jinping's personal initiatives. It now appears before us as a broad road for economic development and for the project of socialist modernisation. It is a broad road also for solving problems that the whole world faces, for the elimination of poverty, and for the creation of prosperity. It is also made of the strength and the wisdom that the Communist Party of China and its members have contributed to the history of humanity…

As the mountain and the sea celebrate with joy the success of such a great undertaking, I can already see also the joyous roiling of the Yellow River! And it is the roiling Yellow River that will make the Helan Mountains and the Liupan Mountains once again stand tall and proud among the great mountains of China, singing boldly and loudly!